THE BRIDE SHIP

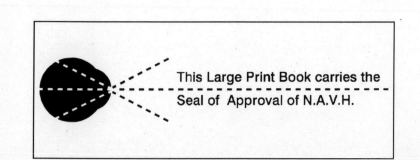

This Large Print Book carries the
Seal of Approval of N.A.V.H.

THE BRIDE SHIP

REGINA SCOTT

THORNDIKE PRESS

A part of Gale, Cengage Learning

GALE
CENGAGE Learning·

Farmington Hills, Mich • San Francisco • New York • Waterville, Maine
Meriden, Conn • Mason, Ohio • Chicago

GALE
CENGAGE Learning®

LIBRARY OF CONGRESS CATALOGING-IN-PUBLICATION DATA

Scott, Regina, 1959–
    The bride ship / by Regina Scott. — Large print edition.
        pages cm. — (Thorndike Press large print gentle romance)
    ISBN 978-1-4104-8213-6 (hardcover) — ISBN 1-4104-8213-8 (hardcover)
    1. Large type books. I. Title.
PS3619.C683B75 2015
813'.6—dc23   2015015656

Published in 2015 by arrangement with Harlequin Books S. A.

Printed in Mexico
1 2 3 4 5 6 7 19 18 17 16 15

She is clothed with strength
and dignity;
she can laugh at the days to come.
— *Proverbs* 31:25

To my Larry, who encourages
me to take the right path,
and to the Lord, who always
lights the way.

CHAPTER ONE

Pier 2, New York Harbor
January 16, 1866

Head high, Allegra Banks Howard held her daughter's hand and marched down the rough planks of the pier to join the queue of women about to board the S.S. *Continental.* In the frigid air that blew up the Hudson, the four-year-old's skin looked nearly as blue as her wide eyes inside the hood of her fur-lined cloak.

"I'm not seeing that fellow who's been following you," her friend Madeleine O'Rourke reported, standing beside Allie on tiptoe to peer through the crowd that surrounded them.

"Neither am I," Allie replied, but she wished she could be certain. She and Maddie weren't tall enough to look over the others' heads. With so many people about, their pursuer might be within a few feet of them, and Allie wouldn't know until he swooped down to grab them. Her hand tightened on her daughter's.

Stay with us, Lord! We're so close!

"And when will we catch sight of Mr. Mercer?" her other friend Catherine Stanway asked behind them. With her pale hair smoothed back under a fashionable feathered hat, she did not appear overly troubled by the absence of their leader. "Will the man miss his own sailing?"

Allie shook her head. All she'd wanted this afternoon was to take Gillian aboard the ship bound for Washington Territory. They would travel with Asa Mercer and the dozens of women who had pledged themselves to live and work in the new city of Seattle, to help make it a community.

She'd already met many of the other travelers, from the ever-so-proper Catherine to the outspoken Maddie. She could hear the women in line now, chatting with excitement. Each had a story to tell, of loss, of hope, of faith. Each believed her destiny lay on the far-off shores of Puget Sound. After all Allie had gone through, she refused to be left behind!

And yet, from the moment she and Gillian had tiptoed out of the Howard mansion in the dead of night in Boston two weeks ago, nothing had gone right. One of the horses had thrown a shoe, delaying the stage at Hartford; someone had stolen the bag with most of Gillian's clothes as she and Allie waited in Danbury; and for the last three days, an older man in a common brown coat had dogged their steps every time they had set foot outside the hotel. Allie was fairly sure she knew his purpose.

She wouldn't go back to Boston. She couldn't. Gillian's future and her own depended on it.

The line crawled forward, far too slowly for Allie, while all around them New Yorkers gathered to see them off, gazes curious, voices no more than a murmur among the calls of the sailors and the creak of hoists. That frost-laden wind tugged at her quilt-lined wool cloak, sending icy fingers even under her gray skirts, and she was thankful she'd decided to put on multiple petticoats instead of the steel crinoline her mother had once favored.

What would her mother and father have said if they could see her now? For the first time she was grateful they hadn't lived to see how their good friends the Howards had trespassed on her nature.

A tug blew its mournful horn as it chugged by, coughing silver smoke. Allie felt as if the sound echoed inside her. She could not fail, not this time. She refused to be the woman the Howards expected, and she would not allow Gillian to be molded into a shape that ill suited her, forced to marry, to live to please the prominent family.

As if her daughter quite agreed, she pulled on Allie's hand. "Let's go, Mother. I'm going to have the vapors."

The vapors. Allie knew where Gillian had learned the word. Allie had been advised by her mother-in-law to use the excuse whenever she felt distaste for a situation. A lady might have the vapors when an unwanted suitor came to call, when a treasured gown no longer fit properly. If a Howard had the vapors, people scurried to fix the problem. But having the vapors would hardly help them now.

Allie bent to lift her daughter into her arms. Gillian seemed heavier even than the day before. She was growing so fast, at least physically and mentally. But life with the Howards had bruised her daughter, and Allie could only thank God for the chance to take Gillian out of that environment.

"We'll be aboard soon enough, sweetheart," she promised. She nodded to the man in a brown coat and cap who stood beside the gangway, sheaf of papers flapping in his grip. "See that fellow? He's very likely the purser, ready to welcome us. And he may ask us some questions. Remember what we practiced?"

Gillian nodded solemnly. She was such a serious child, every propensity for play eradicated by the stern governess her grandmother had hired.

"We are going west because of Papa," she said.

Allie nodded encouragement. After all, it was the truth. Frank's death had been the catalyst to propel Allie from Boston at last. But a casual questioner would likely assume Gillian's father was waiting for her on the West Coast and not connect them with the story that had appeared in the New York papers about the Howards' missing daughter-in-law. It had been a little unnerving for Allie to see her face gazing back at her from the sketch on the page.

She only hoped the purser was less observant as she set Gillian back down and came abreast of him. Could he tell that the hair tucked inside her hood was jet black? If she lowered her gaze fast enough, would he fail to notice her eyes were as deep a blue as Gillian's? Her clothes were wrinkled from travel. She'd traded her velvet coat for this gray wool cloak. She knew she had shed a few pounds of worry with each step away from home.

Did she still look like the daughter of one of Boston's best families?

Apparently not, for all he said was "Name?" with his gaze poised over the papers. He was a small man, clean-shaven, with straight brown hair peeping out from under his cap of office and not much older than her twenty-three years, she thought.

"Allegra Banks and daughter," she replied, using every skill her mother had taught her to keep her voice level, calm and composed.

He scanned down the page, then looked up. His smile warmed her. "You are on the list, Mrs. Banks. I'm Mr. Debro, the purser. We'll provide more information about the journey once everyone has been settled. Welcome aboard."

Heat flushed up her. This was it, their chance. No more arguments with her mother-in-law about how she should live, what she should think; no more pulling her hand from the fevered grip of Frank's cousin as he offered himself as her next husband; no more fighting over who would influence Gillian's future. Perhaps she could even forget the look on Frank's face when he'd marched off to meet his death at the Battle of Hatcher's Run, leaving her a widow.

Allie's foot was on the gangway when a hand came down on her shoulder.

"You don't have to do this, Allegra," a man said.

Allie's breath caught in her chest like a bird in a cage. It couldn't be. Clay was many miles away and nearly six long years ago. Yet she could not mistake that voice: deep as a winter's night and warm as hot chocolate on a cold New England morning. It still had the power to set her to trembling.

She glanced back. The man standing behind her dwarfed the purser. One gloved hand sat heavily on her shoulder, the other was wrapped around the handles of a worn leather satchel as if he'd come at great haste to find her. His fur coat would have made him look like a bear except that the hair escaping his fur-lined hat was as red-gold as the lashes framing those cool green eyes. His skin was more bronzed than she remembered, as if he'd spent much time out of doors, and where once he'd laughed at life, now he seemed to be scowling.

Clay Howard could have only one reason for being here now. Somehow, his family had found him and sent him in pursuit of her. They must have thought she'd bow to his demands. She refused to be the little scared mouse of a girl who had wed his

15

brother because she couldn't bear to follow Clay into the wilderness. She was a widow now, a woman of her own making. She didn't have to pretend she had the vapors.

She drew herself up, looked down the nose her mother had always called entirely too pert, and said in a perfect imitation of Mrs. Howard's prim tone, "You have no call to accost me, sir. Unhand me before I call the authorities."

Mr. Debro took a step closer. "Mrs. Banks? Is there a problem?"

"Banks?" Clay shook his head as he dropped his hand. "I might have known you'd go by your maiden name." He nodded to the purser. "This is Mrs. Howard, and I'm Mr. Howard. I suggest you leave the lady to me."

Clay watched the purser's frown deepen even as Allegra paled. The creamy color suited her more than the angry red she'd worn when she'd first seen him.

Of course, he probably looked just as red. It wasn't often you found your dead brother's wife trying to board a ship of husband hunters. That was the kindest term given to the women foolish enough to join Mercer's expedition to Seattle.

Why would a woman put her faith in Asa

16

Mercer after seeing his ad in a newspaper? By all accounts, he'd only held one meeting with the women. And as for the jobs supposedly waiting for these women when they landed on those verdant shores? He knew from experience they were more likely to find the willing arms of every lumberjack, fur trapper, farmer and prospector starved for female companionship.

Allegra Banks didn't need to go to Seattle to find herself another husband. He hadn't been out of Boston a month before she'd married his younger brother. He was certain the men must be lining up for the chance to be husband number two.

He would never be one of them. His mother and the Boston belles he'd met cherished a picture in their minds of the perfect husband, and he'd soon realized he could not fit that frame. He took too many risks, with his money, with his life, to ever make a good gamble for a husband.

No job held his interest for long. He'd panned for gold in California and shipped lumber from the forests of Oregon Territory. Half the people of Seattle owed him their livelihood because he'd been willing to invest the money he'd earned to take a chance on their dreams. If they didn't make good, he'd be back in the gutter again. What wife would ever put up with such an unpredictable lifestyle? And why should he settle for anything less than his freedom?

If he had the sense God had given him, he'd have refused his mother's request to bring Allegra back to Boston where she belonged. But for once he found himself in agreement with his family. The wilderness was no place for a pampered Boston socialite like Allegra Banks.

As if to prove it, she shrugged out of his grip, blue eyes flashing fire. The black silky fringe trimming her gray skirts positively trembled in her ire. But before she could level him with a word, as he knew she was capable of doing, another voice interrupted. It was thin and reedy and seemed to be coming from the front of Allegra's cloak.

"Papa?"

The word stabbed through his chest, made it hard to breathe. A little girl peered around Allegra to gaze up at him. Curls as golden as Frank's were pressed inside the hood of her cloak. But those blue eyes, like the sea at night, were all her mother's.

"Hush, Gillian," Allegra said, one hand going to pull the child close.

Gillian. His mother's name. No one had said anything about Allegra and Frank having a little girl, but then the mighty Howards

18

were all too good at pretending. If they could forget they had another son besides precious Frank, they could certainly forget an inconvenient granddaughter. He couldn't imagine his father willing anything to a girl, and he doubted his dutiful brother would have risked their mother's wrath by leaving his estate to a daughter. Still, the pier must have been bucking with the incoming tide, for he suddenly found it hard to keep his footing as well.

The purser didn't seem to be having any trouble. "I don't understand," he said. "Aren't you the widow Mrs. Banks?"

He had the widow part right. And like the rest of Boston society, she probably thought Clay was to blame. He'd fought his father all his life. It was only logical that Clay should have been the one to go to war, the one who died fighting. He was the prodigal son who had never managed to ask forgiveness for leaving. No one in his family but Frank would have mourned his loss.

"Mr. Howard is correct," Allegra said, still so stern she could have been a professor at Harvard. "My married name was Howard, but he bears no responsibility for me. I make my own decisions."

And she had every right and capacity to do so. She was of age, and she'd been smart enough to turn down his offer of marriage once. But he couldn't agree with her decision this time.

The purser nodded toward the ship, where a couple of burley sailors had paused in their work to watch the scene on the pier. "In that case, I must ask you to do as the lady asks, Mr. Howard. I believe you will find yourself outgunned shortly."

The sailors were a match for him in size, but he'd tussled with bears twice as furious. "I don't much care what you believe," Clay said. "Mrs. Howard and her daughter are coming with me."

He flipped back one side of his coat. He could see the purser eyeing him, taking note of the size of his shoulders, the way his free hand hung down in ready reach of the pistol on his hip. Mr. Debro had to realize that Clay wasn't one of the proper Boston gentlemen who courted women like Allegra Banks. They would only have protested, promised a stinging letter to the editor of the newspaper, refused to raise a fuss. Clay specialized in raising fusses.

Still, the purser held his ground. "Mrs. Howard, do you wish to speak to this man?"

Allegra frowned at him. She had to wonder at his presence, standing here, bag in hand, as if he'd just arrived on the stage.

After all, the last time she'd seen him, he'd been begging her to marry him, to leave Boston and journey west. Her refusal had stung then, but everything he'd experienced since had told him she had been right to stay in Boston where she would be safe.

And he certainly didn't look the part of a gentleman ready to escort a lady home. His fur coat was patched together in places, his boots were scuffed and dirty, and all he carried with him were a few days of clothing and toiletries stuffed in his satchel. His own mother had refused to allow him in her parlor. Allegra would be mad to accept his help.

Or desperate. As her breath came in short bursts like the puffs of a steam engine, he could almost feel her determination. He couldn't understand what had driven her out of the city of her birth. Surely returning to Boston was preferable to traveling thousands of miles away to a place she was ill suited to live. Why was she so set on leaving home?

"Excuse me." Clay turned to find a pretty blonde in a tailored brown coat behind him along with a narrow-eyed woman in a cloak nearly as red as her hair. Around them ranged several other women, all with heads high and fingers clutching their reticules as if they meant to use the little cloth bags to effect.

The blonde's smile was tight under her trim brown hat. "The tide turns within the hour, sir," she informed him, patrician nose in the air as if even the scent of his soap offended her. "We have a great deal to do before then. You have no right to detain our friend." She flapped her gloved fingers at him as if shooing a chicken. "Be gone."

The other women nodded fervently.

Clay inclined his head. "I'm not here for trouble, ladies. I have only Mrs. Howard's best interests in mind, I assure you."

"Sure'n, isn't that what they all say?" The lady with the red curls clustered about her oval face had a voice laced with the lilt of Ireland. She looked him up and down. "Go on, now. A big strapping lad like you can't be so lacking for female companionship he needs to snatch his women off the pier. Have some respect for yourself."

For once in his life, Clay had no idea how to respond. As if she knew it, Allegra smothered a laugh. Even her daughter was regarding him quizzically.

"Truly, sir," the blonde scolded him, "it's the Christian thing to do."

"It's all right, ladies," Allegra said. "Mr. Howard was just saying farewell."

Now besides the humor, he could hear triumph in her voice. She thought her posse of vigilante females would frighten him off. She expected him to wish these ladies well, to allow her and Frank's daughter to board this vessel and sail off to places that would endanger their values, their faith and their very lives.

Normally, he'd be the last to dissuade anyone from pursuing a dream. He knew the heady feeling of charting his own course, making his own way. Yet he also knew what lay waiting for these women in the wilderness.

Father, how can I compromise my own beliefs and let them go?

He couldn't. Allegra's determination must have been contagious, for he felt his shoulders straightening with purpose.

"Give me five minutes, Allegra," he said. "If I can't persuade you to return to Boston, I won't stop you from boarding the ship."

She held her ground, one hand on Gillian, the other grafted to the rope edging the gangway.

"Mrs. Banks, er, Howard?" the purser put in, pausing to clear his throat as if as unsure of his reception as he was of her true name. "If you intend to speak to Mr. Howard, I must ask you to step away so I can continue the boarding process."

The blonde came to Allegra's side, chin up and pale blue eyes narrowed with purpose. "If you want to go, Mrs. Banks, I'll watch over Gillian." She glanced at Clay as if she didn't trust him. "But if you wish to board, I wouldn't give this fellow another moment of your time."

He couldn't chide her spirit or her practicality. Allegra hadn't seen him in years. She had no way of knowing the man he had become. He tried to smile. She didn't look any more certain of him.

In fact, he could almost see the thoughts behind those deep blue eyes, weighing her options, determining his worth. He'd seen the look before, the calculation of a Boston socialite over whether a person warranted the pleasure of her company. He'd thought he was beyond caring about the conclusion of such an assessment. Once, that conclusion would have immediately been in his favor as a Howard. Now his family couldn't be bothered to receive him. Still, he was surprised by the wave of relief that coursed through him when Allegra transferred her daughter's hand to her friend's.

"Go with Ms. Stanway, Gillian," Allegra said with a sidelong look to him. "I can allow five minutes for your uncle, but no more."

CHAPTER TWO

Five minutes should have been more than enough time to make her refusal to whatever Clay had to say. She couldn't imagine any circumstance that would change her mind about her plans. If she remained in plain view of the ship, he could do nothing to prevent her from leaving. She'd seen Mr. Debro look at the sailors. She knew she could count on help if needed.

But Gillian wasn't content to let her go. She must have slipped her hand from Catherine's, for she darted to Allie's side. "Can I come, too, please? He looks like Papa."

The longing in her voice tugged at Allie's heart. Gillian had been all of two when her father had left for war. Allie had read her all the letters he'd sent, especially the stories he wrote just for her. Gillian couldn't understand the finality of death, the fact that her father would never return.

But to see Frank in Clay? Allie looked him over more closely. Perhaps the color of his hair was similar, but his had always been straighter than Frank's, his eyes more pale and piercing, his body taller and stronger. They had been so different, in temperament, in ambitions. Clay had never obeyed his parents with unquestioning devotion like her husband. Frank had been smooth, polished, proper. Clay had been defiant, commanding, but now everything about him was rough, from the stubble on his proud chin to the dust on his worn knee-high boots. She couldn't see Frank in him.

But at Gillian's statement, he pushed back his hat. "Clever of you, little miss, to notice," he said with a bow. "I'm your father's brother. And I'm here to bring you home."

Gillian's eyes widened. Allie sucked in a breath and stepped between them. How dare he try to use her daughter against her!

"Gillian's home is with me, sir," she informed him. "And I am heading for Seattle." She gave Gillian a hug before patting her back and pushing her toward Catherine. Catherine took the little girl's hand and turned to give her own name to the purser.

"I'm not trying to usurp your place," Clay

said quietly as he straightened and the other women returned to their places in line. "I thought Frank's daughter deserved to know her family."

Guilt whispered; she could not afford to listen. She knew that by taking Gillian to Seattle, she was cutting off everyone the little girl had ever known. But Clay had been away for so long. He couldn't understand how his family had tried to control Allie, to control Gillian. He knew she'd refused to leave Boston once. How could he realize how important this trip was to her now?

"You are wasting your five minutes, sir," she said. "I believe you only have three left."

His mouth compressed in a tight line. He glanced about, then led her through the crowds and a little apart from the gangway to the shelter of a stack of crates awaiting loading. Allie could see Catherine taking Gillian aboard the ship. Some of the tension seemed to be going with them. Whatever happened now, at least her daughter was safe.

She turned to find Clay eyeing her. "Why are you here, Allegra?" he asked.

Though his tone was more perplexed than demanding, she felt her spine stiffening. "I would think that obvious. We're going with

Mr. Mercer to Seattle."

"And you think that's your best choice for a future?" he asked with a frown. "What about Boston? Your place in society?"

Her place in society? Well, she'd once considered it precious, and he had cause to remember. She was the one who didn't like remembering. She'd been so sure then of what she'd wanted. She'd been taught to manipulate to achieve her goals, yet she hadn't realized how easily she'd been manipulated until it was almost too late.

She puffed out a sigh of vexation that hung in the chill air between them. "You honestly think I should be content to stay in Boston? And this from the man who ran away to join the Wild West show!"

A smile hitched up, and it somehow seemed as if the gray day brightened. "I wanted to see the Wild West, not play cowboy in a show," he replied. "And from what I've seen, the Northwest territories are no place for a woman."

"Which is precisely why women are needed," Allie argued. "You can't tell me Seattle won't be improved by teachers, nurses, seamstresses and choir leaders."

He chuckled. "That statement merely shows what little you know of Seattle. There are few children to teach, a single struggling hospital for the nurses, no call for fancy clothes for the seamstresses."

Allie's eyes narrowed. His description hardly matched the information Mr. Mercer had given them. How could Clay know so much about Seattle? If her in-laws had ever received letters from him, they hadn't shared the news with her. And Frank, of course, rarely spoke of Clay. He thought the entire matter too painful for her.

"So you've seen Seattle," she said, watching him.

His gaze met hers. Up close, the changes of time were obvious: the fine lines beside his eyes, the tension in his broad shoulders, the way his smile turned from pleased to grim.

"I've been there," he said so carefully she could only wonder if he'd robbed the bank. But perhaps they didn't have a bank, either!

"Then you must know why we're needed," Allie told him.

"Besides being someone's wife?" he asked, rubbing a hand along his square jaw. "No. Seattle is a scattering of houses in a clearing, five hundred people, give or take. And the outlying settlements are worse. I heard most of these ladies going with Mercer are orphans. They've nowhere else to turn. You have a family, a home, opportunity for a future. I can't see you as one of Mercer's belles."

At least he hadn't used one of the unkind names she'd seen in the newspapers. Cargo of Heifers. Petticoat Brigade. Sewing Machines. The editor of one of the local papers had expressed extreme doubt that any girl going to seek a husband was worthy to be a decent man's wife. What, did the rest of the country expect every woman who'd lost a sweetheart, a husband in that horrible war to simply stop living? That they couldn't find employment instead of decorating a man's home?

Anger bubbled up inside her. "I have no intention of seeking a husband in Seattle. And may I remind you that you had a home and opportunities once, too. That didn't stop you from leaving."

His jaw tightened. "I knew what I wanted and what I was leaving behind. I doubt you do."

Didn't she? How many nights had she lain in her canopied bed, warm, safe, suffocating? How many times had she prayed for wisdom, for guidance? Her prayers had been answered with a dream, a future for her and Gillian that didn't include marrying someone the Howards picked out. When Allie had seen the advertisement in the paper for teachers and other workers in far-off Washington Territory, she'd known it was the pointing of God's finger. She'd been the one to close the door on adventure once. Now He'd opened it, and she intended to follow His lead.

"Save your doubts, Mr. Howard," she said. "Save your breath, as well. You gave up the right to order me about years ago."

Clay's brows went up, and he took a step back to stare at her. Allegra Evangeline Banks Howard would never have spoken to a gentleman that way, particularly not her husband's brother.

"You've changed," he said.

"How perceptive of you to notice," she replied. "Did you think I had no more to worry about than which dress to wear? Motherhood, and widowhood, mature a woman in a dozen ways. And this trip will do more."

He sighed and dropped his gaze to the wooden pier, where his boots scuffed at an iron nail. "I can see you're certain, but I can't let you get on that ship, Allegra. You have no idea how to survive in the wilderness."

She knew he was right. Who was she to take on such a challenge, to brave the unknown? But her will rose up even as her head came up.

"Clayton Howard," she said, breath as sharp as her words, "if you can learn, so can I. Now, you have had your five minutes, sir. Nothing you've said has dissuaded me from leaving. Thank you for coming. Good day."

Before she could push past him, he held up his hands as if in surrender. His words, however, were far from capitulating. "I can't demand that you come with me, Allegra, though I've no doubt my mother expected me to do so. She's ready to welcome you back to the family. Isn't that better than heading off to the wilderness alone?"

So he was willing to admit that he was here on his mother's behest. She couldn't help the frustration building inside her. Was she never to be free?

"I think it's time Gillian and I made our own family," she informed him. "And you can tell that to your exalted mother. And as for the other member of your family, your cousin Gerald, you can tell him that I wouldn't marry him if he was the last man on earth, and sending bullies after me isn't going to persuade me otherwise!"

He cocked his head. "Gerald has been pressuring you?"

That's what he heard? Not that she was

her own person, capable of making her own decisions. Not that she considered him nothing but a bully to chase after them this way. No, he had to fixate on the rival, the cousin who seemed intent on inheriting the considerable estate that would have been Clay's if his father hadn't disowned him when Clay headed west.

"Every day," Allie told him. "In every possible way. He's become extremely tiresome." It was the most polite way to put it. At times, Gerald had looked at her with a glint in his eyes that made her feel as if she had suddenly fallen through the ice on the pond below the house. It was as if he coveted her, as if she were a possession. And Clay's mother had encouraged him. She shuddered just remembering.

Clay must have seen her movement, for he took her arm. "Allow me to escort you back to the hotel," he said. "We can talk further where it's warmer."

Behind her, the *Continental* blew its horn, the blast piercing the cold air. She would not let the ship leave without her. Her bags were already aboard. And she would never abandon Gillian.

She pulled her arm from Clay's. "Your hearing must have been affected by your travels, sir. I am boarding this ship. If you insist on conversing further, you'll have to board it with me." She turned for the ship, keeping her head high, her steps measured. She wouldn't look back, not to Boston, and not to Clay.

For all she had once wished otherwise.

Clay stared at Allegra as she headed for the gangway. She walked gracefully, as if on her way to a ball. She had no idea she was heading into trouble instead.

What am I to do with her, Lord?

The prayer held more exasperation than appeal. He'd ridden, by hired horse and stagecoach, from the Northwest territories to Boston in the last month, hoping to reunite with family after news of Frank's death a year ago had reached him, courtesy of an old family friend. Though Frank was beyond Clay's help, he had considered it his duty to ensure his brother's widow was well provided for. But he'd met failure on all sides. The one task where he'd thought he could still succeed was to convince Allegra to return to Boston where she would be safe. Now even that seemed to be denied him.

But he'd never been one to give up without a fight.

His purpose, as he saw it, was to protect

Frank's wife and child. He'd never be a family man like Frank, steady, reliable, but he could at least make sure Allegra and Gillian had a solid future. If they refused to return to Boston where they belonged, then he had only one way to accomplish his goal. He had to return west in any event.

I know it may be crazy, Lord, but surely this is what You'd want me to do.

He shoved his hat down on his head a little farther and waited in the shadow of the crates as the last of the women filed up the gangway. The purser glanced through his notes with a frown, as if he thought he must be missing someone. Then he shrugged and climbed aboard, as well. As soon as the way was clear, Clay strolled up the gangway and onto the ship.

No one stopped him, ordered him to produce his ticket. With his satchel in his hand, he probably looked like a typical passenger, even if he wasn't one of Mercer's maidens. As it was, the crew and officers were far too busy preparing to sail to pay him any mind.

And the crowds were even denser on the deck than they had been on the pier. He was surprised to see several families aboard, older husbands with wives and children in tow, brothers escorting what were clearly sisters by the similarity of their features. People milled about, looks ranging from excitement to terror. At least some of them knew what they were leaving behind. Going from one coast to the other happened once in a lifetime for most people.

Clay moved among them, keeping an eye out for Allie and Gillian. Even with all the passengers on deck, it shouldn't have been that hard to find them. As far as he could see, the entire ship was about as long as the Howard mansion in Boston but only half as wide.

The main deck circled the ship, with an upper deck above one of the blocky buildings. Though the black funnel sticking up in the center of the deck sputtered a cloud from the steam engine, two masts rose higher into the air. It seemed the *Continental* could sail under wind power, as well. The three buildings along the deck would house the wheel, the captain's quarters and the officers' mess, and the first-class accommodations, Clay guessed. The stairs running down beside them would likely take the passengers belowdecks, where they'd find another salon and staterooms for the ordinary passengers.

And there, just about where the first mast towered over the deck, Allegra stood with some of the other women, faces set resolutely toward the mouth of the North River.

Just then, the horn bellowed, and little Gillian cried out, arms reaching for her mother. Allegra gathered her close, bent her head as if to murmur reassurances. Something hot pressed against Clay's eyes.

That little girl has lost so much, Father. I didn't have a say in the matter, but now that I know about her, I can't see her hurt further.

Neither could Allegra. That much was obvious. She raised the little girl's chin with one finger, smiled at her, lips moving as if she promised a bright future.

How could he take that future from them?

He pushed his way through the crowds to their sides. Allegra looked up, then straightened at the sight of him, eyes widening.

"What are you doing?" she cried. "We're about to sail!"

As if to prove her point, two of the crew began to haul in the gangway.

Clay glanced over his shoulder at the gangway, then back at Allegra. "It seems you're set on going, Mrs. Howard. And that means I'm going with you."

"What are you talking about?" Allie cried.

He couldn't be coming with them. Surely he wasn't part of Mercer's expedition. She'd never heard his name mentioned, hadn't seen him at the hotel with the others. If she had, she might not be here now.

But before he could answer, the ship groaned, heaving away from the pier. Everyone around her rushed to the railing, carrying her and Gillian along with them, and for a moment, she lost sight of Clay.

The sight below them was compelling enough. From the pier, dozens of people waved and cheered. Boys threw their hats in the air. Women fluttered handkerchiefs. After the reception Mercer's belles had received in the New England papers, Allie found it hard to believe so many New Yorkers would stand in the cold to watch them set sail. It was as if she and her friends were making history.

Those on the *Continental* were even more excited. Maddie was blowing kisses to the crowd below. Other passengers raised clasped hands over their heads in a show of victory. Even Catherine unbent sufficiently to give a regal wave. No one seemed bereft at what they were leaving behind. Hope pushed the ship down the bay. Hope brightened every countenance. Even the air tasted sweeter.

Perhaps that was why it was so very painful when hope was snatched away.

"Attention! Attention, please!" Mr. Debro hopped up on one of the wooden chests that dotted the deck and waved his hands as if to ensure everyone saw him. "We'll be stopping shortly at quarantine near Staten Island. Everyone to the lower salon on the orders of Captain Windsor. This way!"

Allie and Maddie exchanged glances, and she saw worry darken her friend's gaze.

"Very likely it's nothing to concern us," Catherine said as if she'd seen the look, as well. "The captain probably wishes to address the passengers before we reach the ocean."

"Of course," Allie agreed, but the frown on Maddie's face said she wasn't so sure. Allie took Gillian's hand, and Catherine and Maddie fell in beside them as they headed for the salon.

It was a simple room, with a long wooden table scarred from frequent use. Around it, smaller tables and chairs made of sturdy wood hugged the white-paneled walls under the glow of brass lanterns. At one end, doors opposite each other led up to the deck, with another opening amidships that must lead to the upper salon. Other doors recessed along the way appeared to open onto staterooms. Across the back, a wide window and narrow door gave access to the galley where copper pans glinted in the glow from the fire in the massive black iron stove.

Already the room was crowded, but there seemed to be fewer women than Allie had expected. She'd heard that the expedition was to include as many as seven hundred female emigrants, yet she estimated at most sixty flitting from one group to another. And still she caught not a glimpse of Asa Mercer.

Catherine excused herself a moment to go speak to Mr. Debro, who was frantically shuffling his papers.

Gillian tugged on Allie's skirts. "Where's our new room, Mother?"

Mother. The formal word always reminded Allie of how she'd nearly failed her daughter. Gillian's first word had been Mama, her second Papa. Allie had spent most of her time with her baby daughter, marveling over each change as Gillian grew into a toddler. But as soon as she was walking well, her grandmother had insisted on a governess.

"A small child can be so challenging," she'd told Allie and Frank over tea in the formal parlor of the Howard mansion. "You've never been a mother before, Allegra. You have no experience with children. For Gillian's sake, we should look for someone older to help you. Don't you agree, Frank?"

Of course, Frank had agreed. Frank never argued with his mother. Allie had already been wondering about her ability to raise such an active little girl, so she'd agreed, as well. Gillian had moved into the nursery suite with a governess, and her next words had been please and thank-you and little else in between. *Mama* had never returned to her petal-pink lips.

"We'll know where to go soon," Allie promised now, taking her daughter's hand and giving it a squeeze. "And we can sail off to adventure."

Gillian nodded, but her frown told Allie she wasn't sure adventure was something to eagerly anticipate.

Catherine returned then, her rosy lips tightened in obvious disapproval.

"This is a shameful state of affairs," she said to Maddie and Allie, where they were waiting with Gillian along one wall. "What sort of ship allows stowaways to sneak aboard?"

Stowaways? Allie immediately glanced around for Clay and spotted him leaning against the far wall, a head taller than any

42

other man in the room. He'd been clear from the start that he wanted them to leave. Surely he'd never paid his passage. Had he caused this commotion?

Just then, the young purser raised his voice from where he stood by the doorway to the upper salon.

"May I have your attention, ladies and gentlemen?" he called, and the other voices quieted as people shifted to see him better. Allie was close enough to notice the sheen of perspiration on his brow under the brown cap.

"There seems to be some misunderstanding as to which people have paid their passage," he said, confirming Catherine's statement. "When I call your name, please accompany me to the upper salon, where Captain Windsor and the authorities are waiting to examine your tickets. If you do not have the appropriate ticket, you will be asked to gather your things and embark on the tug alongside us, back to New York."

Allie felt as if the air had left the room. She pulled Gillian closer as voices rose in protest.

"See here, sir," an older gentleman declared, pushing his way to the front. "I've paid for a wife and five children. I've spent all we had waiting for this infernal ship to

43

sail. If you send us back, where do you suggest we go?"

"Mr. Mercer assured me no money was needed," another woman called. "He cannot go back on his word!"

"Where's Mr. Mercer?"

"Yes, find Mr. Mercer!"

The cry was taken up by a dozen voices.

The purser raised his hand and managed to make himself heard above the din. "Mr. Mercer is presently unavailable, but rest assured, he has been consulted on the matter."

Allie's stomach knotted. She had only a letter from Asa Mercer, assuring her and Gillian of places on the ship. She'd never received an actual ticket. Would the captain count her letter as sufficient evidence to allow them to stay? Was her adventure over before it had begun?

Chapter Three

As soon as Clay heard the reason they had stopped, he knew he had to act. While the room erupted in protest, he slipped out the side door and circled around for the upper salon.

It was a more opulent room, with leather-upholstered armchairs positioned along the paneled walls for conversation and a large table running down the center for meals. Doors with brass latches and louvered windows opened onto spacious staterooms. The scent of fresh paint hung in the air.

Another table had been positioned across the top of the salon, where three men, one seated, two flanking him, waited in the brown-and-gold uniforms of the Holladay line.

Clay strode up to them and nodded to the man at the table. "Captain Windsor, sir. I'm Clayton Howard, and I'd like to report a stowaway."

The captain eyed him. He seemed the very embodiment of the seas he sailed — gray hair, gray eyes, strong body and unyielding disposition.

"Indeed, Mr. Howard," he intoned. "We are here to make that determination."

"I'll spare you the trouble," Clay said. "I haven't paid my passage, and I'd like to rectify that matter. Will you take gold certificates?"

Captain Windsor tilted up the cap of his office. "Certainly. But I must ask why you didn't purchase a ticket beforehand."

Clay couldn't lie. "I came here intending to stop my brother's widow from sailing. Since she is determined to make the trip, I'm coming with her."

The officers behind the captain exchanged glances, but whether they thought him a tyrant or a fool, he couldn't tell.

"Very well, Mr. Howard," the captain said. "Some of the passengers who were supposed to have boarded did not make the sailing, so we should have room for you. Give your money to Mr. Debro when he arrives with our first passenger, and welcome aboard."

Clay inclined his head. "Would you allow me to stay in the room until I'm certain my sister-in-law's documents are sufficient?"

Captain Windsor agreed, and Clay went to sit on one of the chairs along the wall, where he could monitor the proceedings.

He thought it would be a simple matter. After all, how many stowaways could have slipped by Mr. Debro's watchful eye? However, what he saw over the next hour disgusted him.

He knew the story of how Asa Mercer had come by the use of the S.S. *Continental,* which had seen service as a troop carrier in the war. The so-called emigration agent had written home to Seattle to boast of his accomplishment. None other than former general Ulysses S. Grant had allowed Ben Holladay to purchase the ship at a bargain and refit her for duty as a passenger ship so long as he agreed to carry the Mercer party to Seattle on her first run.

Mercer and Holladay had apparently settled on a price for passage, and Mercer had provided the list that Mr. Debro had used to allow passengers to board. But it was soon apparent that Mr. Debro's list did not match Captain Windsor's instructions from Mr. Holladay. Someone had cheated these people, but Clay couldn't be sure whether it was Asa Mercer or the steamship company.

Everyone claimed to have paid or been

told payment was unnecessary, the fare was courtesy of the fine people of Seattle. Mercer must have confessed how he'd accepted money from a number of gentlemen to bring them wives. Clay could only hope Allegra wasn't one of the women with a husband waiting. The fellow was doomed to disappointment, for Clay still had hopes of discouraging her from settling in the wilderness. Surely over the course of their trip he could find the words to persuade her.

But the other passengers were more discouraged. Two men and their families, disappointment chiseled on every feature, had already been escorted downstairs to identify their belongings, along with a few crying women. One, Mr. Debro reported, had barricaded herself in a stateroom, refusing to leave. Others threatened retribution.

Allegra was different. She must have left Gillian below with friends, for when it was her turn, she glided into the room alone, head high, smile pleasant. Her gaze swept the space, resting briefly on Clay. Her look pressed a weight against his chest. She passed him without comment and went straight to the captain, pulling a piece of paper from the pocket of her cloak and holding it out as if allowing him to kiss her hand.

Captain Windsor didn't even glance at her offering as Mr. Debro came to stand beside him. "I need a ticket, Mrs. Banks, not your correspondence with Mr. Mercer."

She was paler than the first Boston snowfall, her profile still. "If you read that correspondence, Captain, you will see that Mr. Mercer acknowledges payment for my passage. I was promised a spot for me and my daughter. I paid Mr. Mercer six hundred dollars."

Six hundred dollars. A princely sum for most people, but a pittance for his family.

"You may have paid Mr. Mercer," Captain Windsor replied. "However, there is no record of Mr. Mercer relaying the monies to Mr. Holladay, the owner of this fine vessel. Have you any way to pay for your passage, madam?"

She shifted on her feet, setting the black fringe on her skirts to swinging. "I gave Mr. Mercer all I had. I've been washing dishes to pay for our board until the ship sailed."

Clay stiffened. How was that possible? Frank must have provided for her. Clay hadn't been surprised to hear that his younger brother had stepped in as soon as Clay had stepped out. Frank had been in love with Allegra for years. Besides, the marriage settlement had been considerable.

He'd seen the papers, even if he'd left before signing them.

But if Allegra couldn't pay her way, did that mean he had an opportunity to return her to Boston, after all?

"We have sufficient help in the kitchens," Captain Windsor said across from him. "I'm afraid I have no choice but to send you back. Fetch up Ms. Madeleine O'Rourke, Mr. Debro."

The purser frowned and glanced around Allegra toward Clay. "Mr. Howard? Will you be escorting the lady?"

Because Allegra had used her maiden name, the captain couldn't know she was Clay's sister-in-law. Clay rose, but she took a step closer to the captain.

"Please," she said, voice low. "Don't let him take me back. I'll do anything."

The tremor in her voice shook him. Had Frank's death made Boston so impossible for her, being reminded of him everywhere she looked? He couldn't conceive that his mealymouthed cousin Gerald had caused such heartache. The Allegra Banks he remembered would have silenced Gerald with a look.

Whatever its source, her pain propelled him to her side, forcing her gaze to meet his. For a moment, he saw fear looking back at him.

Father, what happened to her?

As if she was determined not to allow him to help, she took a breath, collected herself and became the sophisticated Allegra Banks he remembered.

"I don't require your escort, Mr. Howard," she said. "I know my way downstairs."

"I'm not offering to escort you," Clay said. "I'm offering to pay your way." He was taking the biggest risk of his life, disappointing his family once again. *Forgive me, Father, if I've mistaken Your direction, but I cannot help thinking this is the right thing to do.*

As she stared at him, Clay turned to the captain, pulled out his pouch and counted off the last of his certificates. He'd have little to live on the rest of the trip, but if that meant a chance to help Allegra and Gillian, he could make do.

The captain glanced between the two of them. "Under the circumstances, Mrs. Howard," he said, "I should ask you if you are willing to accept this man's money for your fare."

She had to know what accepting such a gift might mean, that she was somehow under Clay's protection. Once more he could see the calculations behind her blue eyes.

"Have you pen and paper, sir?" she asked the captain. "I would have you draw up a contract between me and Mr. Howard."

"That isn't necessary," Clay started, but she whirled to face him, eyes blazing.

"It is entirely necessary," she scolded him. "I will not accept money from you without a contract. And I will pay you back every cent, even if I have to work the rest of my life to do so."

He wanted to argue. Why couldn't he do her this service? After all, the good citizens of Boston thought he'd been the one to abandon her, when he and Allegra had been promised for ages. But she knew the truth. She'd been the one to send him away.

He nodded. "Very well, Mrs. Howard. Let's not trouble the good captain now. I'm sure there's pen and paper belowdecks."

She drew a deep breath, turned to the captain and inclined her head. "I accept Mr. Howard's offer, then. If there is nothing else, gentlemen? I'd like to settle my daughter before we sail."

Captain Windsor handed the certificates to the purser. "You're free to go, Mrs. Howard. Mr. Debro will give you your stateroom number. I hope the trip is to your liking."

She inclined her head again. "Come

along, then, Mr. Howard. Let's settle this between us." She made her way from the room, head still high, steps measured, never doubting he'd be right on her heels, like a trained spaniel.

She thought a simple contract would settle things between them. He was certain it would never be that simple. He caught her arm before she could start down the stairs. "I don't want your money, Allegra."

Her chin was so high he thought her neck must hurt from the strain. "And I don't want your help, Mr. Howard. But it appears that neither of us is going to get our wish." She took a deep breath. "I'll give you ten dollars a month once I'm employed in Seattle."

She was a hopeless optimist. He couldn't imagine what work she'd be qualified to do in Seattle, and she'd be lucky to make that much a month regardless of the job she took. Wasn't this further proof that the wilderness was no place for her?

"It will take years for you to pay me off," he pointed out. "I'll give you better terms." He lowered his head to meet her gaze. "You don't want me around. That's clear enough. But if you allow me to become acquainted with my niece, I'll call us square."

She sucked in a breath. "Spending time

with Gillian? That's it?"

Clay straightened. "That's it. Though it goes without saying that I expect the two of us to try to be civil to each other for the three and a half months it will take to reach Seattle."

She raised her brows. "Three and a half months being civil to you, Mr. Howard? You ask too much." She pulled away from him and clattered down the stairs.

The nerve of the man! Allie stomped down the stairs, fury rising with each footfall. Clay Howard didn't fool her for a second. All that talk about acquainting himself with his niece only to claim he wanted Allie to be "civil." Her days in Boston society had taught her that when a gentleman paid so much money to support a lady, he generally expected a great deal more than civility — fawning gratitude, to say the least.

She did not intend to be civil about it.

Nor was she inclined to grant him any favors. She would find a way to pay him back. She might not be an excellent cook like Maddie or a trained nurse like Catherine, but she could sew a fine hand. All those years of embroidering pillowcases and tatting lace had to count for something. Mr. Mercer had assured her she could support Gillian by sewing for other families. She'd merely add Clay's money to her list of expenses.

She felt him behind her on the stairs, but she refused to turn and look. Too bad she couldn't simply pretend he wasn't there. Her mother and his would have had no trouble doing so. Anyone in Boston society trembled to receive a cut direct from Mrs. Banks or Mrs. Howard. To her shame, Allie had used the gambit more than once on the men who had courted her, looking through them as if they weren't there, refusing to hear their pleas for forgiveness for whatever they thought had annoyed her. She wasn't going to treat anyone that way now.

But she could not help remembering the last time she'd seen Clay. She'd known she'd marry Clayton Howard since she was seven and overheard her mother talking with his. Clay had been thirteen then, an impossibly heroic figure in her eyes, and she'd spent much of the next ten years following him around with Frank beside her.

While her parents and the Howards complained that Clay was too wild, too undisciplined, Allie and Frank had looked up to him, tried to ape everything he did. She had a scar on her knee from where she'd been thrown trying to ride as well as he did. Frank had spent a week trying to master the way Clay tipped his top hat with such a flourish. Clay had just smiled at their antics and gone about his business. She'd never understood why his parents hadn't appreciated him as much as his younger brother.

But when Allie turned seventeen, things changed. Boys who couldn't be bothered to notice her suddenly vied for her attention. She was the belle of Boston, her parlor stuffed with suitors. Instead of her following Clay around, hoping to catch his eye, he was the one who had to compete for a moment with her. Her popularity had been exhilarating, and she'd let it go to her head.

Then came the night he'd confessed his dreams to her. Her mother had been hosting a ball, the house crowded with the very best of Boston society. Clay had looked so handsome, so commanding, in a tailored coat of midnight black that was the perfect complement to her pearly-white ball gown. The string quartet had been playing a lilting waltz, and she'd hoped Clay would take her in his arms and whirl her about the floor. Instead, he'd led her out onto the back veranda overlooking the gardens scented by her mother's prized roses.

Clay had put his arms around her, sheltering her as moonlight bathed their faces, and she'd shivered in delight to find herself the center of his attention at last. But his words had not been the declaration she'd hoped.

"I'm done with Boston, Allegra," he'd said. "I'm heading west, and I want you to come with me."

She pulled away from him, fluttering her fan even as her pulse stuttered. "Clay," she said, "you cannot mean it. Boston is our home. Everyone we know is here."

"And everyone here knows me," he countered. "That wild Howard boy. I feel as if I can't breathe. Out west I can be my own man, a man you can be proud to call husband."

Her heart soared. He wanted her beside him, his partner, his love. It was everything she'd ever wanted. And yet . . .

"I'd be proud of you here, too, Clay," she assured him. "I know you and your father don't see eye to eye, but if you talk to him . . ."

His hand sliced through the air. "I've talked to him too many times. I can't be the man he expects, Allegra, and if I stay under his thumb I'll be no man at all." He caught her close, spoke against her temple. "Come with me. For 'I am certain of nothing but the holiness of the heart's affections and the truth of imagination.' "

She loved it when he quoted the old poets such as Keats. Clayton Howard knew all the ways to turn a phrase and take away her objections. But this time, instead of sweeping her away, his touch raised a panic.

She'd just come into her own. She was somebody. How could he ask her to leave?

She pushed him back. "Clay, be reasonable. Everyone knows there's nothing but wilderness and savages beyond the Adirondacks. Boston society is the best in the nation. If you'd just try a little harder, I'm sure you could fit in."

"That's the problem," he said, his warm voice cooling. "I don't want to fit in, Allegra. I want more. I thought you'd want more, too."

She could not imagine what more there might be. Boston ladies married well, bore children, entertained family and friends, supported worthy causes. How could she do that from some backwoods hovel?

"There now," she'd said as if soothing a petulant child. "I'm sure we can discuss this another time when we've both had a chance to think about it." She'd linked her arm with his. "They should be playing a polka soon. I know you like that dance."

He'd touched her face with his free hand,

fingers tracing the curve of her cheek. "I would take any opportunity to dance with you, Allegra. My feelings won't change."

She'd thought he meant his devotion to her would never change. But two days later, he'd left Boston, and she hadn't set eyes on him again until they'd met on the pier. It seemed Clayton Howard's devotion was to his future, not theirs. Her parents and his had encouraged her to swallow her disappointment and marry Frank. Frank, who had never argued with her, who had been her dear friend as long as she could remember. And so a month later, she and Frank had wed amid the smiling approval of Boston society, a society she could no longer abide.

She didn't remember reaching the bottom of the stairs. The touch of Clay's hand on her arm drew her up.

"Be reasonable, Allegra," he murmured, offering a smile that would once have set her to blushing. "I have no intention of being an annoyance. But I think we both agree it's my duty to protect you."

"Duty?" Allie shook her head. "This journey was my choice, sir. You have no duty to protect me from my future. I can handle myself on the frontier. You forget, my ancestors civilized Boston."

Clay snorted, dropping her arm. "Is that your reason for going? You think the fine citizens of Seattle need to be civilized? There isn't a fellow in the territory who will thank you for it."

"On the contrary," Allie insisted. "Mr. Mercer assured us that we will be welcome additions to the city, serving to bring it to its full potential. He, sir, has a vision."

Clay rolled his eyes. "Spare me. I've spent the last hour watching how easily Mercer's plans fell apart. No one seemed to know who had paid and who hadn't. It wouldn't surprise me if Mercer had skipped town with your money. You've been duped, Allegra. Admit it."

Anger was pushing up inside her again. Why were her ideas never taken seriously? Why was she always the one who had to bend to another's insistence?

"Just because you dream small, Clay Howard," she told him, "doesn't mean other men have the same narrow vision. And neither do I. I will pay you back every penny, I will allow you to spend time with Gillian, but I won't listen to another word against our plans. Do I make myself clear, sir?"

Any Boston gentleman who had borne the brunt of her anger would have begged her pardon, immediately and profusely. Clay merely lowered his head until his gaze was level with hers. Something fierce leaped behind the cool green.

"Don't expect me to jump when you snap your fingers, Allegra," he said. "I paid your passage because this trip seems to be important to you. But I won't nod in agreement like a milk cow to everything you say. I've been to Seattle. I know the dangers of the frontier. I owe it to Frank to protect you from them."

As if in agreement, the *Continental* shuddered, and a deep throb pulsed up through the deck. Allie was tumbling forward, her feet not her own. She landed against something firm and solid — Clay.

His arms came around her, and she found herself against his chest. His gaze met hers, seemed to warm, to draw her in. She couldn't catch her breath. Once, she'd dreamed of his embrace, his kiss.

Heat flared in her cheeks at the memory, and she pulled herself out of his arms. "You owe Frank nothing, Clay Howard. And you owe me less. If you insist on coming to Seattle with us, you'd better remember that."

CHAPTER FOUR

Clay paused while Allegra continued into the salon. In truth, he felt as if the jolt of the ship starting forward had knocked some of the breath out of him. It had been a long time since he'd held Allegra in his arms, and, for the sake of his sanity, it ought never to happen again. Hadn't he learned by now that he was no match for Boston society?

In fact, it was the suffocating chill of Boston high society that had driven him west, far from everything he'd ever known. He couldn't regret it. He'd climbed mountains, tops shimmering with snow, ten times the size of Beacon Hill. He'd crossed rivers wider than the Charles and more swiftly flowing. He'd met Indian chiefs with as much pride as his late father, lady prospectors with more presence than his mother. Riding across the vast prairies, he'd realized how small he was and how big the God he served.

It was God's urging that had propelled him back to Boston when Clay had received the letter telling him about Frank's death. Like the prodigal son, he'd come to make amends. He wanted to explain to his mother why he'd left, to make sure Allegra was doing all right with Frank gone. He'd taken a room at Boston's finest hotel, Parker's; bought a new suit of clothes; even hired a carriage to take him to his family home.

No fatted calf awaited him. Though his father had died several years ago, Clay had hoped his mother would receive him. But the person waiting for him in somber black in the elegant parlor was his cousin Gerald.

"A great deal has changed since you left, cousin," he'd said, his icy blue eyes staring across the space, every blond hair pomaded back from his narrow face. "With Frank gone, I've had to take up the responsibilities you refused to honor."

Clay's hands had fisted at the sides of his fancy suit. "I'm here now. Where's my mother?"

"Indisposed." Gerald had all but sneered. "And quite unwilling to see you. It is my unhappy duty to inform you of the fact."

"She has no interest in where I've been?" Clay challenged. "What I've done?"

"None," his cousin said. "It doesn't matter where you've been. It matters that you weren't here. We all know it should have been you in that field near Hatcher's Run."

Of course it should have been him. He was the oldest, the better rider, the best shot. He'd had the advantage of a year of military training in a school that specialized in turning willful boys into disciplined men. Frank hadn't had to attend that school. Frank was the good son, obedient, a friend to all who knew him. He didn't know why his brother had gone to war, when so many of the wealthy families paid a poorer boy to fight in their son's stead when their son had been drafted. According to the friend who had written Clay, Frank had gone down protecting others who had been wounded, considerate even to the end.

Clay raised his head. "If you've accepted responsibility for my mother and Frank's widow, I applaud you. Just know that I'm willing to help, whatever they need."

His cousin's tight smile was the only answer.

The trip back to the hotel had been mercifully short, for all Clay's emotions ran higher than the horses on the hired coach. He'd been throwing his things back in his satchel when the bellman came to tell him that a Mrs. Howard was waiting for him downstairs.

Immediately his mind had gone to Allegra, and he pushed past the fellow in his rush to see her. But the woman who perched on one of the scarlet upholstered chairs in the hotel's ornate parlor was gray haired, her bearing cool, composed in her silver-colored gown trimmed in black lace and jet beads.

"Mother," he said, going to her.

Gillian Howard's thin lips trembled, but she did not offer her pale cheek for his kiss. "Clayton. I thought that was you when I looked out the window. You came home."

Was he mad to hear hope behind the words? "I wanted to talk to you," he confirmed, sinking onto a chair beside her. "I wanted to see Allegra."

Before he could continue, she reached out and clutched his arm, fingers tight against his sleeve.

"That's why I'm here, son," she said, calm voice belying her hold on him. "Allegra is missing, and you're the only one who can bring her home."

She'd gone on to explain her daughter-in-law's fascination with Asa Mercer's story about struggling Seattle and the chance of making it a paradise on earth.

"It's the same ridiculous pie-in-the-sky tale that sent you west," she'd lamented,

65

dabbing at her eyes with a lace-edged handkerchief. "You came back . . . you must know the truth. Tell her this hope in Seattle is a lie. Convince her to come home. Please, Clay, she's all I have left!"

Her pain had touched him just as Allegra's had today, yet some part of him hurt that his mother could not consider him part of the family. "I thought Gerald was taking care of everything for you," he couldn't help commenting.

She'd lowered her gaze even as she tucked her handkerchief into her reticule. "Gerald has been a great blessing to me. He is very good about seeing that the family carries on. I cannot ask this of him."

But she could ask it of him. Gerald was a gentleman; Clay had thrown off the label. His cousin might not be willing to do all it would take to retrieve Allegra. His mother obviously believed Clay had fewer scruples. Though Clay liked to think he was still an honorable man for all he'd chosen a different path than the one his parents had picked out for him, he could not argue that he was his mother's best tool for the job. He was more than ready to do Allegra a service, particularly if it meant saving her from the mistakes he'd made.

Now he snorted. And wasn't he doing a

jolly good job of saving Allegra? Instead of sending her home to Boston, he'd aided and abetted her in running away! Shaking his head at his own behavior, he entered the lower salon. Those passengers who had not yet been assigned staterooms were clustered around a hatch at the end of the room. Allegra and her daughter were looking on, but he couldn't tell whether they were curious or concerned. He pushed himself to the center, where a pretty, petite blonde was struggling with a brass latch embedded in the floor.

On seeing him, she put on a winsome smile. "Please, sir," she said sweetly, "would you mind helping me with this?"

The others made room for him, their gazes expectant, as if he were about to open a fabled treasure cave. Clay was more suspicious.

"What is this?" he asked, positioning himself over the hatch.

"Access to the coal bin, sir," she replied. "I was told by Mr. Mercer to open it immediately when we set sail out of quarantine. He said it was very important."

Clay couldn't understand why anyone needed to see into a dark, dusty coal bin, but he had to admit to curiosity as to why Mercer had thought it so important. He bent to haul on the ring, and the hatch opened. People leaned around his arm, peering into the gloom. He could see Allegra and her redheaded friend exchanging frowning glances.

"It's safe now, Mr. Mercer," the blonde called into the void. "You can come out."

Allegra stiffened in obvious shock, while others put their hands to their mouths. Coal-dusted fingers waved above the edge of the hole, and Clay bent to tug Asa Mercer to the floor of the salon. He was a slender man, not yet thirty, with a solemn face and a brisk manner. Now his curly reddish hair and whiskers were speckled with black, his long face striped with grime. He tugged down on his paisley waistcoat and beamed at those around him.

"The coal is well stored and sufficient for the first leg of our journey," he reported as if he'd merely climbed into the bin to inspect it. "It appears we are under way. I look forward to a fine voyage, a very fine voyage."

Allegra stared at him a moment, then turned her gaze to Clay's. Very likely, they'd reached the same conclusion.

She had no one to rely on but him, and she had every right to be concerned.

It was not the most auspicious start to their journey. While many of the women welcomed their benefactor, Allie couldn't shake the image of Mr. Mercer rising from the coal bin. This was the man in whom they'd placed their trust?

Catherine evidently had similar concerns. "I'm greatly disappointed in him," she confessed as they all went to find their staterooms. "He paid his own passage, but it seems as if he promised space to anyone who asked. When it became clear not everyone would be allowed aboard, he hid to avoid telling them the truth."

Allie glanced into one of the rooms they were passing. "I don't understand it. There can't be more than one hundred passengers aboard, and there seems to be room for at least three times that. What happened to the other people?"

"Perhaps they saw those wretched reports in the papers," Catherine mused. "The ones claiming we'd be eaten by bears or enslaved by savages."

Perhaps. The editorial articles had nearly made Allie change her mind. But Mr. Mercer had seemed so earnest, his vision of a settled Seattle so clear. She knew she wasn't the only woman who'd put her faith in him. Was he actually a coward? And what about the money she'd paid him? Was he a terrible cheat and liar as well? Or was it the mismanagement of the steamship company that was to blame? She'd read stories in the Boston papers about how ruthless Ben Holladay could be in business dealings.

"I don't care how many rooms he has on this great tub," Maddie proclaimed, "so long as we each get a bed."

Catherine smiled at her. "I'm sure we'll each have a bed, even though we'll likely have to share a room. I'm just glad you and I could produce our tickets, Madeleine."

Maddie stopped at a door at the end of the lower salon and grinned at Allie. "And would you lookie here now! It seems you and me will be together in this room, Allegra, my dear."

"You and I," Catherine corrected her, pausing to peer inside the room, then at the number on the door. "Number thirty-five. As I am number fifteen, I must be on the upper deck. Shall we meet for supper?"

Maddie wiggled her fingers at Catherine. "La-di-da — do you think those of us on the lower floor will be welcomed above our stations?"

Catherine tsked. "I cannot imagine anywhere you would not be welcomed, Madeleine dear." She bent to kiss Gillian on the cheek, then straightened. "I shall see you all shortly."

Maddie sighed as Catherine strolled away. "Not an unkind bone in her body, so there isn't. But she's mad to think I'll be welcomed at her table."

As they'd waited for the ship to sail, Allie had learned a great deal about both her friends. Catherine came from a small town outside Boston, the daughter of a prominent physician. Maddie had been quieter about her background, but Allie knew she had journeyed from Ireland as a child with her father, only to meet prejudice on America's shores. She seemed to expect it now wherever she went.

"The good ship *Continental* is not New York," Allie informed her, leading Gillian into the little room. "We'll be spending a quarter year together. The sooner we learn to live in peace, the better."

"Just you remember that," Maddie told her, "when that handsome Mr. Howard comes calling."

Allie refused to dignify the comment with a response. Instead, she set to work making the room their home.

The cabin was a cozy, white-washed space, with two berths stacked one atop the other along one wall and surrounded by flowered chintz curtains. A narrow padded bench sat opposite with room underneath to stow their trunks.

"And look here," Allie said, leading her frowning daughter to the tall slender wooden cabinet between the bunks and the bench. "There's a mirror on top so we can tidy our hair, and a desk that folds out for writing letters."

Maddie pointed to the wood railing around the top of the cabinet. "And that's to keep our belongings from tipping over when the sea rocks the boat."

Gillian's frown only deepened.

Allie forced a smile as she hung her cloak on a hook on one side of the cabinet. Gillian was used to much finer things, a room three times the size of this one, fancy dresses, fine food, but she was also used to being bossed about every second of her day under harsh discipline no child should have to endure. Changing that situation was more than worth lesser accommodations.

So, she showed Gillian how to make up the berths with the bedding they'd brought, hung a few of their things in the little cabinet, tucked the letters Frank had written her carefully in the back of the trunk. The only time she truly felt a pang of regret was when she arranged her two favorite books and Bible on one end of the bench for easy reach.

She and Frank had devoted one room of their home to a library. How they'd loved to sit and read aloud by the fire or share insights from their private reading. All she'd had room to carry were *Ivanhoe* and *Pride and Prejudice.* Both she could one day share with Gillian.

As they finished setting the room to rights, Maddie stood back and nodded. "Just like home. And we even have a sheet and blanket left over to be charitable to Mr. Howard."

Allie had been stowing her trunk under the bench. Now she paused to glance up at her friend. Because she'd had to sneak away from the Howard mansion, their belongings consisted only of what could fit in the trunk that she had convinced a footman to hide in the carriage house for her.

She'd had a valise, as well, with many of Gillian's dresses, but it had been stolen. Allie had spent the evenings waiting for the *Continental* to sail by taking apart one of her gowns to make clothes for her daughter. With each item they currently possessed so hard won, how could she think of giving any away?

"Mr. Howard can certainly fend for himself," she replied, pushing in the trunk and rising. "I see no need to rescue him from his own choices."

Maddie cocked her head. "Even when he was so kind as to try to rescue you from yours?"

"Don't you find that just a bit overweening?" Allie asked with a grimace.

"Oh, to be sure. But a man will be a man, so they will. And as men go, he's a charming one. What other gent would set his own plans aside to further yours?"

Allie stared at her. She'd been so busy arguing for her right to take this trip that she hadn't considered why Clay was taking it. He must have had plans for the next three months, and Boston could not have been part of them. She knew what little fondness he carried for his former home. Yet he'd said his mother had sent him to find Allie, so he must have been to Boston. He couldn't have reached the ship in time any other way. Why was he willing to come with them now?

She did not have a chance to ask him until the next day. After she and Maddie finished setting up their stateroom, they joined Mr. Debro for a tour of the ship. They started on the lower deck, which was completely enclosed in hickory, the passageways lit by the golden glow of lanterns along the way. The deep thrum of the steam engine vibrated the floor and made her feel as if she'd wandered into a cozy hive.

"But you mustn't enter the engine room, ladies," the purser warned as they paused before the open door. "The crew works hard to keep the boilers burning, day and night. They have no time for pleasantries."

Allie was more interested in the activities aboard ship, for she was fairly certain keeping up their small room would not require all their time. She was pleased to find that the lower salon had games like checkers and ninepin, and the upper salon had a piano just waiting unpacking.

The upper deck was exposed to the elements. Already a cold breeze whipped about the buildings along the planking. But Allie knew once they reached warmer weather she and her daughter could promenade there.

"The wheelhouse is in the stern," Mr. Debro explained, pointing as he talked. "And the officers' quarters are in the bow. You will have no need to visit either."

"Is that an explanation or a warning?" Maddie whispered to Allie, twinkle in her brown eyes.

"But the officers will dine with us, won't they?" another woman asked, and Allie could see many countenances turned hopefully to the purser's.

Mr. Debro reddened. "That is up to the captain, madam. But I believe, as he has his family with him this trip, he intends to dine in the upper salon."

Maddie looked at Allie as if to say *I told you so.* She was equally amused when Mr. Debro pointed out the larger cabins in the central building on the upper deck. The beds were bigger, the upholstery finer, the space brighter from the latticed windows overlooking the sea.

"These may appear more elegant," Allie whispered to Maddie, "but they are likely colder on a winter's night than our room."

Maddie nodded as if that were fair enough.

Above the rooms on the upper deck was another space railed in iron chain, a longboat lashed to each corner.

"This is the hurricane deck," Mr. Debro told them, one hand to his head to keep his hat in place. "As you will notice, it's most often windy here, but it is a fine place to take your constitutional in the morning."

They climbed down the narrow stairs in

time to see Clay exiting one of the upper-deck staterooms. He tugged off his hat and inclined his head to the ladies, several of whom giggled behind their hands as if they'd never seen a gentleman before. He went so far as to wink at Gillian, who turned her head to watch him as they passed. Allie kept her own head high.

"I'll see you at dinner tonight, Mrs. Howard," he called after her.

"Someone's made a conquest," one girl said with a laugh.

Allie ignored her. In fact, she did her best to discourage any conversation with Clay when they gathered for dinner that evening and he sat himself nearby. She set Gillian between them at the table, then directed her attention to Catherine and Maddie on her left. She slid the platter of salted beef to him along the table to avoid any chance their hands or gazes might meet. And she answered any questions put to her as shortly as possible.

"You're working far too hard," Catherine told her after dinner had ended and the three women and Gillian were clustered around one of the small tables along the wall. "Simply ignore the fellow. He seems clever enough to understand your intent."

"Oh, to be sure," Maddie agreed with a

glance at Clay, who was leaning against the opposite wall. "And if you're certain you're uninterested, you won't mind if I should cast my net in his direction."

"Madeleine," Catherine scolded, "if Allegra has determined the gentleman to be lacking, we would be wise to look elsewhere."

Allie bit her lip to hold back hasty words. In truth, she'd once admired Clay, although she knew some in Boston had been shocked by his behavior — racing his horse against his friends', spending his money on wild schemes and strange inventions. And he criticized her for following Asa Mercer!

Still, no matter her opinion, she could not fault Clay's behavior that night. The passengers had been divided between the upper salon and the lower, and it seemed that Maddie was right, because finances and connections clearly played a part as to which person went where. Most of the people in the lower salon with her and Maddie were common folk, clothes presentable but worn, and the common language made Catherine raise a brow from time to time at the mismatched verbs and colorful adjectives. Catherine and Clay had been given spots in the upper salon, but both had come downstairs to dine.

Though Clay didn't go out of his way to introduce himself to any of the other passengers, he always spoke politely to anyone who approached him, Allie noticed. He had helped one of the older widows to dinner when she couldn't manage the hard wood chairs. He swapped stories in the corner with a group of older gentlemen after dinner, casting no more than a glance and a smile at a passing lady. She couldn't tell if he had truly changed since the days she'd known him, or whether he was merely putting on a good show for the other passengers.

"Good night, Mrs. Howard, Ms. Gillian," he said when she started for her stateroom with Gillian in hand. "Sweet dreams."

Her cheeks warmed, but she managed a nod and kept walking.

Their first night aboard ship was bitterly cold, and she was thankful for their inside stateroom, where heat from the lower salon seeped around the door. The warmth of Gillian's body pressed against hers on the little berth helped, as well. But even as she lay cuddled beside her daughter, Clay once more intruded on her thoughts.

Was he freezing in an outer berth where the wind whistled through the latticed windows? Was his only covering that pieced-together fur coat? How would he even be able to fold his length onto the narrow berth? She finally found sleep by assuring herself she would do her Christian duty and check on him in the morning.

Having left Maddie dressing Gillian, Allie found him on the upper deck, where many of the women were enjoying a moment in the rare January sunshine. Like her, they were bundled in coats or cloaks that reached past their hips, full skirts swinging as they walked. The *Continental* was out into the Atlantic, Allie knew, and steaming south. She looked for the familiar sight of the coastline and found only the rolling blue-gray waves. How amazing, when all her life she'd seen no farther than the islands dotting Boston Harbor.

Clay might also have been admiring the view. He was wearing his heavy fur coat, his hands deep in the pockets, his breath making puffs of the cool air as he spoke. Three female passengers were clustered around him, all chattering and flashing smiles, their faces turned up to his like flowers before the light. Allie stiffened, then immediately chided herself. She had no claim over Clay. If another woman thought she could tame him, Allie only wished her luck.

He looked up just then, and their gazes

met. The smile that brightened his face made her stomach flutter. How silly! She wasn't a debutante meeting the mighty Clay Howard for the first time. She squared her shoulders and marched toward him.

He met her halfway. "Good morning, Allegra," he said with a nod of welcome. "How did you and Gillian fare your first night aboard?"

One of the older women nearby cast them a look with raised brows. She couldn't know their past history and family connections gave him the right to use her first name.

"Tolerably well, Mr. Howard," Allie said, making sure to use his last name. She took his arm and drew him a little farther away from the others toward the deck chairs that rested along the wall of the first-class quarters. "And you? Ms. O'Rourke wondered whether you had all you needed."

She couldn't confess that she'd wondered, too, but he didn't question her. Instead, his smile deepened, showing a dimple along the right side of his mouth. "Give her my thanks, but tell her not to worry. I'm set up fairly well. I'm bunking with Mr. Conant, a reporter from the *Times,* and he was kind enough to offer me the lower bunk so I can stick out my feet. And Ms. Stevens and the widow Hennessy provided me with sheets and blankets when they heard I had none."

She should be relieved that he had been so well supported. Yet some part of her was disappointed she hadn't been the one to make sure he was comfortable.

"Well, then," she said, removing her hand from his arm. "It seems you have no further need of us. Answer me one question, if you will, and I'll leave you to your promenade."

He cocked his head. The breeze pulled free a strand of red-gold hair, and she had to fight the impulse to smooth it back from his face. "And what question would that be?" he asked with a smile, as if confident of his ability to answer it.

"Why did you join us on this trip? You can't have been planning on spending three or more months at sea."

"No, indeed," he said with a chuckle. "But make no mistake, Allegra. I joined the company of the *Continental* because of you."

There went her stomach fluttering again. "Because of me, sir?" Her question sounded breathless, and she cleared her throat.

"You and Gillian," he clarified. "It's a long way with more dangers than you can know. Someone has to protect you."

Oh, but he was impossible! "Did it never dawn on you, sir, that I might be able to protect myself?"

His shrug did nothing to stem the rise of her frustration.

She stepped back from him. "I will have you know that I'm fairly self-sufficient. Should you need *our* help on this trip, you can find Gillian and me in stateroom thirty-five, on the port side of the lower salon. We'd be more than glad to protect *you.*"

CHAPTER FIVE

Clay watched as Allegra turned and swept away. Even bundled in her wool cloak, there was something defiant in the height of her head, the set of her dainty boot against the deck. She was so very determined to do this on her own.

He couldn't blame her. He'd felt the same way when he'd left Boston. He couldn't wait to put distance between him and everything connected with the name of Howard — arrogance and greed and overbearing authority. What he had now, little as it might seem to her, he'd earned with the brains and brawn the good Lord had given him. He wasn't about to change that, for anyone.

"Now, there's a fine-looking woman." A gentleman strolled up to Clay, the golden lion's head on the handle of his ebony walking stick glinting in the sunlight. He offered his gloved hand. "Josiah Reynolds. I understand you're a Howard."

Clay didn't accept the man's hand. "How can I help you?"

Reynolds lowered his arm. In his gray sack coat hanging loose about his shoulders, he looked short and sturdy, and only the bristling brown mustache over his thick lips prevented him from resembling a bulldog.

"No help required but the honor of your company," he assured Clay, pulling his coat closer against the icy breeze that puffed off the ocean. "The way I figure it, those of us who are bachelors must band together if we're to survive this trip unshackled."

Clay grinned at his joke. "I thought all the ladies were set on finding a husband in Seattle, not aboard ship."

Reynolds smiled. "I hope you're right. My home is in San Francisco. I may yet escape the noose." He glanced at a passing lady who had prominent front teeth and shuddered.

"If you ask me," Clay said with a shake of his head, "you could do worse than to marry one of these women. They have more gumption than half the men I know. It isn't easy leaving everything and everyone behind."

"True enough," he agreed, giving his walking stick a thoughtful twirl. "But any lady who has to cross a continent to find a husband must have something wrong with her."

Clay scowled at him, and the fellow excused himself to find other company. Clay shook his head again, this time at his own attitude. Only yesterday, he had been equally certain that only the desperate would take advantage of Mercer's offer. But the ladies he'd met so far challenged that theory.

Allegra's friend Ms. Stanway was as fearless as she was fetching. Ms. Stevens, who had offered him the blanket last night, was as sweet-tempered as she was sweet-faced. Any number of these women could have found beaux even in the war-ravaged East. Why take a chance on Seattle?

"And a pleasant morning to you, Mr. Howard," Ms. O'Rourke said as she sashayed up to him. The breeze had turned her cheeks a pleasing pink, and her brown eyes sparkled as she grinned at him, arms buried in the sleeves of her rust-colored wool cloak. "Still unengaged? Such a slacker, you are."

She must have overhead his conversation with Reynolds. Clay chuckled. "I'm sure you'll have no trouble finding a gentleman to propose, if that's what you're after."

She leaned against the railing. "And isn't

that what every lass is after? A nice rich lad of good family who's kind on the eyes."

Clay's surprise must have been showing, for she laughed and said, "What — don't all you gents pine for something similar? A pretty girl who will cook and bake and clean for you?" She fluttered her cinnamon-colored lashes. "Some of us have better ways to spend our time." She pushed off the railing and all but skipped down the deck.

"You'll find Ms. O'Rourke quite outspoken," Ms. Stanway said in her wake. She offered Clay a smile that did not seem to warm her blue eyes, which were a few shades lighter than Allegra's. "But she is correct. Not all of us are hoping to marry when we reach Seattle." She nodded to two of the women who were standing farther along the railing, gazes out to sea. "The Prescott sisters worked in the cotton mills in Lowell. Those were shuttered during the war and don't look to be opening soon."

"So they're seeking employment," Clay surmised. "And what about you, Ms. Stanway? Why are you going so far from home?"

That smile remained frozen on her face. "I lost my brother and father to the war, sir. There is no home to return to. Excuse me."

She continued past, head high, carriage serene. The ocean breeze no more than ruffled the feather on her hat. He had a feeling if she had debuted in Boston they would have dubbed her the Ice Princess. But then, they wouldn't know the story of her losses.

He'd thought he knew Allegra's story. She'd been born into a well-respected though slightly less affluent family than his. She'd risen to the top of Boston social circles. She'd married Frank; they'd had a child together. But though she'd lost her husband in the war, she still had a home to return to. As much as he'd fought with his family, he knew they would never require her to find a job to support her and her daughter, if for no other reason than such uncivilized behavior might harm their social standing. With a place assured her, why was she so set on Seattle?

Allie spent most of her second day aboard ship learning the routines of mealtimes, setting up her own routine with Gillian and determining how she and Maddie would share chores in their little room. Mr. Mercer also gathered his little flock and expressed his concerns for their safety.

"The eyes of the world are upon us, my dears," he told them as he paced before them in the upper salon, the tails of his coat flapping with each step. "We must do all we can to prove we are endowed with the utmost of taste and civility."

"He should have thought of that before he hid in the coal bin," Maddie murmured to Allie.

Mercer must have heard her, for he clasped his hands behind his frock coat, gazed at his charges and explained. "I am certain some of you were concerned about our little contretemps leaving New York. Rest assured that matters have been resolved."

Many of the women seemed to accept that, but Allie could not keep silent. "Then you've determined what became of the missing money and will reimburse those who paid twice."

Mercer adjusted the black cravat at his throat. "As I said, madam, the matter has been resolved, and I apologize for any confusion or consternation it may have caused. Now is the time for every lady under my escort to focus on her future in Seattle." His gaze swept them again. "And there will be no fraternizing with the officers."

Several of the women stiffened at that, and two went so far as to argue with him.

"Mother?" Gillian asked, turning to glance up at Allie from her place in Allie's lap.

"What's fraternizing?"

"Nothing that need concern you for a good number of years," Allie assured her. Maddie smiled at that, but Allie couldn't help wondering about their benefactor's motives. She had been willing to give him the benefit of the doubt concerning the tickets, but his vague assurances were not satisfying. Besides, when he had lectured in the Boston area, he'd said this trip would help the women start over after their losses in the war. If they wanted a husband and found one aboard ship, why did that concern him?

She found herself looking forward to dinner and the chance to ask Clay about the matter. Very likely it was that anticipation that set her heart beating faster when she sighted him entering the room.

Before she could question him, however, she had to take care of her daughter. She focused on cutting the slab of salty beef into smaller chunks Gillian could lift with her fork. Several of the other people were poking at the beans, mouths twisted in disgust, but Gillian sat beside Allie spooning up the brown blobs and chewing thoughtfully.

"Do you like them?" Allie couldn't help asking.

"No, thank you," Gillian said. "They're icky."

Maddie, who was seated on Gillian's other side, shook her head. "They're filling at least. But you're a good girl to eat them."

"Good girls eat everything on their plates," Gillian said woodenly, as if repeating a lesson. "Good girls say please and thank-you."

"Kind people say please and thank-you," Allie replied, hurting for her daughter. "What you decide to eat has nothing to do with whether you are a good or bad person."

Gillian frowned at her. "Then may I please have a piece of cake instead?"

Maddie laughed as she gave Gillian a hug. "Sure'n, me darling, I'd bake you one right now if we had the proper ingredients."

"And I'd let you eat it," Allie promised. "As it is, this seems to be the best the *Continental* can do. When we reach Seattle, I'll bake you a cake myself."

Gillian nodded and returned to her beans.

Allie nodded, as well. She'd never baked a cake before in her life, but surely Maddie or one of the other women could teach her. She hadn't washed dishes or made beds before, either, and she was managing that. It wasn't talent that was required but determination, and the Lord had given her plenty of that lately.

That was why she turned to Clay, who was sitting just down the table from them and looking no more pleased with the fare.

"Mr. Mercer said he had resolved the financial issues," she told Clay. "Have you been reimbursed?"

He smiled at her, and she could not help smiling back. "Mr. Mercer hasn't said a word to me, but your presence and Gillian's are all the reimbursement I need."

It was a charming thing to say, and she felt her cheeks heating. Enough of that!

"Then I can only hope to take up the matter with Mr. Holladay," she promised Clay, "when we reach Seattle."

He shrugged, and she wasn't sure if it was because he thought she'd never convince the wily transportation king to part with the money or if Clay truly didn't care. She made herself focus on the conversation around her, which, thankfully, was generally more satisfying than the food. She found it amazing how many people from all walks of life had decided to make this journey to Seattle.

Mrs. Boardman, for example, was blind, and her husband was particularly solicitous of her because, he told Allie with great joy, she was expecting their first child.

"Though it does concern me that we have

only a dentist abroad for medical assistance," Mrs. Boardman told Allie, one hand on her swelling belly.

"Ms. Stanway is a nurse," Allie assured her. "I'm certain she'd be glad to help."

Clay spoke up. "You may want to settle in San Francisco if a doctor's care is important to you, ma'am. There's only one in Seattle, and he treats natives as well as the settlers, so he tends to be busy."

Mrs. Boardman thanked him for his advice, but Allie couldn't help her frown. Only one doctor in the growing town? What if Gillian became ill or was injured? Would Catherine's skills be enough to save her?

"Mortality on the frontier is notably high," a young lady named Ms. Cropper put in as if she found the matter fascinating. "Cholera, typhus, dysentery, scalpings."

Allie shuddered. Time to turn this conversation back to the pleasant. "New lands to discover," she countered. "Opportunities for new friends, family."

"Husbands," Maddie put in with a wink.

"Employment," Catherine added.

Others chimed in then with their plans to teach, to establish businesses. Allie caught Clay watching, a slight frown settled on his brow. Had they given him as much food for thought as he'd given them?

The meal ended with optimism restored. Everyone seemed in an excellent mood and so excited about their journey, the sights they'd see along the way, the hopes they had for their destination. But as the evening wore on and groups formed to read aloud, talk or play cards, Allie began to feel a change in the ship. Saltcellars slid from one side of the table to the other. Pots clanked in the galley. When she stood, she had to put out a hand to steady herself before taking a step.

One by one, the other women grew quiet, turned ashen. Some dashed up the stairs to the deck, and Allie caught a quick glimpse of them leaning over the railing before the door swung shut behind them and cut off the light. Others retired to their bunks. Clay helped more than one to the kitchen in search of hot water or empty bowls.

Allie was only thankful she, Maddie and Gillian were spared the bouts of seasickness. They retired a short time later and passed the night listening to the dishes clatter against each other in the galley. More than one woman called out that the ship must be sinking. Gillian clung to Allie with a whimper.

Allie had been that afraid many times — when she'd realized her answer at the ball had driven Clay out of Boston, when Frank had marched away to war, when Mrs. Howard had advised her in that cold voice that Allie's only choice was to marry Gerald. Now she could not fear. Despite Clay's comments about medical care in Seattle, she knew she was on the right path.

"The ship isn't sinking," she assured Gillian, stroking her daughter's silky hair in the dim cabin. "Captain Windsor is very wise, and every sailor we've met is strong and able. They'll see us safely through this storm."

"But it's so bumpy," Gillian said, huddling closer.

"Think of it like a carriage ride along a country road," Allie advised. "Just a few bumps and then we'll be at our destination."

"Seattle?" Gillian piped up hopefully.

"Seattle," Allie promised. "But not for a while yet. We must be patient."

Just then someone pounded on their stateroom door, and she recognized Mr. Debro's voice. "Mrs. Howard! Mrs. Howard! Come quick! It's Mr. Howard, and he's in a bad way!"

Clay couldn't remember being so miserable. He kept his eyes tight shut as the ship bucked and rolled. With a *whoosh,* a wave heaved up over the bulkhead and doused the door of his stateroom. An answering slosh told him that some of the seawater had forced its way under the door and was spilling across the hardwood floor.

Father, if it's Your will that I die tonight, I'm ready.

A moment later, he heard the door click open.

"Shut it, Conant," he ordered. "Or we'll drown."

"No one will drown today, Mr. Howard," Allegra said.

Clay's eyes snapped open. In the dim light of the brass lantern teetering atop the cabinet between the berths, she stood in her wool cloak with her friend Ms. Stanway beside her. Neither had donned a hat, and their unbound hair streamed down around their faces, bright blond and midnight black, the strands glistening with the rain.

He tried to sit up, despite the protest of his stomach that persisted in heaving along with the waves. He hadn't done more than yank off his boots before falling into bed and pulling up the covers, but he didn't want Allegra to see him like this.

She darted forward. "None of that, sir. Lie down, if you please, and let Ms. Stanway have a look at you."

"I'm a nurse," her friend reminded him, venturing closer. As Clay lay back, she felt his forehead, the touch cool and moist. "Give me your hand, Mr. Howard."

Clay pulled his fingers out from under the blanket and was ashamed to see them shaking. Ms. Stanway didn't so much as raise a brow as she pressed her own fingers against his wrist, holding it steady. Around her, he could see Allegra watching, her white teeth worrying her lower lip as if she was concerned.

It had been a long time since anyone was concerned about him. Warmth bathed his frozen limbs.

Ms. Stanway released him and straightened. "No sign of a fever, though his heart seems to be beating a bit fast," she reported to Allegra before turning to Clay. "Are you in distress, Mr. Howard?"

"I'm fine," Clay assured them, then had to clamp his mouth shut a moment as his stomach threatened to climb out of it. "There are others worse off. Go tend to them."

The ship rolled, and Allegra and her friend grabbed the wooden posts of the berths to keep from toppling over. Clay felt the bile rising with the waves.

"Out!" he ordered.

"Basin," Ms. Stanway countered, hanging on to the bed with one hand and pointing with the other.

Allegra allowed herself to fall across the cabin onto the bench, then braced herself against it to wrestle open the bottom compartment on the cabinet. Inside lay a porcelain-lined cast-iron pot.

Again the ship rolled, and she tumbled against the cabinet. Her face twisted with the impact.

"Just go!" Clay begged.

She ignored him, tugging up the pot and pushing it across the floor to his side.

Clay tightened his lips, hands pressing against his gut. He was supposed to be the strong one. He knew how to best the odds. He'd crossed the continent, twice. He'd survived the illness, hardship and treachery of the goldfields. He'd helped build dozens of businesses in Seattle. He was here to support Allegra, not the other way around. Even his bunk mate, the reporter Roger Conant, was out helping the moaning women.

"You'll feel better if you let it go," Ms. Stanway advised.

He knew he'd feel much worse.

"It's all right, Clay," Allegra murmured, shifting across from the bench to kneel beside him, one hand braced against the wall to hold herself steady. "I've tended Gillian when she was sick, and after Frank went to war, I helped at the hospital. I don't mind."

She should. Tending the sick might be a noble calling, but she hadn't been born to it. She should be arranging dinner parties, skating arm in arm with a handsome suitor on the pond at Boston Common, dancing the night away, not kneeling at his side. Yet he knew another minute and he'd have no choice but to accept her help.

"Please go," he told her and nearly winced at the pleading tone in his voice.

Her gaze was as unyielding as the sea pounding the ship. "I am going nowhere, sir, until I know you're all right."

He wanted to tell her to forget about him, that he'd done just fine alone up until this point, that he didn't need anyone and preferred it that way.

But his stomach had other ideas.

"There, now," she said after he'd finished coughing over the pot. Her hand rubbed strength into his back. "You'll feel better shortly." As if the sea agreed with her, it calmed a moment, and Ms. Stanway took the fetid basin to toss its contents into the waves.

Clay lay back and closed his eyes. Gentle

fingers smoothed the hair from his brow.

"Take deep breaths," Allegra murmured. "Everything will be all right now."

Her voice was so soft, so tender, he felt as if she'd wrapped him in fine wool. He wanted to snuggle into it and never come out. "Forgive me," he managed to say.

She gasped, and he opened his eyes again. She was staring at him as if he'd asked her to swim to the bottom of the ocean. "For — for what, sir?" she stammered.

He realized too late that she would remember he needed forgiveness for more than his sorry display a moment ago, but also for leaving Boston, and for abandoning his family and her. He was only glad when Ms. Stanway blew in the door again and shut it firmly behind her with a shudder.

"Have you the ginger, Allegra?" she asked, returning the pot to its place beside Clay as if she expected a repeat performance.

Her question obviously reminded Allegra of why she'd come. "What the cook would part with," she admitted, pulling a pale, plump root from the pocket of her cloak. She broke off a piece and handed it to him.

The spicy scent struck his nostrils, and Clay pressed his head deeper into the pillow to escape it.

"It's all right," she assured him as if he

were a child afraid of a spider on the wall. "It's just ginger. Father always made us chew some before sailing out to the islands. He said it settles the stomach."

He'd tried buffalo and rattlesnake as he'd crossed the country, so ginger couldn't be so bad. Clay accepted the chunk, his strong fingers brushing hers before he ate the ginger. As if she'd been the one to take a bite, she swallowed as she leaned back. The taste reminded him of the cookies the Howards' chef used to bake in the fall.

"Now, lie back," Allegra advised, and he was obeying before he thought better of it. She pulled the blanket up, smoothed it over his chest. Either her hands were trembling, or the ship was rocking again. Her eyes were certainly as deep and stormy as the sea. He could easily drown in her gaze.

"Take slow, even breaths," Ms. Stanway instructed. "In and out, and count to four between each." She put her hand on Allegra's shoulder. "We should go. There are others who need help."

Allegra nodded. She rose, then suddenly bent and put her hand to his cheek, her face soft, but voice firm. "Don't be concerned, Clay. Everything will be all right. God won't let the ship go down."

She was up and out the door before he could ask her how she could be so sure.

CHAPTER SIX

It was another day and night before the *Continental* reached gentle seas again. Leaving Gillian in Maddie's care, Allie worked with Catherine and others who hadn't been affected to ease the discomfort of those who had. Some took quite a while to gain their sea legs, as Mr. Debro called their condition.

If Clay suffered again, he refused to show it, for he was up and about by the next morning. In fact, he recovered so quickly that Allie could almost think she had dreamed the night in his stateroom.

Still, she could not forget the way he'd clung to his pride, or the way he'd looked afterward. She'd never thought to see Clay Howard vulnerable, yet those green eyes had pleaded for understanding, for acceptance of him at his worst. She'd felt the brush of his fingers, and it had shaken her.

Why? She was a widow. She had gained

her independence. She didn't need a man in her life. Why had she wanted to throw herself into his arms? Just because Clay Howard had softened for a moment didn't mean she had to follow suit.

She was almost thankful that there was nothing soft about the man who emerged from his bunk. He answered the breakfast gong with few others, but Allie noticed he didn't take more than tea and then only with a grimace.

"You don't look well, Mr. Howard," the widow Hennessy remarked, patting his hand. "Why don't you return to your berth?"

As a passenger in the finer part of the ship, he had every right to pass his time sitting safely in the upper salon, Allie knew. But Clay shook his head. "I'm fine, ma'am. Thank you for your concern." His gaze met Allie's down the table. "And thank those who came to the rescue last night."

Her face felt hot, and she dropped her gaze to the biscuit she was breaking apart to share with Gillian.

She was glad Catherine requested her help after breakfast, for surely such work would keep her mind off Clay. But everywhere she went, she ran into him. He brought water from the galley for Dr. Barnard and his wife,

104

both of whom had been felled even though the dentist kept trying to rise. When Allie peered in on the widow Chase and her two children, all of whom were ill, she found Clay sweeping out their stateroom for them.

It wasn't only the passengers he helped. Allie and Catherine were clinging to the walls of the first-class accommodations in a rising wind when she spotted Clay right there among the crew, wrestling with a pair of longboats. The vessels had apparently broken loose in the roaring waves, and the crew was trying to save them before they were pulled out to sea.

That night at dinner, the other women named him their hero.

"There's not a family aboard ship that doesn't owe you thanks," Maddie proclaimed, raising her cup of tea in salute.

"I think they're more thankful for Ms. Stanway and Mrs. Howard," Clay countered with a smile to Allie. "Fetching and carrying is easy work compared to nursing."

She could not argue with him there. She had the utmost respect for Catherine's brisk, no-nonsense manner, her calm approach to the groaning passengers. Allie found it hard enough to leave Gillian in Maddie's care while she helped her friend where she could. How could she not respect how readily Clay turned his hand to help those in need?

Of course, some of the other men also offered help. Mr. Debro, the purser, was willing to answer any question she put to him, whether on the workings of the ship or the stages of their journey. Young Matt Kelley, an orphan from Boston who was traveling on a scholarship, watched Gillian when Allie and Maddie were both needed.

Allie had just finished checking on the condition of one of the older widows and was coming out of her first-class stateroom when she nearly collided with another gentleman. He immediately caught her arm to keep her from falling, his walking stick clattering to the deck.

"Forgive me, madam," he said, releasing her to bow. "I should not have interrupted your errand of mercy."

"And I should watch where I'm going," Allie insisted. Indeed, some of the passageways on the ship were so narrow the ladies who preferred steel crinolines had been forced to abandon them to storage in the hold and hemmed up their skirts to fit over petticoats instead.

He tipped his top hat to her. "Josiah Reynolds of San Francisco, at your service."

"Mrs. Howard," she returned. She

purposely did not state her hometown, but he immediately brightened.

"Of the Boston Howards, I presume. Charming family."

Allie's smile felt colder than the wind. "So I have heard. If you'll forgive me, Mr. Reynolds, I should go. I have other passengers I must see."

"Of course." He bent and retrieved his walking stick. "Good day, Mrs. Howard."

It seemed for a time that good days would be difficult to find. But at last the waves quieted, the skies cleared. The passengers ventured out onto the deck again, and the officers relaxed enough to smile and chat before going about their duties. Allie hung out her cloak to dry after her many soakings and tried to turn her mind to her daughter and their future once more.

But even there Clay intruded, for it seemed Gillian could not get her fill of him.

Allie knew she should not have been surprised. There didn't seem to be an unmarried female aboard who was immune to his charm. The widow Hennessy, who had to be approaching her seventieth year, would pat the chair beside her at meals and insist on his company, and he would always join her with a pleasant smile and a friendly word.

Maddie had offered to do his laundry, and without charge, though she was putting aside pennies from the other passengers for similar services.

"But would he take my offer, oh no, not him," Maddie told Allie as her friend swept their stateroom, Gillian standing at the ready with the little wooden dustpan. "He says he'll settle up with me when we reach Seattle." She leaned against the broom as she glanced at Allie. "The darling boy has the money, doesn't he? He wasn't having me on?"

Allie paused in making the bottom berth. "He had money enough to pay for Gillian's and my passage as well as his own."

Maddie smiled. "Well, if he had money once, sure'n he'll have it again. That's good enough for me."

It ought to have been good enough for Allie, too, but she couldn't help wondering. What did Clay do for a living now that he no longer had the Howard income to fall back on? And where exactly did he live? Questions about him continued to pile up, but she couldn't get answers if she persisted in speaking to him only when spoken to. Besides, she found plenty to keep her busy aboard ship. Clothes always needed mending, it seemed. Maddie asked her assistance with the laundry. She'd noticed several of the passengers reading, so she'd offered to set up a schedule for trading books, a suggestion that had met with approval on all sides. Truly, did she have to involve herself with Clay?

Gillian made the decision for her. No matter where Allie set out to go on the ship, her daughter tugged her in Clay's direction as unerringly as a compass pointing north.

Whenever they came upon him actually sitting on one of the deck chairs for a moment between tasks, Gillian would lean against his knee until he set her on his lap and told her stories. When he took his exercise around the deck, as he did each morning and late afternoon, she'd walk behind him until he noticed and hefted her up on his shoulder, where she perched like a parrot and called out things she could see from her vantage point.

"That cloud is dark," she'd say, pulling one hand from his head just long enough to point to the offending puff above them in the wide expanse of sky. "I think it will rain."

"On your ocean?" Clay would say. "Never! See if you can find us a mermaid to consult on the matter, Captain Howard."

Captain Howard. It was a silly name, for her tiny blonde daughter resembled a fairy more than she did the captain of a ship. But his pet name for her never ceased to brighten Gillian's face, and for that, Allie could only be grateful.

So, though she found it hard to be in Clay's company without quizzing him or having him quiz her about things she had no desire to discuss, she allowed herself to be drawn to his side because her daughter so obviously enjoyed being with him.

"I can't very well forbid her to see him," she explained to Maddie one evening as they were sitting on the bench in their nightgowns, Gillian asleep on the bunk beside them. "He is family, and I did promise to allow him to become better acquainted with her."

"Seems a bit odd he knew nothing of her birth, so it does," Maddie mused, arms wrapped around her knees where she'd pulled them up under her red flannel hem. "Did no one think to write him?"

Allie shrugged. "I don't suppose they knew where he was. He just disappeared from Boston one day and reappeared on the dock."

"Just in time to sail away with us." Maddie frowned. "I'm thinking you'd best be keeping a closer eye on him. We wouldn't want him disappearing in the middle of the ocean!"

Allie laughed at that, but she knew she had no choice but to keep a much closer eye on Clay. Gillian would have it no other way.

The very next day Allie had no sooner set her daughter's booted feet on the planks of the deck for a constitutional than Gillian scampered toward the first-class accommodations, where Allie now spotted Clay leaning against the whitewashed wall.

Gillian dipped a curtsy, cream-colored wool skirts spread wide. "Good morning, Uncle."

Clay saluted her. "Good morning, Captain Howard, ma'am. I am happy to report your ship sails well and to the south as directed."

Gillian did not so much as look at the water as Allie drew to her side. "Thank you. Please, will you tell me about Seattle?"

Besides searching for mermaids, quizzing her uncle seemed to be Gillian's favorite game. Allie supposed it was a step forward from the passive waiting that had marked her daughter up until now, but she wondered what Clay thought of the frequent, often disconnected questions.

She also continued to wonder how he knew so much about a city he'd only visited.

111

It was becoming clearer all the time that either he'd learned to tell tall tales or he was quite intimate with Seattle.

He chuckled at Gillian's question. "More about Seattle? You must be an expert by now."

"What's an expert?" Gillian promptly asked.

"Something your uncle appears to be on any number of subjects," Allie replied for him. "Especially on Seattle. And why would that be, Mr. Howard?"

"You're asking why a Howard could be an overblown windbag on any subject?" Clay shook his head. "Madam, I thought you were better acquainted with my family than that."

Even though she was too acquainted with his family, Allie couldn't help her laugh. She turned to Gillian. "What did you want to ask your uncle, sweetheart?"

Gillian stood very tall, up on the toes of her black boots, as if she was trying to meet Clay's gaze. "Are there any girls in Seattle like me?"

Clay bent to ruffle her curls. "I doubt there are many girls like you anywhere in the world, Captain Howard."

"Are there any boys to play with, then?" Gillian asked as Allie took the deck chair nearby, resigned to a lengthy conversation between the two. Besides, if she listened, she might hear a few answers herself. Clay was more cautious with Allie, but he responded to Gillian's questions quickly enough.

"Oh, there are a few boys and girls," he replied, straightening, "but they're mostly on the outlying farms. You'll be something special, Captain."

Allie smiled at that, but to her surprise, Gillian puffed out a sigh as if she didn't like the answer.

"Is Seattle big?" she asked.

He didn't question the change in topic. And once again, he had a ready answer.

"Depends on what you mean by big," he replied, rubbing his chin with one hand. "It's got hills higher than Beacon Hill in Boston, but only a few houses and none so grand as your grandmother's house."

Gillian wrinkled her nose. "I didn't like Grandmother's house. People were mean there."

Clay frowned, but Allie's heart ached. All she'd wanted was for Gillian to forget that dark time. She reached for her daughter, pulled her onto her lap and held her close.

"They didn't mean to be unkind, Gillian," she said, mindful that she was speaking about Clay's family and servants. "They were used to raising boys. They didn't know how to take care of a sweet little girl like you."

"I imagine not," Clay rumbled, pushing off from the wall. "After all, I was quite a handful." He bent to meet Gillian's concerned gaze. "What do you say, Captain Howard? Shall we go look for mermaids again?" He opened his arms, and Gillian all but dived into them.

How could Allie protest? Clay knew just how to make Gillian happier, and though Allie had yet to hear her daughter laugh, she had hopes that that glorious sound was not far off. Perhaps his care for Gillian was the reason she listened when Clay knocked on their door a few nights later and asked to speak to her.

They were all still dressed, Gillian in her plaid dress, Allie in blue and white and Maddie in green, their hair held back from their faces by matching ribbons. Allie set aside the book she'd been reading with Matt Kelley and bid Clay to enter.

He nodded in greeting, then frowned as if surprised to see the young orphan perched on the bench beside Allie. She could see Matt's closest ear turning red where it stuck out of his thatch of thick brown hair.

114

"Good evening, Mr. Howard," Allie said. "Did you know Mr. Kelley shares our love of literature?"

Matt ducked his head, but Clay's frown cleared. "A fine thing, books. 'The very stuff of dreams and fire.' "

She recognized the quote from Vaughn Everard. It seemed Clay still loved the old poets. She wasn't sure why that so warmed her.

Matt didn't seem to know what to make of the statement. He scrambled off the bench. "I best be going." With a nod to Allie and Maddie, he hurried past Clay and out the door.

"It's kind of you to teach the boy," Clay murmured in the quiet that followed.

"Not at all," Allie assured him. "He's quite sharp. It's a privilege to show him the wonders he can find in books."

"And what wonders can we be showing you this fine evening?" Maddie asked Clay.

He regarded Allie a moment longer, as if she'd done something quite unusual. Then he turned to Maddie. "It's the dark of the moon tonight, and a fine set of stars. The sea's a little choppy, but I thought perhaps Captain Howard would like to see the sky."

Why was Allie disappointed he'd come for her daughter and not for her?

"Strolling the deck after dark with a handsome fellow," Maddie said with a grin. "How could we refuse?"

Clay's mouth hitched up in a grin. A few minutes later they all climbed the stairs to the upper deck.

The *Continental* had been sailing to the southeast, leaving America far behind. Allie knew their first stop was to be Rio de Janeiro in Brazil, so she guessed they would be at the equator in a few days. Even at sea the air had warmed so that no cloaks were necessary. Clay had traded his bulky coat for a navy jacket cinched at his waist and trousers tucked into his knee-high boots. The breeze from the water, thick with salt, brushed her cheek as she and Maddie settled on the wooden chairs along the deck and spread their skirts.

Clay stood beside them, back to the wall of the building, hand braced against the movement of the sea. Gillian leaned against his knee. The light from the bow outlined him in gold.

"See there?" he said, pointing just ahead of the ship with his free hand. "That's the Southern Cross. Sailors use it to tell where they're going."

In the glow of the stars, Gillian's eyes were wide. "Really?"

"I promise," Clay said. He nodded toward the west. "And that's what we call Orion. The ancient Greeks thought the stars made a picture of a mighty hunter, but the Indians in the Dakotas think they outline a bison."

"What's a bison?" Gillian asked.

Even in the dim light, Allie could see Clay's brows go up.

"You mean, your mother never taught you about bison?" he teased. "What's a fine Boston education coming to these days?"

Allie shook her head at his silliness, but Gillian straightened. "Mothers don't teach. That's what governesses do."

Allie's cheeks felt hot. Would he realize how little influence she'd had on her daughter until recently?

Clay merely chuckled. "And what Boston governess would know about bison? They're a big brown shaggy cow with a massive head and a humped back, Captain Howard. If you look close, you can see his tail, just there."

Gillian hurried to the bulwark as if to get closer. Away from the bow light, she was merely a shadow against the wall of the ship.

"So is that where you settled? Dakota?" Allie asked, trying to keep an eye on her daughter.

"I passed through," Clay replied, leaning

against the wall beside her. "The Dakotas, Texas, the California goldfields. It took a while for me to find where I belonged."

Oh, Father, I know how he feels! Allie had to take a breath to still the emotions that rose at his words.

Maddie must have sensed her trembling, for she spoke up. "And where would that be, then, Mr. Howard?"

"Seattle, Ms. O'Rourke," he answered. "I've lived there for the past two years."

At last he admitted what she'd been suspecting. How odd that he'd chosen the very town she had determined to make her and Gillian's home. Even though she crossed the continent to avoid her late husband's family, she'd still have a Howard living near her. For some reason, that fact did not seem so terrible as it would have even a few days ago.

"And what do you do in Seattle?" Allie asked.

He shrugged. "This and that. I was one of the few who arrived with a stake, so people came to me when they had an idea that needed funding. I helped them build their businesses. I'm more than a little surprised to find that I now own pieces of a number of enterprises in Seattle. It's a far cry from what I would have done in Boston, but I have the privilege of working with people who respect me for my insights, not pander to me because of what I'm named. When Seattle grows, I'll grow with her."

She could hear the pride in his voice, the longing for a place she had yet to see. Maddie elbowed her in the side.

"Well, then, you'll have no trouble paying me for the doing of your laundry, will you?"

Clay chuckled again, a warm sound that raised gooseflesh on her arms. "Unless half of Seattle falls into the sound before I return, Ms. O'Rourke, I should be able to lay my hands on the money."

"So you settled in Seattle," Allie marveled. "And by the sound of it, you like it. Why were you so set against us going there?"

Clay opened his mouth to respond, and a shout sounded from the bow.

"Man overboard!"

He jerked toward the call, but Allie's heart jumped in her chest. She thrust herself from the chair to clutch his arm and keep him at her side.

"Where's Gillian?"

CHAPTER SEVEN

Feet pounded from every direction, nearly as loud as Clay's heart. As if greedy to grab another victim, a wave crested the bow, spilling water down the deck. He seized Allegra by the arms and set her back against the wall of the upper salon.

"Stay here," he ordered. "I'll find her."

Immediately she pushed off the wall, chin up. "No! I'm coming with you."

"We'll both come," Ms. O'Rourke insisted, voice equally determined as she gathered her skirts and climbed to her feet.

He had no time to argue. He grabbed Allegra's hand and tugged her after him while her friend scurried to keep up.

"Gillian!" he shouted, feeling as if the freshening breeze snatched the word from the air.

"Gillian!" Allegra cried, voice piercing the night.

Ms. O'Rourke added her cry to theirs.

Ahead of them, Clay could see that the sailors were focused on a point to starboard. He managed to catch the arm of a passing officer, pulling them all up short.

"Who is it?" Clay asked. He was almost afraid to hear the answer. Allegra's fevered grip on his arm told him she was as fearful. *Please, Father, help me protect that sweet little girl!*

"One of the crew, sir," the officer replied, and Clay felt guilty for the relief that shook him. "The sea is rising. Best you and the ladies get inside."

"My daughter is missing," Allegra told him, voice calmer than her demeanor.

He tipped his cap. "Then find her quickly, Mrs. Howard. We'll have our hands full rescuing Mitchells." He dashed off.

Allegra turned to Clay, her face as pale as the moon. "Now what?"

Now he could take a deep breath. "We'll search the deck," he said. "She couldn't have gone far."

"I'll take the port side," Maddie offered. "Sometimes she likes to sit under the longboat there." She hurried off about the bow, skirting the crew who were gathering.

"How could she have wandered off?" Allegra fretted. "I didn't take my eyes away from her for more than a minute!"

The panic was rising in her voice, and Clay felt a similar fear rising inside him.

"We'll find her," he promised Allegra. "Call her again."

"Gillian! Gillian!"

The sob in her voice cut through him. Here he'd put himself aboard to protect them, and what good had it done? What kind of man let a little girl fall into the sea while he chatted with her mother like a lovesick swain?

Then he heard it, no more than a whisper blown on the wind. "Mother!"

Clay honed in on the cry. A darker shadow huddled by the railing. Before he could move closer, a wave crested the bulwark, sloshing across the deck, and he nearly slipped. Allegra clung to him as much to help him as to keep her own feet. Head down, he towed her toward the railing.

Gillian raised her hands, face shining from the water streaming down it. Allegra scooped her up and held her close, and Clay led them both back to the companionway to the lower salon, shutting the door on the wind and waves. He leaned against the barrier, feeling as if some part of him had dived into the sea and only now was coming up for air.

Father, show me how to keep her safe in

122

the future!

In the light of the lantern that was kept burning all night in the lower salon, he could see that Allegra's color was returning. She bent and kissed her daughter's forehead. Then she held her at arm's length as if to be certain she was unharmed. "Gillian, what happened?"

"I — I — I only went a li-li-little way," the girl said through chattering teeth. "I wanted to see the bison."

Allegra hugged her closer again. Water dripped to the floor around them.

Clay pulled off his jacket and knelt to wrap it around Gillian. "Come along, Captain Howard," he said, lifting her up as Allegra stood. "Let's get you back to your room so your mother can change you out of these wet things. The other officers can take care of your ship for now."

Allegra raised her arms. "Let me see to Gillian. Perhaps you'd be so good as to locate Ms. O'Rourke. I'm sure she's worried, too."

He handed over her shivering daughter with a nod. Her eyes met his over Gillian's head. Allegra wanted to say more. He could see it in those deep blue eyes. What was going through her mind?

"Thank you," she said, and her smile

warmed him more than any jacket.

Clay found her friend easily and returned with her just long enough to take back his jacket. Then he spent the next half hour with the crew, trying to locate the lost sailor in the waves, throwing out ropes and the cork rings of life preservers only to reel them in, empty. Reynolds, Conant and several of the other men helped, as well.

Each toss made him feel as empty as the rings. *I nearly failed You tonight, Father. I already failed my family by setting out on my own. But I had to go. You know what I would have become if I'd stayed.*

But though he offered prayers for the lost man, as well, Mitchells was never found.

"Goes to show that life aboard ship can be more dangerous than these ladies want to believe," Reynolds told Clay as they headed back inside, chilled and dripping. "They have no idea what they've let themselves in for."

Clay had the same concern. Wasn't that why he'd boarded the ship to begin with? Yet what more could he do? At the moment, all he wanted was a cup of hot water from the galley.

But when he and Reynolds entered the lower salon, they found far more waiting.

"Come along, gents," Ms. O'Rourke

called, motioning them to the head of the table where warm blankets lay ready. Steaming cups of tea rested on the scarred wood along with cold biscuits. Clay dropped into a seat, grateful even for the food of the *Continental.* Someone draped a blanket about his shoulders. He looked up to thank his benefactor only to find Allegra bending beside him. Her eyes were downcast, her mouth pressed tight.

"I know I told you I didn't need your help," she murmured. "But I'm very thankful you helped us tonight. We could have lost her."

She rested a hand on his shoulder, and he covered her hand with his. "We didn't."

She glanced up, and he followed her gaze to where Gillian sat in the door of their stateroom, watching the tableau with solemn eyes. She was draped in a blanket, as well, her round cheeks pink.

"And we must thank you, Mrs. Howard," said Reynolds, who must have overhead Allegra and Clay's exchange. He took the seat beside Clay and reached for a biscuit. "You and Ms. O'Rourke went to some trouble."

Maddie flashed him a grin. "I'd like to take the credit, so I would, but all I did was solicit blankets. Mrs. Howard organized us, convinced the cook to share and worked it all out."

Allegra straightened, leaving Clay cooler. "It was no trouble. Ms. O'Rourke and I managed the lower salon, and Ms. Stanway is arranging tea for the officers in the upper salon. We take care of our own, sirs."

She made it sound as if they were family. He knew how thin the connection had grown. He had a chance to strengthen that bond on this trip, if she'd let him. He could only hope that tonight was a good start.

Allie believed what she'd said, that they took care of their own. She'd always wanted sisters, and now she felt as if she, Maddie and Catherine were becoming more of a family than the Howards had ever been. They all mourned the loss of the sailor, but as the first week passed aboard ship, life settled into a welcome routine.

The gong sounded at seven each morning, summoning them to a breakfast of biscuits and tea. One of the women organized a school in one of the longboats, and ten boys and girls sat on the little seats under the tarp to continue their studies. Gillian wanted to join them, but Allie held her back.

Her daughter already knew how to read, even at four, and Allie thought Gillian's greater need was time to have fun rather than undertaking more studious pursuits. Of course, the other pursuits aboard ship were largely as confining.

She and Gillian could join the women passengers in sewing and darning and chatting in the salons or on the deck chairs, sharing stories about their past, their hopes for the future. Mr. Conant could always be counted upon to read aloud in his clear tenor voice while they worked. She could visit the passengers who were still a little under the weather, read her Bible or do her chores. She could snuggle in the corner of the bench and reread *Pride and Prejudice.*

But Allie didn't want to see her daughter so confined, not after the strict discipline Gillian had endured in Boston. So she set out to teach her daughter how to play. She started with Scotch-hoppers.

"Pretend each of these planks is a square," she told Gillian one sunny day as they stood on an empty space of deck near the bow. Maddie was perched on a chest of ropes nearby, leaning against the bulwark, brown skirts spread around her, hand shading her eyes from the sparkle of the waves.

Allie tossed one of the brass washers she'd requested from the purser onto the first plank while Gillian watched with her usual frown. "You toss your marker at a square, then hop in a pattern like this."

Allie grabbed a handful of petticoats and hopped up the planks. She could feel her gray wool skirts with their black silk fringe bouncing with each step. When she reached the top plank, she turned and hopped back. "Like that."

"Why?" Gillian asked.

Though it was becoming her daughter's favorite word, the question took Allie by surprise. "It's a game, Gillian. It's fun."

Gillian's frown grew. "Why?"

Allie blew out a breath and glanced at Maddie in exasperation.

Her friend lowered her hand. "You're more serious than a vicar, Gillian, me love."

"What's a vicar?" Gillian asked.

"A very wise man who studies the ways of God," Clay said, ducking under a line stretched across the deck as he joined them. He nodded to Maddie and Allie, before continuing to Gillian. "And they are known for disapproving of fun, while you should be having more of it." He crouched beside her and held up his hands. "Pat-a-cake?"

"Pat what?" Gillian asked.

Clay glanced up at Allie in obvious surprise. Allie lowered herself beside him, skirts pooling about her.

"It's another game, sweetheart," she explained. "Like this." She slapped her palms on her thighs and held her hands up to Clay's. He met hers with a smile and joined her in the rhyme.

"Pat-a-cake, pat-a-cake
Baker's man
That I will master as fast as I can.
Pat it and prick it and mark it with a . . ."

"G," Allie improvised.

Clay nodded, and they finished together. "And put it in the oven for Gillian and me."

At the last clap, Clay caught her hands, grinning so hard his dimple popped into view. His fingers were firm and warm, his gaze warmer. She couldn't look away.

"May I learn, please?" Gillian asked politely.

Face heating, Allie pulled back to rise. "I'm sure your uncle will be glad to teach you. Give Mama a moment in the shade, and then we can try together."

Allie could feel Clay's gaze on her as she went to sit by the railing under the cool of a sail's shadow.

"Take a deep breath now," Maddie murmured beside her. "Sure'n any lady would be flustered to have the likes of Mr. Howard holding her hand."

"Really, Maddie," Allie scolded, knowing

she sounded too much like Catherine. "It's only a game."

"And a fine one at that," Maddie assured her with a wink that made Allie laugh despite herself.

She thought Clay might join them in their play more often after that. He seemed to find the salons too confining, for he was more often to be seen on deck, helping the crew or talking with the captain or one of the gentlemen passengers. As she had teased him, he appeared to know a little about everything, from handling the wheel to the finer points of Milton. She told herself she should be glad he kept himself so busy instead of hovering over her and Gillian.

He saw it as his duty to protect her. She didn't want to lean on his strength. She had to build her own strength, for her sake and Gillian's. And she didn't much like the way she reacted when he was around, growing breathless at his glance. Yet now she had a more important reason to wish his company.

He knew about Seattle.

She had read everything she could about the place in the newspapers and emigration pamphlets, but she couldn't help thinking that the accounts were biased. The newspapers either thought it an excellent place poised for growth or a horrible backwoods where one was likely to meet an untimely death. The pamphlets, and Mr. Mercer, for that matter, touted only the wonders to be found there. She wanted more. She wanted facts.

She was still thinking about the matter their first Sunday at sea when the rumor spread that Mr. Mercer intended to officiate at church services in the upper salon.

"Sure'n his time in the coal bin must have given him a glimpse of eternal punishment," Maddie teased as she helped Allie dress Gillian in her best gown, a rainbow-striped satin with black cord trim across the shoulder and hem. "Perhaps someone should be telling him that he'd do better kneeling at the altar than presuming to stand upon it."

Allie smiled as she straightened the pink satin bow at the back of her daughter's head. If God could forgive her for her fears in the past, He could certainly forgive Mr. Mercer his cowardice. The other women had, for the most part, forgiven him. Whenever Allie saw him, he had one or more ladies with him, asking him about Seattle, listening to his advice. She still couldn't make up her mind about him. Either he was a cunning charlatan or the most put-upon man of her acquaintance.

Regardless, she was quite looking forward to singing the Lord's praise that morning for sending her and Gillian on this journey. She'd even donned one of her nicest gowns, a sky-blue silk with wide panels of white edging the bodice, overskirt and cuffs, and a neat white collar trimmed in lace. Maddie had also changed into her best dress. The russet color of the fine wool brought out the fire in her hair, and the black lace shawl that crossed the bodice showed her figure to advantage. With Catherine in a white gown trimmed in blue with a blue jacket on top, Allie thought they made a handsome group.

The other ladies in the upper salon looked just as fine, with many a taffeta and velvet among them. Someone had taken the trouble of polishing the woodwork; she could smell the lemon in the air as she took her place beside Mr. Conant. She was only disappointed to find that the piano was still in its packing case. That would hinder any music.

But Mr. Mercer, in a brown coat and striped waistcoat, stepped in front of the group and began to sing.

"He leadeth me, He leadeth me. By His own hand, He leadeth me . . ."

The ladies' sopranos rose to the beamed

ceiling in the familiar words. Mr. Conant's tenor blended nicely, but Allie was all too aware of the rumbling bass behind her. Clay's voice underpinned the score as surely as granite supported the foundation of a chapel. She was almost sorry when the song ended.

"Dear Lord," Mr. Mercer prayed, head bowed and eyes fervently shut. "Thank You for the many blessings we have received from Your mighty hand. Keep watch over us as we make this sacred journey to that most blessed place, Seattle. Amen."

"Blessed place?" Clay muttered behind her, skepticism clear in each syllable. Several people glanced his way with grins. Allie's face felt hot.

Mr. Mercer then pulled a newspaper from his pocket and began to read a sermon. The text was uplifting, but she thought it would have sounded more edifying if it had been spoken by an impassioned preacher.

"That was one of the Reverend Henry Ward Beecher's sermons," Catherine whispered beside Allie after Mr. Mercer finished the concluding prayer. "His sermons are reprinted in the newspaper. If that is the best Mr. Mercer can do, perhaps we should organize the service next Sunday."

"We have more than Sunday services to arrange," Allie replied to Catherine as she took Gillian's hand and headed downstairs. "We need to know what we're facing when we reach Seattle."

Maddie joined them as they reached the lower salon. "I can't be arguing with you there, Allegra. I always thought that Mercer was too full of himself to tell us all the truth, so he is."

Catherine frowned at her. "Then why agree to join his expedition?"

Maddie shrugged. "Seattle couldn't be any worse than where I was, laundering in New York for pennies, living in a garret." She leaned closer and lowered her voice. "Seattle could be far better. The *Independent* had it that men outnumber the women twenty to one!"

Catherine raised her platinum brows. "I know you enjoy the gentlemen's company, Madeleine, but surely you do not intend to accept the first man who proposes."

Maddie nudged her shoulder. "Oh, off with your airs, now, Catie, me love. I've seen you eyeing that handsome lad in Engineering."

Catherine raised her chin with an eloquent sniff. "As if I would marry a sailor. My father raised me to expect a husband among the professions, but I think Seattle is more in need of my nursing services than as a wife."

"For a wee bit, at least," Maddie predicted with a wink to Allie. "And what of you, Mrs. Howard? Will you turn your hand to husband hunting when we reach Mr. Mercer's blessed shores?"

Allie smiled at the reference to the service. "I have no need of another man to guide my life. I think it high time I guided my own."

Catherine nodded. "Quite right. Do you know one of the women told me she felt the same way? She already wrote to Governor Pickering requesting that she be designated the Old Maid of the Territory, exempt from any marriage proposal. She carries his letter granting her request in her reticule."

"Let's be hoping it's worth more than Allegra's letter from Mr. Mercer," Maddie replied.

Allie shook her head. "I want no more of Mr. Mercer's assurances. We have someone in our midst who is keenly aware of everything Seattle has to offer and quite unlikely to varnish the truth he speaks."

Maddie nodded. "Mr. Howard. But I'm thinking he may not be wishing to share everything he knows with us. For all that he's a charmer, he tends to keep his own council."

"I've noticed that, too," Catherine said. "There is a wall he will let none behind."

She sensed it, as well. But she'd known Clay as long as she could remember. He'd said he wanted to protect her. What better way than to arm her with information? She couldn't find the facts she sought in a book, worse luck.

She glanced around at her friends. "I know Mr. Howard seems unapproachable, but I still say he's our best hope for learning more about Seattle. If we put our heads together, I'm sure we can find a way to convince him to tell us everything."

CHAPTER EIGHT

Clay's first inkling that Allegra and her friends were up to something was the tantalizing smell of fresh-baked bread. He'd been out in the sunlight, helping Mr. Debro inventory the life preservers on the hurricane deck, when the aroma drifted past. It brought back memories of breakfasts at home, their chef beaming down on him as Clay dived into the fluffy eggs and warm toast dripping with butter. Funny. He hadn't thought he could be homesick for Boston, not after all these years.

He hadn't thought he'd be so attracted to Allegra, either. What need did he have for a fine Boston lady in his ever-changing life? She would never put up with his mad starts, as his mother used to call his ideas. It should be easy to keep her at a distance, think of her only as his brother's wife, meant to be cherished and protected. Yet he couldn't stop remembering her smile, the touch of her fingers, the tender way she looked at little Gillian. Some part of him wanted a similar look directed at him.

Perhaps she was best protected at a distance. When he returned to the territory, he didn't need her memories following him about.

But it was soon obvious that memories hadn't brought back that aroma. Mr. Debro laid a hand on the stack of cork rings and drew in a breath through his nose.

"Do you smell that?" he asked, closing his eyes and sighing. "It's like my mother's cinnamon rolls." He opened his eyes and frowned at Clay. "That can't be coming from the galley."

Clay had to agree. So far, the food aboard the *Continental,* at least in the lower salon where he generally ate with Allegra and Gillian, was plentiful but uninspiring. It mostly consisted of hard biscuits, fried salt beef and parboiled beans, with little other vegetables and no fruit. Sometimes he thought the tea was being steeped in seawater, for he couldn't seem to wash the salt from his mouth. He could only hope they might do better when they put in to Rio for supplies.

The purser was as inclined as Clay to investigate the scent, so they followed their

138

noses to the lower salon, where a number of the passengers and several of the officers were already gathered around Allegra's friend Ms. O'Rourke. The redhead was standing at the top of the table in her green wool gown, eyes twinkling with merriment as if she knew the dreams she'd inspired with her baking.

"And there is the man we've been waiting for, so we have," she declared as Clay shouldered his way forward. She patted the checkered cloth mounded on the table, the edges of a pewter platter just visible under the cloth. "Did you have something you wanted to say, Mr. Howard?"

Clay couldn't seem to take his eyes off that platter. "Only that whatever is under there smells mighty tempting, ma'am."

The others around him murmured their agreement, and several shuffled closer. Matt Kelley went so far as to duck under Clay's arm for a better look.

Ms. O'Rourke's smile widened. "I'd be happy to show you what's beneath, Mr. Howard. But first we have a wee proposal for you."

"Indeed we do," Allegra said. Clay turned to find her coming out of her stateroom, one hand in Gillian's. Her other friend, Ms. Stanway, marched at her side. Both had their heads up, and their skirts swung accompaniment to their brisk walk as they approached the table. Once again she wore the gray gown with all that black fringe. Her friend's brown taffeta dress was far more somber. Clay had a funny feeling he was in for trouble.

As if the other passengers sensed it, too, they glanced between Allegra and Clay. He felt like an actor onstage at the Boston Theatre, all gazes waiting for his next move.

"And what proposal would that be?" he asked, standing tall and crossing his arms over the chest of his navy jacket.

While Ms. Stanway took Gillian and went to stand on one side of Ms. O'Rourke, Allegra glided to the other side and nodded to Clay. Her look was polite and precise, and he waited to hear what she was going to demand of him. If she ordered him to leave the ship at Rio and stop bothering her and Gillian, he knew he'd have some tough talking to do.

"Why, you have knowledge we need, sir," she said, gaze meeting his in challenge. "About the territory, about Seattle. We propose a trade. You teach us what we'll need to be successful there —" she nodded to Ms. O'Rourke "— and we'll keep you supplied with sweets."

The redhead whipped the cloth off the platter, and the scent of cinnamon danced in the air. Clay couldn't tear his eyes off the treasure lying there. Clustered on the rough pewter were hot cross buns, snowy icing dripping down their sides. Several of the passengers gasped out an "Oh!"

Clay had to swallow before speaking. "A mighty fine offer to be sure," he started, but another man pushed forward.

"Don't listen to him, Ms. O'Rourke," he begged. "I've five pieces of silver right here. Give me your platter."

"I'll give you eight," someone yelled.

"I'll go ten and make them gold!"

Ms. O'Rourke's smile turned up, and she reached for the edge of her platter.

Allegra put herself between the redhead and Clay and raised her hands in supplication. "Friends, friends, please!"

"Our Savior said that man cannot live by bread alone," Ms. Stanway reminded them from the other side of the platter.

"I'll bet the good Lord never smelled those buns," Mr. Debro muttered, gaze fastened on the sweets.

Even Gillian licked her pink lips as if she was having a difficult time being good for once and only wanted to gobble down those buns.

Allegra stiffened her spine and glared at each of the men in turn. To Clay's surprise, gazes bowed, fellows stepped back.

"These were baked solely for Mr. Howard," she informed them. "He can determine how to apportion them, if he accepts our request to teach." She met Clay's gaze, and the deep blue softened even as her tone grew more imploring. "Well, Mr. Howard? You could do a great deal of good here. Won't you please help us?"

Now every gaze was on him, some as entreating as hers, others more threatening. He didn't care much for either. Nor did he think that Allegra and her friends would listen to what he had to teach. She'd argued with him every time he'd tried to tell her about Seattle. They'd all started this journey with idealistic dreams, and he couldn't help wondering how they'd react when those dreams met the cold reality of the frontier.

But if Allegra wanted to hear the truth about Seattle at last, who was he to deny her?

"I accept your proposal, Mrs. Howard," he replied. "Cut those buns as small as possible so everyone can have a taste, then grab a chair and meet me on the hurricane deck. We have a lot of studying ahead of us."

■ ■ ■ ■

A short time later, Allie, Gillian, Catherine and Maddie, along with several of the other interested women, joined Clay on the hurricane deck. Allie couldn't help feeling a sense of pride that they'd managed to convince Clay to teach them. She wasn't sure why he had been so reticent to accept their offer, but she couldn't wait to hear more.

She and the other women arranged the white slatted wooden deck chairs they'd carried up from the lower deck into a half circle surrounding Clay, who stood with his back to the massive black funnel rising from the boiler room. The hurricane deck was the highest point any passenger could reach on the *Continental*, topping the upper salon and the first-class staterooms. A railing of black chains surrounded the whitewashed deck, and longboats were strapped at each corner, making Allie feel as if they'd all cozied up inside a little nest.

The weather had been turning warmer each day, and the crew had slung a sail over the top of the deck to shade it from the sun. Today, however, it was holding back a gentle rain. Allie could hear the drops pattering down on the canvas as she settled into her seat next to Clay, with Gillian cuddled close in her lap.

"Perhaps we should have conducted class in the upper salon," Catherine said on the other side of the circle. She pulled her paisley shawl more tightly about the shoulders of her high-necked brown dress as if to ward off the cool breeze that skipped under the sail.

Clay smiled as the others found their seats, as well. "I'd accustom myself to the rain if I were you, Ms. Stanway. It rains a great deal in Seattle. Some days, it's nearly impossible to cross the street for the mud."

"Mr. Mercer says the streets in Seattle are paved with opportunities," one of the women piped up.

"Mr. Mercer has his head in the rain clouds, I'm thinking," Maddie answered her, hands on her green wool skirts, and perched on one of the trunks toward the bow end of the deck. Allie decided not to point out that her seat was clearly marked Gunpowder. "It sounds as if the streets aren't paved at all."

Some of the women laughed at that, but Allie turned to watch how Clay would react. Though one corner of his mouth turned up, bringing his dimple into view, he didn't join in their laughter.

"She's right," he said when they had quieted again. "None of the roads in town are paved, and those outside town are little more than deer paths. Many of the men live in boardinghouses or the Occidental Hotel. Last count, we only had around seventy-five houses, all told, some board, some log."

Seventy-five houses? That was a neighborhood in Boston. And she'd never seen a log house.

"Then you have a sawmill," a man called from the back of the group, and Allie noticed that a few of the male passengers had climbed up on the deck, as well. In fact, more people kept filing up the stairs, until the deck was nearly packed with passengers, jostling to hear more about their new home.

"Henry Yesler has a mill," Clay confirmed. "The first steam-powered sawmill in the area. But most of the lumber he cuts he ships away, either to other parts of the territory or to San Francisco."

"But you have the territorial university," Catherine put in. "Surely the territorial capital is not far behind."

Allie smiled at her friend's insistence, but she knew Catherine was right. Once Seattle hosted the legislature, there would be no telling how quickly it would grow.

Clay's smile only widened. "The territorial legislature voted for the capital to remain in Olympia, three times now. And as for the university, it has thirty students, only one of them old enough to actually graduate any time soon." He bent to tweak one of Gillian's curls. "A few could play happily alongside Captain Howard."

Gillian wiggled in Allie's lap, and she could see that her daughter had brightened at the thought. The others took the news harder. All around her, shoulders sagged, mouths drooped. They'd all pinned their hopes on the stories Mr. Mercer had spun, of prosperity, of opportunity. The picture Clay was painting was of another place entirely.

She wasn't willing to give up so easily. "You settled in Seattle," she pointed out to Clay. "Two years ago, you said. Coming from Boston, why would you choose such a place?"

He straightened and rubbed his chin, the shadow of the sail turning his eyes to jade. "I saw quite a few places coming west. Some were grand, some beautiful, some bursting at the seams with opportunity. But truth be told, there was something about Washington Territory. It's the most magnificent country you're ever likely to see."

A few of the passengers perked up at that.

"Go on," Allie urged him. "What's it like there?"

"Is there good farmland?" a man called out.

"Plenty of water?" another asked.

Clay spread his hands. "Imagine a narrow plain crossed by streams, fertile, forested, the air scented with the resin of fir, fish leaping out of streams and into your nets. Behind it rises the highest mountains in the country, deer grazing their sides, the rocky tops brushing the sky, white even in the summer. And at its front stretch miles of blue-green waters where whales and porpoises play." He smiled down at Gillian again. "I wouldn't be surprised to find a mermaid or two."

Everyone was watching him now, as if afraid to blink and miss something. He was a twopenny artist on the streets of Boston, sketching pictures of exotic places on the pavement. Yet while those men embellished their pictures to suit their audiences, she knew Clay would never lie about such matters.

Somewhere, three months away, lay a fertile land of snowcapped mountains and deep forests. And she had a chance to make her place there.

Catherine must have been thinking along similar lines, for she straightened from where she'd been reclining on a deck chair. "Mr. Mercer said nurses were needed, but Mrs. Howard told me you claim there's only one hospital."

Clay dropped his hands and shrugged. "Doc Maynard tried starting one in a house, but he's had trouble keeping it open. Most folks couldn't pay for their care. You see, in Seattle, we're what you call land rich and dollar poor."

Allie frowned.

"Why?" Gillian piped up.

As always, Clay showed no annoyance with the question, though some of the other passengers frowned as if indignant a child would interrupt. "The federal government gave each man one-hundred-sixty acres to prove up, Captain Howard," he said. "Three hundred and twenty if he had a wife. That means all they had to do was live on the land for five years, build a house and make some improvements, and the land was theirs free and clear."

"Riches aplenty, I'm thinking," Maddie murmured.

"Then why did you say people were

poor?" Allie challenged.

Clay turned his smile her way, and her gown felt too warm.

"Because there're few people willing to buy the land when they can grab their own free," he explained. "The money that came west went into building houses, bringing out supplies. Anything else we pretty much barter for."

Catherine stared at him. "Do you mean to say you have no stores, no means of procuring goods?"

"We have stores," Clay assured her. "Goods brought across country, around the Horn and up from San Francisco or across the sea from the Orient. But a lot of what we need we trade for. I might swap salmon or timber for cloth, my fresh-picked blackberries for your fancy shawl."

Catherine clutched her shawl closer still. "That's medieval!"

Clay chuckled. "That's Seattle."

Allie couldn't help thinking he was painting things a bit too darkly again. "But all that will change as the city grows and open land becomes more scarce," she said, and had the satisfaction of hearing other grumbles quieting. "As more people come to the area, you can sell parts of your land, bring additional monies into the economy."

Clay inclined his head. "Well said, Mrs. Howard. That's the hope of Seattle, as well."

"Only right now," Maddie put in, leaning forward as if to make sure she understood, "there's little money left to be paying a laundress or a baker, you're saying."

"Only when Yesler pays his men," Clay agreed. "The loggers' payroll goes a long way toward keeping money flowing. Of course, the money tends to stay close to the mill."

"Why?" Gillian asked.

More people frowned, but this time Allie thought it was because they had the same question.

Laughter lit Clay's pale green eyes. "Because shopkeepers cater to their tastes. The fact is, we have more grogshops than grocers."

Allie put her hand over her daughter's mouth before she could ask what a grogshop was, as all around them faces turned crimson.

"I do believe you're exaggerating, Mr. Howard," she told Clay.

He held up one hand. "My word of honor."

"So are we to live in such an uncivilized place?" Catherine protested. "We were given to understand that Seattle was settled and cultivated, requiring only our contributions to flourish."

Clay nodded to her in respect, but his tone was firm. "We're an outpost of civilization, Ms. Stanway. We have the same challenges as any other frontier town — securing enough clean water and food for everyone, keeping the peace, building for the future with limited resources."

Allie dropped her hand from Gillian's mouth. "Why must you always play the pessimist!"

Clay's face hardened. "You said you wanted to learn the truth about Seattle, Mrs. Howard. Don't blame me if it's not to your liking."

Oh! Another moment of this and she'd have to put her hand over her own mouth or risk saying something harsh. Of course she wanted the truth, and she'd thought he'd give it to them. But it was all too apparent that Clay Howard was set on shading the truth every bit as much as Asa Mercer had with his stories of blessed shores.

She thought she understood why Mr. Mercer had been so boastful when he'd first lectured to them in Boston. He'd wanted to convince them to come. He believed in the future of Seattle. Having such a compelling vision, he'd been blinded to anything that might hinder their acceptance of his offer, even to using the funding appropriately.

But Clay? Why was he so set against them all going to Seattle? It sounded as if he owned pieces of nearly every industry there. Wouldn't more citizens merely mean a greater profit? Weren't teachers and seamstresses, and yes, wives for those who could stomach the role, a good thing?

Any way she looked at it, Clay Howard was still keeping a secret, one that could well spell their success or downfall in Seattle.

So, what would she have to do to get him to share it with them all?

CHAPTER NINE

Clay couldn't help being pleased by the time the Seattle School, as Gillian called it, broke up for the day. Already he could see that the other passengers were rethinking their decisions.

If they enter the territory with a little caution, Lord, I'll count my time in these classes well spent.

Allegra, however, did not seem as pleased. She handed Gillian to Ms. Stanway and remained behind as the other passengers filed down the stairs to the lower parts of the ship.

"That was not as useful as it could have been," she informed him. The breeze tugged a strand of midnight black hair loose from the braid around her head to tickle her cheek, but those deep blue eyes were far from amused.

Clay shrugged. "You wanted me to tell them what I know about Seattle. I did."

She shook her head, lips thinning. "You told them what you wanted to tell them. They need the truth, sir. They need information on which to base decisions." She peered up at him. "You could do better."

He felt his cheeks heating. What, was he going to be discomposed by a Boston socialite? He'd faced down outlaws and claim jumpers alike.

"What do you want, Allegra?" he demanded.

"A little more discipline," she said, raising her chin. "I'll ask each of your students to think of a question and bring it to me after dinner tonight. Once I compile them, I can give them to you a few at a time for you to compose your lessons."

Clay blew out a breath. "I've no need to compose lessons. I'm not a schoolmarm."

"Which is why you need my help," she countered. She picked up her skirts and swept down the deck.

Clay shook his head again. What had he gotten himself into? For a moment, he was tempted to tell her the deal was off. Then he remembered Ms. O'Rourke's hot cross buns. With a groan, he knew he was going to submit.

He thought perhaps Allegra would let him off that night, as she, Gillian and Clay had been invited to dine with Captain Windsor and Mr. Mercer in the upper salon. All the officers were there in their brown-and-gold uniforms, smiles as bright as their brass buttons. Mercer's black frock coat could have graced the best Boston dinner party. Every lady who had been invited must have chosen her best gown, as well, for Clay hadn't seen so many silks and velvets since he'd left Boston. Even Allegra looked as if she'd dressed for the occasion.

Her dark hair was pulled back in a chignon at the nape of her neck, with two red velvet bands crossing the top and back of her head as if to keep every curl in place. Her white satin gown was trimmed in red velvet, and the red velvet bodice was fitted to her form. Clay thought he wasn't the only man having difficulty keeping his eyes off her.

"It's wonderful having you dine with us," Catherine told her from where she sat on Allegra's other side. The tall blonde was dressed in a blue satin gown. "And you, as well, Mr. Howard," she added with a smile that stopped at Clay and did not venture down the table to where Mercer was prosing on about some matter.

"Yes, Howard," Reynolds put in from across the table. "About time you stayed upstairs where you belong. Though, mind you, I can't blame you for wishing to see the sights belowdecks."

He laughed at his own joke, but Catherine merely eyed him.

Allegra went one further. "You might consider joining us downstairs yourself, Mr. Reynolds. I promise you excellent company. And Mr. Cummings has promised to serenade us with his concertina, so we shall shortly have music, as well."

"Then you are indeed ahead of us, Mrs. Howard," Reynolds assured her with an eye to where the baseboard of the upright piano was strapped against the far wall. Clay made a note to offer to the captain to set it on its legs the next day, when he wasn't conscripted for Allegra's classes.

The company was better than the meal, he had to own, for even the captain, it seemed, dined on beef and beans. The dinner was even less appetizing after having had a taste of Ms. O'Rourke's masterpieces that morning.

"How exactly did your friend manage to bake when the cook can't seem to do better than hardtack?" Clay asked Allegra after they'd finished eating and were taking a turn about the room. Gillian was sitting on one of the leather-upholstered chairs with Ms. Stanway and listening in her solemn manner as one of the officers tried to woo the pretty blonde. Neither Gillian nor Ms. Stanway looked amused.

"The cook has the proper ingredients," Allegra assured him. "He simply has no idea how to use them."

"Then by all means," Clay said, "have pity on us all and teach the fellow."

Allegra shook her head, dark hair glinting in the candlelight. "He has no interest in learning. We were fortunate that he also has a sweet tooth and was persuaded to let Maddie bake from time to time. That and the fact that Captain Windsor was willing to allow us to use ship's stores." She slanted a glance up at Clay. "I understand she's planning on ginger cookies tomorrow."

Clay's mouth promptly began watering again.

As if she knew she had him, Allegra began searching in her beaded reticule. Like many of her gowns, it was made of fine material with an excess of satin bows and silk fringe. He tried to picture it on the wrist of any lady in Seattle and failed.

She lifted several pieces of paper into the candlelight from the folds of her bag. "We must talk about tomorrow's lesson, sir," she said.

Clay nodded to the chief officer as they

passed the spot where the man leaned against the wall. By the scowl on his face, he apparently hoped to distance himself from all the flirtatious conversations going on around him.

"I wouldn't think we had all that much to discuss," Clay said to Allegra. "How hard can it be to stand up and talk about my home?"

"Not nearly as easy as you'd suppose," she protested. She stopped him and shook the papers in her gloved fist. "I promised everyone I would give you their questions, but some of these are ridiculous." She plucked one from her hand. "Listen to this — 'Are there many men of your stature in Seattle?' "

Clay couldn't see why she was so upset. "I'd say there are any number who have achieved a level of success by making the most of opportunities."

Allegra rolled her eyes. "Knowing the lady who raised the question, I doubt she was asking about your prospects." She selected another. "What about this one — 'Do you have any brothers?' " She threw up her hands, and the pages fluttered like the wings of a startled bird. "You offer them an excellent opportunity to prepare themselves for the future and all they can do is flirt!"

Clay hid a smile. If Allegra had raised her eyes above her papers for a moment, she'd have seen any number of her compatriots engaged in flirting at that very moment. The two engineers, Mr. Tennant and Mr. Rowland, had a lady on each arm as they promenaded, and Mr. Debro stood by the head of the table, surrounded in skirts. Even Reynolds was up against the opposite wall as he attempted to fend off a pair of determined gray-haired spinsters.

"Perhaps they're merely practicing their conversations," Clay suggested to Allegra, "before they reach Seattle and start hunting for a husband."

"They'd do better to consider how to farm the opportunities than to hunt for husbands," she insisted.

Clay gazed down at her. The color in her cheeks was growing, her chest rising and falling in her velvet bodice as if the very idea of searching for a husband incensed her.

"Oh, come now, Allegra," he said. "You know the pattern. A young lady is expected to accumulate a certain set of accomplishments and then find a husband who appreciates them."

Now her eyes were narrowing as well. "If she is so very accomplished, why must she need a husband?"

Clay frowned. "Did you take up with those women agitators after I left Boston? I can't believe Frank's death caused these changes in you."

She dropped her gaze before answering. The ship must have taken a wave sideways, for the floor rolled, and Clay caught her elbow to steady her, the silk of her evening gloves soft under his grip. She did not pull away.

"I have read a few of their treatises," she admitted. "And I can appreciate most of their arguments. But it was Frank's death that made the decision for me."

Her fingers plucked at the velvet edging her short cap sleeve. "When you left Boston, our parents expected me to marry him, so I did. Everyone expected us to take the house next door to your parents, so we did. When Frank died, everyone expected me to move in with your mother, wear black, stay indoors and shrivel away for a time before marrying again. All my life I've done what people expected of me. Perhaps I decided to do the unexpected for once."

It could not have been that simple. He'd known her to send a swain off for a cup of punch or her shawl on a whim, but to leave Boston? That had to have taken foresight and planning.

"You said you paid Mercer all you had for your tickets," Clay said. "How could that be? Frank left you well off."

Her smile was sad. "So everyone assumed, but everything except a small household allowance was put in trust for Gillian. She'll have all she needs once she reaches her majority." Her look turned fierce. "She can marry who she pleases. Or not marry at all. She can be her own person."

The ship rolled again, and the few dishes left on the table chimed against each other as they slid. Allegra swayed, and Clay put an arm about her waist to keep her from falling. Her gaze met his, and the surprise melted into something more. He felt himself slipping into the depth of her eyes as he leaned closer.

"Isn't it a fine evening, Mrs. Howard?"

Clay jerked away from Allegra to find Asa Mercer standing beside them, smiling pleasantly. What, had Clay been about to kiss Allegra, his brother's widow, in front of half the ship? What was he thinking?

Allie saw the color flame into Clay's face before she attempted to focus on their leader. She found it difficult to even respond to Mr. Mercer's question. For a moment there, time had turned back. She'd been a debutante again, and Clay Howard was bending closer, as if he meant to kiss her. The planes of his rugged face had softened, his golden lashes drifting closed as his lips neared hers. And her heartbeat had sped just as it had all those years ago.

Why did these memories persist? She wasn't that person anymore. Wasn't there a Bible verse about how anyone who set his hand to the plow and looked back was good for nothing? She'd set her face toward Seattle. She shouldn't be looking toward Boston, for any reason.

"Yes, Mr. Mercer," she managed to say, pasting a smile on her face. "It is a lovely evening. Thank you and Captain Windsor for inviting me and Gillian to dine."

"Oh, of course," he said, tugging down on his waistcoat. "I am a man who can admit mistakes. And clearly a lady of your refinement deserves to be among her own kind."

She could not have understood him. "I assure you, sir, I am well pleased with my accommodations belowdecks." She glanced at Clay. "I don't have to worry about seawater trickling under my door."

Clay's color had returned to normal, and now he smiled as if he too remembered the day he had been seasick. Mercer, however, waved a hand.

"A rumor only, my dear lady. I can assure you the first-class accommodations are superior in every regard, and a much better place for you and your charming daughter."

Allie glanced across the salon to where Gillian was playing pat-a-cake with Catherine. She hoped her daughter's frown marked her concentration this time.

"Gillian has a routine now and is comfortable in our stateroom," she told Mercer, returning her gaze to his. "I would prefer not to change things."

Mercer took her arm and patted her hand. "I fear I must insist. How else can I keep an eye on you?"

Allie yanked back her hand. "I might ask the same question, sir. I wasn't the one who misplaced funds, confused boarding instructions. If you feel the need to oversee someone's life, I suggest you start with your own."

She had the momentary satisfaction of watching Mercer's mouth open and shut wordlessly.

"I believe Ms. Stanway requires your assistance," Clay said to her, and Allie could hear the rumble of laughter behind his words. "Allow me to escort you."

"It's only across the room, Mr. Howard,"

Allie replied. "I very much doubt I could lose my way. Just see that you are prepared tomorrow to discuss the tribes living near Seattle. That at least seems a real concern among the ladies."

Clay nodded, but as she passed him, she caught a glimpse of Mercer's face, skin mottled and bushy brows tight. It seemed her response had gone down even less well than the *Continental*'s salted beef. She could not summon sufficient regret. He had no right or reason to act as if he were her father and she was a child in need of his guidance. Besides, what could he do? He couldn't very well force her off the ship for insubordination when they were in the middle of the ocean!

But as it turned out, she'd underestimated him.

She and Gillian rose the next morning in time to help Maddie bake her ginger cookies, then had to fend off more offers to buy the sweets as they carried them from the galley up to the hurricane deck. It was a lovely day, the sky above the sail blue with puffy white clouds like tufts of cotton waltzing in the air. The same women who had attended class the previous day had returned, many bringing friends and relatives with them. As it was, the space was so crowded Clay had to elbow his way to the funnel.

Allie settled back in a deck chair with Gillian on her lap, Maddie on one side and Catherine on the other as Clay passed around the plate of cookies. The rest of the students had taken up their places when Mr. Mercer appeared at the back. Once more his brows were drawn down as he stood and listened, arms crossed over his narrow chest.

"I understand you have some concerns about the natives in the area," Clay said, his voice a deep rumble over the thrum of the engine. "I imagine the idea of living next to an Indian village might sound pretty primitive."

Several people nodded; others exchanged glances as if they weren't sure what to believe.

"I'm here to tell you that you have to start from a different perspective," Clay said, resting one hip against the chest of life preservers near the funnel. "Living among the Indians isn't so very different from the way you lived back home. Chances are, wherever you're from, you found all kinds of people — Swedes, the Irish, Germans and more."

"We came from a town with a fine set of

Christians," one woman remarked. She glanced at Maddie and put her nose in the air.

Allie stiffened at the slight to her friend. She knew some people distrusted the Irish, acting as if they were some sort of brutes, but she'd always considered such prejudice ridiculous.

"They may have been fine Christians," Clay put in smoothly, "but they probably didn't all attend the same church."

More voices sprang up, extolling the virtues of this group over that. Clay's frown was growing, and Allie feared his patience was fading in direct correlation. She set Gillian on the deck beside her chair and stood.

"Friends! Friends!" she called, raising her hands above her head to get their attention. "Let Mr. Howard speak, if you please. I believe he's trying to make a point."

Clay nodded his thanks to her intervention. "Indeed I am. You wouldn't look at a town of people and think them all identical to each other, yet many people make the mistake of looking at the Indians in the area and thinking they're all the same. They aren't. There are peaceful tribes who hunt and fish and even farm like the next man."

"They farm?" Catherine asked, pale brows high.

"Indeed they do," Clay assured her. "There's a fleshy root called the camas they cultivate and harvest just like a potato."

"They must have learned that from an Irishman," Maddie put in with a triumphant glance at the woman who had nettled her.

Allie hid her smile. "Go on, Mr. Howard," she encouraged Clay.

His smile seemed to raise the temperature under the shade sail. "However they learned it, Ms. O'Rourke, it's part of their traditions. Other tribes have other traditions. Some are warriors who pride themselves on what they can take from weaker tribes. Some live off trade, some prefer to be self-sufficient and some are insulted if you try to barter. You have to know who you're dealing with."

Allie glanced around the group and found many nodding or looking thoughtful. *Thank You, Lord, that they're willing to listen!*

Then she noticed that one member of their group was turning redder by the moment. Mr. Mercer pushed his way to the front.

"This nonsense must stop, sir," he said, shaking a bony finger at Clay. "These ladies will have no call to deal with savages. You will frighten them."

Allie drew herself up. "Better that we

know the truth, sir, before we embark on your so-called blessed shores."

"Mrs. Howard," he scolded, speaking slowly, as if she would have difficulty comprehending him should he speak at a normal pace. "You have no need for concern." He turned to the others, putting his back to Clay. "Indeed, none of you have any reason for concern. You must not listen to such stories. They will only damage your delicate sensibilities."

Allie's temper rose with each word. She tapped him on the shoulder, forcing him to turn once more and face her. "Perhaps we aren't the shrinking violets you think us, Mr. Mercer. I, for one, would like to be prepared for the dangers I might face in Seattle."

"Dangers?" Mercer spread his hands with a laugh. "There are no dangers in Seattle, dear lady, unless you count the danger of losing your heart to a charming gentleman."

"And if you believe that," Clay said, straightening to tower over their benefactor, "then you probably believe that bilge water tastes like lemonade. I wouldn't advise drinking it any time soon."

Mr. Mercer's long face darkened above his whiskers. "You may not have entered Seattle before the Indian Wars, Mr. Howard, but it is well known where your sympathies lie. A man who would forsake his own people to champion an immoral band of lazy heathens does not deserve to teach impressionable young ladies, in my book."

Forsake his own people? What was Mercer talking about? Did he know Clay had left his family behind in Boston? Or was this something else?

Clay dropped his chin and gazed at Mercer from under his brows. His voice was no less powerful for its quiet. "And a man who lies to further his own gain has no business teaching at all."

Mercer tilted back his head to meet Clay's gaze. Whatever he saw there made him pale. He took a step back and tugged down on his waistcoat before turning to the other passengers, who were watching wide-eyed.

"I cannot, of course, keep you from speaking," he said, though he did not look at Clay. "I can, however, insist that the ladies under my escort spend no more time in your questionable company. Come along, my dears."

He raised his head so that the breeze ruffled his reddish curls and marched back through the company. What a humbug! Surely the others would see through his posturing.

But, to Allie's dismay, several of the women gathered their things and rose to follow him.

"Stop them," she begged Clay, putting a hand on his arm.

His muscles were tight under her hand. "Let them go, Allegra. They have no interest in the truth."

"And that's precisely why we must insist that they hear it," Catherine said, rising to join Allie at Clay's side and bringing Gillian with her. Maddie stuck out her tongue at Mercer's retreating back before doing the same.

"You're making a mistake," Allie called as several more fell into step behind their leader. "We need to be prepared."

Mercer turned and raised one finger above his head. "Mark my words, Mrs. Howard. You are the one who is making a mistake, by aligning yourself with this naysayer. I only hope you don't live to regret it."

CHAPTER TEN

That day marked a rift in the company of the good ship *Continental.* Clay wasn't sure whether to feel grateful for the reprieve of having to deal with Mercer directly or guilty for his part in the problem. His mission from the first had been to protect Allegra and Gillian. Surely helping Allegra and her friends understand what they would face in Seattle would protect them more than the ignorance Mercer seemed so set on. Clay couldn't regret that some of the women had chosen to listen to him instead of their so-called leader.

He could be sorry they were tarred with the same brush of prejudice.

"His mind has the depth of a teaspoon," Allegra said, shaking her head and drawing in a deep breath as if to still her temper as she watched Mercer and his band leave the hurricane deck.

"Aren't you the kind one to be thinking

he has any mind at all," Ms. O'Rourke murmured beside her.

Catherine Stanway was regarding Clay with head cocked. "And what did he mean, Mr. Howard, that you had forsaken your own kind?"

Clay drew himself up, but to his surprise, Allegra pushed between him and her friend. "His own kind? For shame, Catherine! Are we not all God's children?"

Catherine colored and dropped her gaze. "Of course we are, Allegra. Please forgive me." She peered up at him through golden lashes. "And please forgive me as well, Mr. Howard. I didn't mean to imply that . . . well, I don't know what I meant!"

"It's all right, Ms. Stanway," Clay assured her. He glanced around at the few women who had stayed. "You all have a right to know. The Indian Wars of ten years ago may have been over when I joined the citizenry of Seattle, but their effects still linger. Those who push beyond the boundaries are deemed visionaries or fools."

Maddie shivered. "Is it so very wild there, then?"

"It can be," Clay told her.

"But surely there are treaties," Catherine protested, "reservations."

"Oh, the territorial government negotiated treaties and arranged reservations for many of the tribes," Clay agreed, "but less than two in ten of the natives in most cases have moved to the new lands. Would you leave your home because a government you didn't recognize told you that you had to?"

"Some of us did just that, so we did," Maddie murmured, gaze going off into the middle distance.

"Then you'll understand why those of us who can see both sides of the question are sometimes dubbed Indian lovers," Clay told her.

Allegra shook her head. "But how unfair! They call you names on the one hand but come to you for funding on the other."

Catherine put her nose in the air. "We won't behave so uncivilly, will we, ladies?"

They all assured him they thought quite highly of him indeed. He knew he shouldn't care what they thought. His ability to ignore the slurs to his reputation and sanity had stood him in good stead over the years. Yet when Allegra laid her hand on his arm and gazed up at him, he felt as if he'd grown another foot taller.

"We want to hear what you have to say, Clay," she said, voice firm with conviction. "Please don't listen to Mr. Mercer."

Though he could see her friends nodding

fervently and Gillian gazing up at him expectantly, somehow Allegra's look was the brightest. Clay smiled and put his hand over hers. "I haven't listened to the likes of Mercer for most of my life. I wouldn't want to set a precedent now."

And so the classes continued. The much smaller group met on the hurricane deck each morning. The ladies brought out their parasols against the stray bit of sunlight that managed to skip under the sail stretched above them. Even the ship's officers found a moment or two from their duties to lounge on the deck and listen.

Though they were always respectful to any passenger, the officers had told Clay enough that he knew they bore Mercer little love. They couldn't understand why the emigration agent had forbidden his charges from interacting with any member of the crew, including them. Of course, Mercer's edict hadn't stopped the ladies from flirting, just as it didn't stop some of them from attending Clay's classes.

Mercer, however, was not content to merely protest. The women who approved of his approach clustered around him on the main deck, promenading or strolling. Some made sure to stand just below the hurricane deck and talk loudly, as if trying to drown out anything Clay had to say. He'd never been more pleased with his deep voice, for it wasn't hard to top the higher-pitched voices floating up from below.

At the dinner table, those supporters of Mercer who dined in the lower salon sat at one end, and Clay's students sat at the other. He pitied the people like Matt Kelley who sat in the middle, for they bore the brunt of hostility from both sides.

"This is ridiculous," Clay told Mercer when he came upon the fellow one afternoon on his constitutional. "Do you really think I'd harm any of these women by telling them the truth about Seattle?"

Mercer clasped his hands behind his coat and raised his head to meet Clay's gaze. "If you were telling the truth, sir, I would be the first to endorse you. As it is, I can only reiterate my demands that you cease immediately."

Clay shook his head. Mercer and his cronies seemed to have a vision for the future of Seattle — fine clapboard houses, Sunday services in a whitewashed chapel, promenades up Main Street. That might be Seattle someday, but they didn't much want to hear it wasn't Seattle today.

"They remind me of the early pioneers," Clay told Allegra. "They originally named the city New York Alki, meaning New York by and by. But Mercer isn't willing to admit that the by and by isn't the here and now."

Allegra met with Clay each night after dinner to plan the next lesson. They sat under a lantern at a little table along one wall of the lower salon while Catherine or Maddie kept an eye on Gillian. Clay would have preferred to simply teach about whatever was foremost on his mind that day, but Allegra had a more strategic point of view.

"Edibles," she said at one point, tapping her pen to her lips as she studied the latest notes his students had submitted to her. "There's an excellent topic." She glanced up at him, dark brows drawn down over her nose. "Exactly which plants native to the area are edible and which should be considered poisonous? I think if we were to arrange them by seasonal availability, that would be most useful."

"Most useful to whom?" he couldn't help teasing. "I'll have you know, Mrs. Howard, that all plants in Seattle are edible and grow every day of the year. They even pull themselves from the ground, wash themselves and present themselves to your table precisely at dinnertime."

Gillian had been sitting on Allie's lap that evening. Now she regarded him with wide eyes. "Really?"

Allegra smiled at Clay over her daughter's head. "Your uncle is teasing us, Gillian. He thinks that's something Mr. Mercer would say about the plants in Seattle."

"Mr. Mercer is silly," Gillian said as if that was the worst complaint she could imagine.

Clay chuckled. "There's something to be said for silliness, Captain Howard. But I'll write down a list of plants in season if that pleases your mother."

By the way Allegra smiled, that pleased her very much indeed.

He couldn't help thinking, however, that she'd be far less pleased if she knew the primary reason he continued teaching the class. He liked Maddie's baking well enough, and he knew he was helping the other women prepare for their new home. But the truth of the matter was that Allegra didn't fight him so much when he was teaching. Standing on the hurricane deck pontificating was the perfect way to watch over her and Gillian.

He realized Allegra would balk if she knew. When had she grown so fiercely independent? Frank couldn't have been such a miserable husband that she felt she had to do everything herself.

He was fairly sure she wouldn't answer

him if he asked a third time why she'd chosen to leave Boston. So he decided to ask someone else instead.

"Ms. O'Rourke," he said as class was ending one day. "A moment of your time."

Allegra raised her midnight black brows at him as she herded Gillian toward the stairs. Clay tried to ignore her as well as the warmth that was rising in his cheeks. Her friend strolled up to him, put her hands on the hips of her green wool dress and tilted back her head to look up at him. Those brown eyes sparked brighter than the waves around them.

"I did my lessons neat as you please, teacher," she said. "Please don't go rapping my knuckles."

Clay shook his head. "I have no reason to treat you so shabbily, Ms. O'Rourke."

She rolled her eyes. "And haven't we known each other long enough that you could call me Maddie?"

Clay felt himself grinning. "I suppose we have, Maddie. Feel free to call me Clay."

She giggled. "And wouldn't Mrs. Howard think poorly of me if I did, you and her being related and all?"

"You think Allegra would mind if you called me by my first name?" Why did that thought so please him?

She slapped at his arm. "Well, of course she would! She's told me the story. You were her affianced at one time."

"But she married my brother," Clay reminded her. He glanced over the top of her to make sure Allegra had gone down the stairs, then took her arm and drew her closer to the stack from the boiler, where their words were more likely to be hidden under the engine's throb.

"As you know the story," Clay said to Maddie, "tell me, was Frank cruel to Allegra?"

Her reddish brows shot up, then she giggled again. "My, but you sound like me, Clay. Most folks would have tiptoed up to a question like that."

Clay shrugged. "Maybe I've been eating too much of your baking, Maddie." He glanced over the edge of the deck in time to see Allegra gazing up at them, a frown on her fair face. He shuffled back a few steps and focused on her friend again.

The redhead was regarding him out of the corners of her eyes. "You needn't worry yourself about Mrs. Howard and your brother. From what I've heard, he loved her true."

That didn't surprise him. Who wouldn't love Allegra? "Then why did she leave

Boston?" he demanded. "She had everything a woman could need."

Maddie shrugged. "I suppose that depends on the woman, so it does. From the sound of it, she had a fine home, only it wasn't truly her own. She had gowns and shawls, but someone else had the choosing of them. She helped the poor and attended events, but only when she was allowed. Sure'n it was a fine life."

Clay frowned. "You make her sound like a prisoner."

Maddie beamed at him. "And haven't I always said what a clever man you are! Perhaps that's why you ran away from Boston, too."

"I didn't run." He felt himself stiffening at the slur and forced himself to relax. "I told my father my concerns. He had a future planned for me that suited me not at all. Had I done what he wanted I would have been an abject failure. He wouldn't bend, I couldn't stay."

She peered up at him. "And that's why you and Allegra rub against each other sometimes. You're too much alike!"

Clay opened his mouth to protest, then shut it again. If his family's dictates had driven Allegra out of Boston, she did have a lot in common with him. But Maddie was wrong when she said they were too much alike. Allegra was fixed on her future. He couldn't forget his past.

What was he doing? Allie stood on her tiptoes on the main deck, but all she could see was the very top of Clay's head, the salty breeze fingering his red-gold hair. With the noise from the engine, she couldn't catch a word of what he and Maddie were discussing.

"I wouldn't worry," Catherine said beside her. "Very likely he's just putting in his next order for sweets."

"Of course," Allie said, feeling foolish. And really, Clay could speak to whomever he liked. Maddie wasn't the first one to cast a glance in his direction, and she wouldn't be the last.

Allie was merely glad he was willing to keep teaching. Every day his words opened up a new world, challenging her vision. When she'd first heard Mr. Mercer extol Seattle's virtues, she'd been sure of God's leading and her own ability to take care of her and Gillian with her sewing. Many a woman in Boston had supported herself or family that way. She'd met several who had sewed for her mother or the Howards over the years.

Now she could only wonder. From what Clay said, there would be little call for fine sewing in Seattle, and nearly every woman aboard was skilled in that area. She'd seen the embroidery and tiny stitches they put onto their clothes as they whiled away the time on deck most afternoons. They wouldn't need to pay for such services.

So what else could Allie do? She supposed she could teach, but several women already had experience and stellar references in that area, and by all accounts there were few children. She didn't have the money to start her own store; she wasn't suited to be a logger or fur trapper.

There must be some job she could take to keep her from having to marry!

She was still considering the matter when she brought Gillian to play the piano in the upper salon that afternoon. Clay and some of the other men had fixed it onto its legs at last, and now it was seldom silent as the ladies took turns entertaining. Gillian had learned the rudiments in Boston, and now Allie showed her how to play some simple songs.

"That man is utterly contemptible," Catherine declared, coming to stand beside the piano with a mutinous look in her eyes.

Gillian regarded her with a frown, but Allie ran her fingers up the keys to distract her daughter. "And who has earned your wrath this time?" she asked her friend.

"Mr. Mercer, who else?" Catherine sat on a chair near the piano. Though her color was high, her back did not so much as slump as she folded her hands properly in the lap of her gray gown. "A New York publisher donated an entire library of books for our enjoyment on this trip, and Mr. Mercer has appropriated the best of them — Chaucer, Milton, Shakespeare, Everard. He says we will only damage them. He seems to think we do nothing but sit around and drool all day!"

"And so we do," Maddie said, coming to join them, as well. "Drool over the officers, that is, or so he fears. His lordship definitely prefers to see us gainfully employed. This morning he brought out a trunk of yarn and set a bunch of lasses to knitting. He says he'll be holding a great fair in Seattle after we arrive and sell our makings to help pay our expenses."

Catherine's eyes narrowed.

"What's to become of the donated books when we reach Seattle?" Allie asked Maddie, helping Gillian position her fingers properly on the keyboard.

Maddie shrugged. "I haven't heard, but

I'm thinking Mr. Mercer will likely be selling them, too."

"Without allowing us the contentment of reading them?" She wasn't sure why that thought so incensed her, but the insult of it pushed her off the bench. "Those books were donated for our use, and I intend to make use of them."

Catherine rose, as well. "Protest, dear sister. We are behind you."

As if to prove it, Maddie rolled up her sleeves.

"Gillian, wait here," Allie told her daughter. Then she turned and with her two friends started toward the other side of the room.

The space was largely empty so early in the afternoon. Clay and Mr. Reynolds were playing checkers at a little table along one wall. The chair must have been a tight fit or too hard, because she'd noticed earlier that Clay kept shifting this way and that as if he couldn't get comfortable. Now he glanced up, and his gaze met hers.

A slow smile grew on his face, and she had to fight to keep from answering it. She was no flirt! But she couldn't help noticing that he leaned back as if to watch her as she and her friends approached Mr. Mercer, who was standing by the whitewashed bookcase along the opposite wall.

"Alphabetical order by author, if you please," he was dictating to one of the younger women who was helping unpack the boxes. *"I before E except after C."*

"That is only for spelling, sir," Catherine informed him as they came to a stop beside the pair. "Not for alphabetizing."

He smiled at her. "It was a test, dear lady, only a test. And of course you passed it perfectly. How fortunate I am to be among such ladies of refinement."

"But not of education, it would seem," Allie told him. As Gillian began plunking out a tune, Allie bent and picked up one of the books the other woman was about to put on the shelf. "Are we fit for nothing but children's readers?"

Mercer took it from her hand as if he feared her mere touch would damage it. "You may borrow it later, if you like, Mrs. Howard. If you learn it by heart, you can read it to your daughter."

He thought she couldn't read anything more than a primer? And she had hoped to leave tyranny behind in Boston! Words utterly failed her.

As if he thought her in need of support, Clay rose and strolled closer. Oh, no, she needed no rescue in this case.

185

She drew herself up and fixed her glare on Asa Mercer. "My daughter," she informed him, "mastered this text three months ago. And I am more partial to Blake."

Clay's voice was like a rumble of thunder. " 'A truth that's told with bad intent beats all the lies you can invent,' " he quoted.

Mercer turned red, but the line only steeled Allie's spine. She held out her hand. "I understand you kept back a number of books, Mr. Mercer. I'd like to see them."

"Now, now," Mercer said, smile so firmly in place it might have been chiseled from stone. "They are very fine editions, and I should not like to see them injured."

"And would you prefer to be seeing yourself injured?" Maddie asked sweetly.

Mercer blinked.

"I'd be careful if I were you, Ms. O'Rourke," Mr. Reynolds warned as he joined Clay at their sides. "We're crossing the equator tonight, and ladies who misbehave have been known to receive a scold from Father Neptune."

Father Neptune? What was this? Allie knew her frown matched Mr. Mercer's.

Clay, however, stiffened. "That's enough, Reynolds," he said, voice low and forceful. "I doubt any man aboard this ship would

186

countenance harm to a lady."

"Who precisely is this Father Neptune?" Catherine demanded.

"It's all in good fun," Mr. Reynolds assured her. "An old naval tradition that welcomes those crossing the equator for the first time."

"I don't call dousing people with seawater welcoming," Clay countered.

Maddie raised her reddish brows. "Would you be threatening me, Mr. Reynolds?"

Reynolds held up his hands. "Never, ladies! My apologies! It was merely a joke."

Mercer assured him no offense had been taken, but Allie couldn't help wondering if some mischief was planned.

"I'll expect to see the rest of those books on the shelves by tomorrow, sir," she informed Mr. Mercer. Then she took Catherine's arm and motioned Maddie with her free hand to return with them to the piano. She could feel Clay's gaze on them, but she refused to meet it.

"Father Neptune," Maddie sneered as they gathered together beside Gillian. "He'd do better to fear Mother Maddie!"

"No one should have anything to fear tonight," Allie told both her friends. "And we're going to make sure of it."

CHAPTER ELEVEN

Clay prowled the ship that evening, unable to settle. He'd heard from others who had come to Seattle by ship that sailing crews could sometimes be merciless to those crossing the equator the first time. It wasn't unknown for pollywogs, as they were called, to be doused in seawater or struck with ropes. He didn't think any of the sailors aboard the *Continental* would try such tactics on a lady, but when it came to Allegra and Gillian, he didn't like to take chances.

"Have you heard anything about a line-crossing ceremony?" he asked Roger Conant when the reporter passed him on the way to dinner that evening.

A tall, slender, brown-haired man with a dapper style and cutting wit, Conant raised a brow. "Concerned, Howard? Tell me, what dastardly deeds have you performed to earn Neptune's wrath?"

Clay knew anything he confessed would find its way into the man's next report to his newspaper. "Nothing," he promised. "I'm more concerned about how the lady passengers will feel if they are the target."

Conant shrugged. "All I can tell you is that something is afoot. The junior officers have been muttering among themselves all day, and I hear salt water is to play a part."

Clay resigned himself to a long night.

He wasn't sure whether Mercer understood the potential for trouble or whether he was merely continuing in his quest to separate the ladies from the officers. Either way, the emigration agent made a great show of heading for his room at ten o'clock, insisting that any lady in his charge would do so, as well.

A few agreed, and any number of rooms were shut tight by that hour, with no light shining through the slats on the doors. As if to make a point, Allegra, Gillian and Maddie remained in the lower salon. Allegra was sitting with Gillian on her lap as Matt Kelley attempted to teach the little girl checkers. Maddie perched on a chair next to their table to watch. Clay wandered over, as well.

Mr. Debro joined them, his smile pleasant as usual.

"Ms. O'Rourke, Mr. Howard," he said

after greeting Allegra, Gillian and Matt. "I simply wanted to say what assets you've been to this journey. Those molasses cookies today were the best I've eaten in years."

"It's just in how you mix the flour and molasses," Maddie assured him, though Clay caught sight of Matt licking his lips at the memory. "But I'm happy to hear you enjoyed them, so I am. Only, don't be expecting more after tonight, for we put the last of the molasses to other uses." She glanced at Clay out of the corner of her eye.

Interesting. What other baked good required extensive amounts of molasses? He could hardly wait to find out.

"Just as well," Mr. Debro said, patting the flat of his stomach. "Many more of those cookies, and I would have popped a button."

"Why?" Gillian said, and Allegra smiled as she pointed her back to the game.

"As for you, Mr. Howard," the purser continued, face reddening just the slightest from Gillian's question, "I don't think I've ever served another passenger so ready to work. Captain Windsor says I'm taking advantage of your good nature. I hope that isn't the case."

"Not at all," Clay replied. "I suppose I've grown used to working. Once I left Boston,

I learned that you do the best you can, but there're always times when you need another set of hands, another point of view. I've received such help often enough that I'm glad to give it back."

"That's because you're nice," Gillian said. She jumped one of Matt's checkers and glanced over at him as if to make sure he didn't mind. Matt grinned in encouragement.

"Your uncle can be both kind and generous," Allegra said with a smile to her daughter as if to encourage her, as well.

He was going to end up bumping his head against the ceiling if they kept praising him this way. "Isn't it your bedtime, Captain Howard?"

To his surprise, Allegra's look darkened, and she glanced at the ship's clock on the far wall, where the hands showed a few minutes after ten. "Not just yet," she said.

"Mother says we are protesting," Gillian informed him. She jumped two more checkers and frowned. "There aren't any more spaces."

Matt started explaining the next stage of the game, dark head bent over the board and slender hands moving, but Clay could not shake his concern. Allegra and her friends intended to show Mercer he had no control over them. Would their actions end up bringing trouble on their heads tonight?

As it was, Allegra and Gillian stayed up until half past ten before glancing about and bidding the company good-night. Clay thought Allegra's gaze rested on him the longest, but he wasn't sure why. Matt followed them to their stateroom before taking his leave, as well.

Others, like Maddie, continued to occupy the lower salon in direct defiance of Mercer's orders, talking with friends or promenading on the arm of one of the unmarried senior officers. Clay settled himself into a wooden chair along the wall and waited.

As the hour grew later, the crowd thinned. One by one, the women bid their friends good-night, the men made their excuses, until only Clay, Maddie and Mr. Debro remained. As the purser went about extinguishing the candles in most of the lamps, she strolled over and plunked herself down on the chair beside Clay's.

"Sure'n you've no call to defy Mercer's orders," she said with a smile. "They don't apply to you. So what would be keeping you up?"

Clay leaned back in his chair. "It must be the excitement of crossing the equator."

She chuckled. "Excitement, he calls it. And why would that be cause for celebration? It isn't as if they painted a big red line across the ocean, you know. It's just a silly made-up thing."

"I cannot agree, by your leave, Ms. O'Rourke," the purser said, coming to take down the lantern nearest them. "You may not see the equator, but it divides our world. Crossing from one hemisphere to another is a rare thing, even for some sailors."

"Aye, and so is crossing the Atlantic," she countered. "But I did that at me da's knee. No one celebrated that. I'm not thinking the going south is any grander than the going west."

"I cannot argue with you there." Mr. Debro nodded to them both. "I'll be turning in now. Leave the lantern burning by the kitchen in case there's need of it." He tipped his cap to Maddie. "Good night, Ms. O'Rourke."

"May you be having pleasant dreams, Mr. Debro," she replied. She rose from her chair as the purser moved off, then nodded to Clay. "I'm thinking it's time I turned in meself."

Clay rose as well. "Good night, Maddie."

Before she could answer, a board creaked to their right, and Clay swung his gaze in

193

that direction. The glow of the last lantern left a circle of light around the door to the galley. The rest of the room was sinking into twilight. Did something move along the far wall?

"Who are you expecting?" Maddie murmured as if she'd seen his look.

"Trouble," Clay murmured back. He kept his gaze on the darker shape that seemed to be gliding toward the kitchen.

She stood on tiptoe to speak in his ear, blocking his view for a moment. "Rest easy, Clay. We're expecting trouble, too. But I own a derringer, and I'm not afraid to be using it." Dropping back onto the balls of her feet, she headed for the room she shared with Allegra and Gillian.

Clay started forward toward the shadow he'd seen, then realized that the way to the kitchen lay empty. He glanced around, ears straining for any sound. A snort from one of the rooms told him someone was about to commence snoring.

He ought to go to bed himself. Maddie claimed they were ready for trouble. And a derringer? He shuddered thinking how the temperamental redhead would use such a pistol. He'd handed his over to Captain Windsor to be stored in the ammunition locker.

Of course, she could well have cause to be so prepared. There was still an unreasonable belief in the East that anyone of Irish descent was somehow less than human. He'd seen cartoons in the paper depicting them as bulldogs or apes. Based on comments he'd overheard, some aboard ship still harbored the prejudice. Would their misguided feelings cause them to strike out against Maddie tonight? Would Allegra and Gillian be hurt in the process?

Clay shook his head. What was wrong with him? Was he so determined to protect Allegra that he saw danger around every corner? She'd proven herself more than capable of taking care of herself and Gillian aboard ship. Was he trying to find a way to justify his presence here?

And then there was the matter of Seattle. He knew a number of the women were looking to find employment. Maddie intended to bake and Catherine to nurse. Others clearly hoped for husbands. Allegra hadn't mentioned what she hoped to do. As determined as she was to stand on her own, surely she wasn't seeking to remarry.

He sighed as he glanced around the room. The shadows appeared to be drawing closer. He'd thought he was only being practical to keep watch. Now his concerns about the future seemed to darken the room, and he felt as if a dozen gazes were following his every movement with malevolent intent.

"I'm ready for you," he said aloud and immediately felt foolish. The only answer was the slosh of the waves against the ship, the only smell the burning tallow from the candle in the lantern. He was completely alone.

Somewhere behind him came a soft click.

Clay whirled, staring into the darkness. Was that the sound of a door being opened? Was trouble even now closing in on his family?

There was only one way to know for sure. He crept across the salon, eyes and ears on the alert. Putting his hand to the latch on Allegra's door, he turned it just the slightest. It moved quickly, smoothly, as if someone else had just turned it as well. Heart stuttering, he eased open the door.

Something fell with a clatter, and mud seemed to trickle into his ear. Even as he clapped one hand to his cheek, he heard Allegra cry, "Light the lamp!"

The lantern flared to life, brightening the space. White tuffs of feathers floated in the air.

"Is everyone all right?" Clay demanded, waving the fluffy cloud away from his face.

Allegra and Maddie were staring at him. Allegra looked dismayed, her mouth open. Neither of them had changed for bed, and the deep pockets on the bunks told him they'd been sitting up, waiting for such a moment. Gillian peered down from the upper berth at him, frowning.

"But Mother," she protested, "that's not Father Neptune. That's my uncle."

"Father Neptune, eh?" Clay asked, but his cheek and jaw felt stiff. Reaching up, he felt feathers and something sticky.

"Oh, Clay!" Allegra rushed forward. "I'm so sorry! We heard some might play pranks tonight, so we decided to protect ourselves." She plucked a feather off his chin with trembling fingers.

Clay stared at it. "Did you just tar and feather me?"

Allegra blushed.

Maddie shook her head. "Sure'n it's just molasses and feathers from the pillows. It will wash right off."

Clay started to laugh, then choked it back as the congealing molasses pulled at his skin. "Serves me right, I suppose, entering a lady's room unannounced. In my defense, I was just trying to make sure Father Neptune hadn't played any tricks on you."

"I don't like him," Gillian said. "He

sounds mean."

"You'd ban him from your ship, I know, Captain Howard," Clay assured her. "But don't you worry. Your mother can protect herself. She'll make sure he doesn't come anywhere near you. Now, if you'll excuse me, I think I better go peel this off before it gets any harder."

Perhaps it was because he had admitted she could take care of herself. Perhaps it was because she'd been the one to devise the trap for Father Neptune that had snared Clay instead. Whatever the reason, Allie felt compelled to offer her help. She thought Clay might refuse, but he waved her ahead of him out into the lower salon.

"Ms. Gillian and my own self will be right here," Maddie promised, keeping the door open and narrowing her eyes as if she still expected someone to play some trick on them.

Allie had been equally concerned Mr. Reynolds or one of the ship's officers would think it a grand joke to tease Gillian or Maddie. She'd considered Mercer, as well, for the antipathy between them was growing, but she rather thought any man who hid in a coal bin to escape confrontation wasn't likely to be brave enough to try a prank. Surely anyone tiptoeing about tonight would do nothing if they saw her and Clay standing in the salon.

"Wait here," she told Clay as he paused at the nearest end of the dining table. He settled himself with one hip against the wood as she went to the galley. Mindful of the cook sleeping at the back of it, she found a rag and wet it with the water that was always kept hot on the stove.

Clay was watching her as she returned. Her plans had worked far better than she'd expected. One side of his face was obscured by a shining brown mass that would have made him look like a gingerbread man except that feathers stuck up at odd angles. She pressed her lips together to keep from laughing.

"Go ahead," he said, though his usual deep voice came out strained as the molasses dripped off his lips. "The joke's on me, I know. Someone might as well enjoy it."

She couldn't help her smile as she held the heated cloth against his cheek. "I'm really very sorry. You must know this wasn't meant for you."

As she removed the cloth, he reached up to run his fingers over the molasses. He found the upper edge below his eye and began to roll the mess down his face. His day's growth of beard seemed to be coming with it; she could see specks of gold among the brown. The skin left behind was a shiny pink.

"So sorry," she repeated.

Clay kept working at the molasses. "You were only protecting yourself and Gillian. I understand."

"Telling a lady she can take care of herself twice in one hour," Allie marveled. "I shall have to be careful, Mr. Howard, or such praise will go to my head."

He grimaced, but she didn't know if the look had been caused by her words or the pull of the makeshift tar. She went to wet the cloth again and brought it back for him.

This time he took it from her hand and pressed it against his face himself. His gaze met hers over the material, his eyes in the dim lamplight were the color of the cool green waters. "You should be praised, Allegra, every hour of every day. You're raising Gillian alone, helping others advance themselves, making sure your friends have the knowledge they need to survive in Seattle. You amaze me."

She thought her skin must be as pink as his. "Anyone can be amazing, Clay, if you give them a chance."

"Now, *that* I highly doubt." His fingers, so

strong, wiped away the last of the molasses. She plucked a stray feather off his chin. He caught her hand, held it tight.

"What are you going to do when we reach Seattle, Allegra?" he murmured. "You've fought to get this far. You have to know it will only get harder from here."

She shook her head. "But it can't, Clay. The hard part was making up my mind to do something, to go somewhere. Now I just have to keep moving, and everything will be all right."

"I envy your optimism." His thumb caressed the back of her hand, raising goose bumps along her arm. "But I can't help thinking you're going from the frying pan into the fire. How do you expect to support Gillian?"

Fear flared inside her like a wick brought to life. No! She would not give in. *This is Your leading, Lord. Help me remember that.*

"I'll find a way," she told Clay. "I had hoped to open shop as a seamstress, but I can see now there won't be enough work."

Some part of her hoped he would argue that point, but he nodded instead. She could feel her spine straightening.

"There must be some need for an educated woman in Seattle," she insisted. "Perhaps something you teach us will strike a chord. Or perhaps it will come to me when we get there." She took the cloth from his other hand.

He peered at her as if trying to gauge how she was going to react to his next words. "You're starting to sound like me, going where the wind blows you. Most folks can't handle that way of life."

"You did," she pointed out. "You seem to have done well."

He eyed her as if she'd never thought to hear her admit his success. "I admire your determination, Allegra. But what if you're wrong? What if the only choice left to you is to marry to keep you and Gillian from starving?"

Frustration pushed her back from him, pulled her hand from his. "If you have to ask, you really don't know me at all." She started past him to return the cloth to the galley, and he caught her arm.

"I won't let you starve," he promised. "If the worst happens, come to me. I'll make sure you and Gillian are cared for."

It was a noble gesture. She knew that. He was being the gentleman everyone had always hoped he'd be, the kind person Gillian had named him. She laid her free hand against his cheek and was surprised to find it as soft as the silk of her gowns.

"Thank you for the offer," she murmured. "I know it is sincere. But perhaps, Clay, it's time I cared for myself."

He was silent a moment, but she could feel the tension in him. His broad shoulders strained against his coat; every plane of his face was tight and controlled. At last he drew in a deep breath and looked away.

"You asked me to compromise my beliefs once and stay in Boston," he said, deep voice as gentle as a caress. "I couldn't do that. Now you're asking me to compromise again, and I'm finding it just as hard." His look speared back to hers. "I returned to Boston to protect you, Allegra. I jumped aboard this ship to protect you. Don't ask me to stop."

She laid a hand on his arm. "But I must ask you, Clay. If you protect me from every mistake, how will I learn?"

He took her hand, cradled it in both of his. The warmth of his touch made her own muscles feel as soft as the molasses. "And how can I stand by and watch you and Gillian get hurt?" he murmured. "I'd sooner cut off my own arm."

"I understand," Allie told him. "I struggle to know when I should keep Gillian close and when I should let her try her wings. But that's different. I'm her mother. It's my duty and privilege to guide her steps. You aren't my father, Clay. It's not your responsibility to save me from myself. Frankly, it's not your responsibility to save me at all."

Oh, but she was going to have a mutiny on her hands any moment. She could almost see the arguments mustering behind his eyes. It wasn't in him to give up on something he believed. Perhaps that's one of the things she admired most about him.

But she wasn't about to give up, either.

She pulled away from him. "Let me offer you a compromise, though I know how much you hate the concept."

He cocked his head. "I'm listening."

That was more than she'd once thought possible. "Give me the opportunity to make my own mistakes," she said, "to chart my own course, just as you did when you left Boston. And I promise, if I feel myself incapable of resolving a problem, I'll come to you for advice."

She held out her hand. "Do we have a bargain, sir?"

He hesitated a moment, then swallowed her hand in his grip. His fingers were as firm as her convictions. "We have a bargain, madam, though I have my doubts that either of us can keep it."

CHAPTER TWELVE

Who was this woman who called herself Allegra Howard? Clay had always found her beautiful, from her thick raven tresses to her sculptured figure. Now her determination seemed to light her from within like a candle in a lamp. The glow only served to draw him closer.

And that would be a mistake for them both. She was journeying to Seattle to make a fresh start, to provide for her daughter. His life held no stability. Oh, Allegra claimed to be willing to improvise, but he thought that was optimism talking. They'd both been raised to expect a husband to be a steady, reliable force in the home. He'd long ago realized he could never be that man. The best he could do was comply with her wishes and give her room to try her wings.

He even thought he was dealing fairly well with the idea, at first. He listened to her advice on what to teach, from medicinal uses of the local plants to the best clothing for wet, cold winters. He watched her shelve the books she had insisted Mercer allow the women to read and only carried the heaviest box from storage for her, even though she hadn't asked. He didn't intercede when she stood up against Mercer on an increasing number of topics.

But when they reached Rio de Janeiro in the middle of February, he knew he'd have more trouble merely standing by.

After more than three weeks aboard ship, Clay was itching to set his feet on land again. He wasn't the only one. It seemed every woman on board was leaning over the bulwark to catch a glimpse of the red-clay roof tiles of the city. That was about all that could be seen from the harbor, for around them the masts of other ships, thick as a forest, reached for the sky. Clay knew that Captain Windsor had already sent messages to his fellow captains offering to exchange dinners and the like.

"It appears we are not to be allowed ashore," Allegra told him when he asked if she'd like to visit the city. She was sitting in her stateroom, Maddie curled up on the upper berth with one of their hard-won books, while Allegra sat on a bench plaiting a ribbon into Gillian's golden curls.

"We have to wait," Gillian told him, lower lip trembling.

"On whose orders?" Clay said, hearing his voice sound suspiciously like a grumble.

Allegra's mouth tightened. "Mr. Mercer's and Captain Windsor's. They've gone ashore to make sure the city is safe for us."

She sounded nearly as annoyed as he felt. Clay knew the orders would make for a long day. He could have taught a session of the Seattle School, but no one wanted to think about the territory when such an exotic city waited across the harbor.

So they all clustered on the deck and took turns pointing out places of interest, from the rugged mountains that looked like a man's face staring at the sky, to the deep green waters of the harbor. Tall palms lined the beaches and brightly plumed birds soared overhead.

"Are we to be kept captive aboard this ship?" Allegra asked as she and Gillian stood beside him at the railing. "Unable to partake of all this glory?"

Clay couldn't help smiling at her. "I'll talk to the captain. There must be a way to go ashore."

She shook her head. "It was merely a complaint born of boredom, Clay. I'm perfectly capable of speaking to Captain

Windsor myself."

As it turned out, however, Captain Windsor and Mr. Mercer didn't return until late, so it was the next morning before anyone could request a moment of the gentlemen's time.

Clay had dressed in his navy jacket, tucked his brown wool trousers into his boots and come down to breakfast in the lower salon when he saw Mercer step to the head of the table. Allegra in her blue-and-white gown looked up from where she'd been dividing an apricot-colored muskmelon for Gillian. At least some fruit had found its way aboard from the captain's excursion.

"My dear ladies," Mercer said, raising his hands as if to issue a benediction, "may I have your attention?"

The diners quieted as Clay made his way to stand behind Allegra and Gillian. Mercer smiled as if in appreciation that they had listened to him for once.

"I fear I must be the bearer of ill tidings," he confessed, hanging his head. "The city is besieged by cholera."

Gasps rang out, and Allegra covered the pieces of fruit with her hand before Gillian could take another bite.

"Yes, yes," Mercer said as if he agreed with their dismay. "And smallpox, as well. In epidemic proportions, I fear. The place is most unhealthful, ladies. I cannot advise you to brave the dangers."

Allegra was the first to speak up. "Advise us or allow us?" she asked.

Mercer turned his smile her way. "Why, both, dear lady. It is my duty to protect you."

Clay nearly groaned aloud. Hadn't Mercer learned his lesson by now? If Allegra had refused to allow Clay to protect her, with their family connections and shared past, she wasn't likely to approve of the emigration agent taking that role. But to Clay's surprise, murmurs ran through the group like thunder before a storm. Seemingly oblivious, Mercer excused himself and headed for the upper salon to make his report there, as well.

Allegra lifted her hand to stare at the melon. "The nerve of the man. Are we to be his prisoners?"

Clay ruffled Gillian's silky hair. "If Captain Windsor agrees with him, I'm afraid we will be. What do you think, Captain Howard?"

Gillian was frowning. "What's coller-a?"

Allegra wrapped her arms around her as if to protect her even from the word. "A very nasty disease, Gillian. One none of us wishes to catch."

"And one very unlikely to bother a sweet little girl like you," Reynolds said, strolling up to them. He nodded in greeting to Allegra as he thumped his walking stick down on the floor as if to make his point. "I wouldn't let Mr. Mercer's report stop you from visiting Rio, Mrs. Howard. In fact, I'd be delighted to escort you and your daughter."

Clay scowled at him. "And what if Mercer's telling the truth for once? You could kill your entire party."

Allegra puffed out a breath as if she was thoroughly vexed, but at him or Mercer, he wasn't sure.

Reynolds took a moment to smooth his mustache down either side of his smile. "There were no reports of an epidemic before we sailed," he pointed out. "And I see no quarantine signs on any of the other ships in port. Old man Mercer is merely trying to scare you." He put a hand on Gillian's head. "I say bring the girl ashore. Make it a party. You'd like that, wouldn't you, my sweet?"

Gillian ducked under his hand and scrambled off Allegra's lap to wrap her arms around Clay's leg. "I want to go with my uncle."

Reynolds frowned, but Clay loosened her grip and swung her up on his shoulder. "What, go ashore and abandon your ship, Captain Howard?" he teased, trying to lighten the mood.

"Captain Windsor went," Gillian protested, wiggling to settle herself on her perch. "Please, Mother?"

Clay could feel Allegra's indecision in the tension across the shoulders of her blue gown, the compression of her lips. She had to be as tired of the small ship as he was. And it wasn't as if they were likely to come this way again. Yet was she so determined to try her wings that she'd risk Gillian's health and her own?

"I'd be willing to go ashore if Captain Windsor thinks it advisable," she said at last. "I trust his judgment. Would you ask him, Mr. Reynolds?"

Clay stiffened, but Reynolds bowed as if he'd been given a royal errand. As soon as he'd left the salon, Allegra rose and held up her arms to her daughter.

"Come down, Gillian," she said. "We need to make sure you're ready if we're going ashore."

Gillian obligingly tumbled into her mother's grip, and Allegra bent to put her down on the floor. Motioning to Maddie, who hurried closer, she whispered instructions. With a grin to Clay that somehow told him trouble was coming again, Maddie led Gillian off to their stateroom.

"You, sir," Allegra declared the moment they were out of hearing, "are going back on your promise."

Clay spread his hands. "What, because I stated my opinion? I don't have to agree with everything you do, Allegra. Part of blazing your own path is being willing to stand up to those who oppose you."

"I'm not afraid to stand my ground," she replied. "But when you state your opinion over mine in front of Gillian, you put her in the middle. I will not have it."

Clay shook his head. "You may be able to order your thoughts to suit yourself, Allegra, but you cannot order the world to fall in line. However, I think you're smart to get another report about the matter besides Mercer's. We both know he's likely to say anything so long as it keeps his hens in their coop."

She deflated. "There we can agree. Oh, but the man is maddening! If the city is infested with cholera and smallpox, of course Gillian can't visit. I would never expose her to such dangers."

Only the danger of moving to the opposite

side of the country, it seemed. Yet he knew he could not point that out, not when the fire was only just beginning to fade from her eyes. "I'll come with you if you like."

The fire sprang to life once more. "Did I ask for a nursemaid?"

Clay shook his head. "Did I offer to be one? It's a strange place, Allegra, in a strange country. It makes sense for several of us to go together for protection."

"Protection again." She sighed more forcefully. "Oh, very well. I suppose you're right. But do not dictate to me, Clay Howard, or you may well find yourself alone on that beach, and you'll have no one to blame but yourself."

As soon as the words left her mouth, Allie regretted them. Clay had only been trying to be helpful, and she'd lashed out. She couldn't say she was surprised by her reaction. It seemed at every turn someone stood between her and her goal, and all in the name of protecting her!

Before she could apologize, however, he inclined his head and strode out of the lower salon. She could understand his reaction. Running away had to be preferable to dealing with her flaring temper.

There was definitely a trick to this

independence, and she hadn't mastered it yet. Surely she could find a way to state her opinion and evaluate the thoughts of others without becoming a shrew!

Mr. Reynolds appeared in the doorway from the deck just then and headed toward her. He was a compact fellow, powerful chest, strong jaw, head set squarely on his shoulders. He moved with assurance, as well, as if completely certain he was in the right. Several of the women glanced his way as he passed as if interested. Allie knew if he hadn't been coming to tell her news she'd asked him to retrieve, she probably wouldn't have noticed him. Clay had ever been the only man to command her attention the moment he entered a room.

"Captain Windsor gives his blessing," Mr. Reynolds assured Allie as he joined her. "He agrees that Mr. Mercer's assessment of the situation might be biased a bit too high."

"Too high, but not out of the question," Allie surmised. "So there is cholera and smallpox."

"There's cholera and smallpox in every city of this size," Reynolds replied with a smile that said he found her concerns amusing. "Rio boasts more than four hundred thousand souls. That's nearly ten times the size of Boston." His smile grew as he leaned

214

closer. "Trust me, Mrs. Howard. I would never let anything happen to such a lovely lady."

The spicy scent of his cologne singed her nose, and Allie stepped back from him. "Thank you for the information, Mr. Reynolds. I'll let Maddie and Gillian know we're going. Please tell Mr. Howard, and see if he can find Ms. Stanway."

She started around him, and Reynolds moved to block her way. "Must we invite the others? Couldn't I have you and your charming daughter all to myself for once?"

Allie met his gaze. His smile was warm, but his gray eyes seemed so cold. Was he truly attempting to flirt with her?

"Mr. Reynolds," she said, trying to be kind, "I value your friendship to me and Gillian, but you must know that I will entertain no thoughts of courtship. I never intend to marry again."

A shadow crossed behind his eyes, and he straightened. "Of course, Mrs. Howard. Forgive my presumption. I'll tell Mr. Howard you'll be ready shortly." His walk was stiff as he moved away, and the sound of his walking stick hitting the floor was louder than usual.

Allie sighed as she went to fetch Gillian. She'd managed to depress two gentlemen in a quarter hour. That was not a promising beginning to the day.

She hated to hurt Mr. Reynolds, but she had no feelings for him and couldn't see herself developing any. She could only take comfort in the fact that she was no longer the type of woman willing to keep him dangling with sweet promises she had no intention of keeping.

Thank You, Lord, that I have grown.

When she joined Clay and Mr. Reynolds at the longboat a short time later, she found a group waiting. Catherine and Maddie had been persuaded to come along, and Mr. Debro and another officer were going to row. The purser would be staying onshore to arrange for more fruit and vegetables for their table.

Allie held Gillian close as the boat skimmed over the water, the air warm as summer. The breeze still held the brine of the sea, but over it she fancied she caught the scent of oranges.

"Where shall we go first, Captain Howard?" Clay called from his place near the bow.

Gillian's gaze followed a flock of parrots wheeling overhead. "May I see the birds, please?"

"Best make for the market, then," Mr. De-

216

bro advised from his place amidships. "I hear the botanical gardens are nice, but they're outside the city, so you'd need to hire a hack to visit them."

Allie wasn't sure what to expect as the sounds and scents of Rio wrapped themselves around her. The sun seemed so much brighter here, even on the narrow, crooked streets along buildings of creamy stone. She had to squint to see Clay at the head of their cavalcade as he pushed through crowds of dark-skinned men who called questions in a language she could not understand. Mr. Reynolds walked at the back of the procession, with Allie, Gillian, Maddie and Catherine in the middle. That didn't stop people from pointing at them. They seemed to find Maddie's red hair particularly intriguing.

Allie and the others passed stone churches with sweeping spires and then the long, low line of the imperial palace with its many windows like eyes gazing back. Dust from the street drifted upward, making it seem as if the very air was sparkling. Gillian walked beside her, clinging to her hand and staring about in wonder.

They found the market easily enough by following the trail of those with baskets, some balanced amazingly on their heads.

The stalls hugged the buildings on either side, with barely enough room to walk two abreast between them. Golden bracelets as wide as the white cuff of her blue gown gleamed in the light; chickens clucked from makeshift pens; the scent of onion and garlic spiced the air.

"Come up here, Captain Howard," Clay called, and Allie led Gillian to him. The stall he stood beside was made of a series of reed cages. In each perched one or more parrots with feathers of emerald, scarlet and sapphire. Allie bent to put her face on a level with her daughter's.

"What do you think?" she said over the raucous cries echoing around them.

Gillian stared at the birds, their beaks stained red or yellow, hooked and long, their feathers iridescent in the sunlight. One of the sellers offered her a pale nut and nodded toward the nearest bird. Gillian held the shell out on her open palm, and the parrot reached out to pluck the nut from her hand. Her eyes widened as he cracked the shell and ate the meat.

"He has very nice manners," she told the seller. "Thank you for letting me play with him."

Allie looked up and met Clay's gaze. The smile on his face warmed her more than the sunlight. It was as if he knew how much such moments meant to her and Gillian. She felt tears coming and blinked them back.

They managed to make their way through the market with little loss to their funds. Clay purchased a straw hat and linen shirt at a bargain. Catherine had succumbed to a fan painted with exotic birds and Maddie was cradling a gourd carved to look like a monkey's face. Allie kept tight hold on Gillian's hand as they ventured out onto a square where a stone fountain sprayed water into a massive basin in which dozens of women were doing laundry.

"Fancy that," Maddie said with a shake of her head. "And I had to lug water up two flights of stairs back home."

Mr. Reynolds had been quiet the whole trip. Now he tipped his hat to Gillian. "What do you say, Ms. Howard? Would you like a closer look at how they wash clothes in Brazil?" He held out his hand.

Gillian pressed herself close to Allie's skirts. "No." Her voice came out muffled. "Go away."

"Gillian!" Allie put her hand on her daughter's head. "I'm sorry, Mr. Reynolds. She knows better than to behave so rudely."

Gillian glanced out from Allie's skirts, face

pale and anguished. "Am I to be punished, Mother?"

Allie's heart twisted. Of those in their little group, only she and Gillian knew how harsh punishment had once been. She bent to cuddle her daughter close. "No, Gillian, but I think you owe Mr. Reynolds an apology."

Gillian kept her gaze on Allie's. "I don't like him."

Mr. Reynolds must have heard the exchange, for when Allie glanced up, she saw that his face had darkened.

Clay knelt beside her and Gillian and tipped back his straw hat. "She's just unsure of a new situation," he murmured to Allie. He took Gillian's hand. "Let's set our sails for the botanical gardens, Captain Howard. You ought to find those to your liking. I bet they're as big as your grandmother's garden in Boston."

Gillian peered at Allie as if for permission. Allie nodded, rising, and Gillian deigned to go with Clay in search of a hack. Mr. Reynolds tipped his hat and excused himself.

Allie shook her head, watching her daughter walk with ladylike tread beside Clay, who had obviously shortened his stride to allow her to keep up. "I don't know what got into her."

"She certainly seems to have taken Mr. Reynolds in dislike," Catherine agreed. She opened her new fan and fluttered it before her face as children began dancing in the spume from the fountain.

"He's not such a bad sort," Maddie mused, watching as he disappeared among the crowds. "He seems to mean well, so he does."

"I fear she can tell he has feelings for you," Catherine said, snapping her fan decisively shut. "She doesn't relish the idea of sharing you."

Allie frowned. "But she shares me with you two. She shares me with Matt Kelley. She shares me with Clay."

"A very wise young lady, to be sure," Maddie said with a smile. "Perhaps you should be asking yourself why she feels more comfortable with Mr. Howard than Mr. Reynolds."

"Indeed," Catherine added. "And why you, my dear Allegra, do not."

"I'm perfectly comfortable with Clay," Allie protested. Her face felt hot, but she was certain the warmth was caused by the powerful equatorial sun.

"Oh, aye," Maddie said with a look to Catherine. "So comfortable you bite the poor fellow's head off when he so much as opens a door for you." She poked a finger at Allie. "Admit it, my girl. You're sweet on the man."

"I most certainly am not!" Allie stared at her two friends. They were both nodding, but she knew they were not agreeing with her. "I'm not!"

"So you say," Catherine replied, moving toward where Clay was waving to them, having procured two of the small wooden carts that were used for transportation in the city. "But if I were you, Allegra, I would ask myself why you feel the need to protest the matter so stridently."

CHAPTER THIRTEEN

Catherine's question remained much on Allie's mind as the *Continental* weighed anchor and steamed south. What was it about Mr. Reynolds that made Gillian so distrustful? Had her daughter's animosity colored her own view of the man?

She watched him more closely after they set off to sea again and their routine returned to normal. He was always quick to tip his hat to a lady, provided she was pretty, young and modest. If she had some physical flaw such as frizzy hair or an unfortunate nose, was older or spoke her own mind, he was equally quick to give her a set down or ignore her completely.

"I begin to think Gillian is right," she confessed to Catherine as they promenaded around the ship. "He has a mean spirit."

"It seems to me," Catherine replied, studiously avoiding glancing in the fellow's direction, "that our choice to leave home disgusts him. Of course, I wonder sometimes if your friend Mr. Howard doesn't feel the same way."

Allie glanced to where Clay had Gillian up on his shoulders by the railing, her daughter's rainbow-colored skirts bright against the navy of his jacket. From the intense look on her daughter's face, Allie knew they were playing Gillian's favorite game — hunting for mermaids in the blue ocean waves.

"You're wrong," she said to Catherine. "He thinks Seattle isn't safe for a civilized lady, but he doesn't belittle us for trying to better our lot."

"Perhaps it's time the Seattle School started up again," Catherine mused.

Allie agreed. With Rio behind them, it was easier to turn their sights once more on their destination. She decided to approach Clay that very evening to discuss his next lesson.

"I suppose I should be glad your friends have so many questions, but what more can I tell them?" he asked, rubbing his chin with one hand where they sat in the upper salon listening to one of the ladies play a complicated sonata on the piano while the officers lounged around her and Gillian leaned against the instrument, obviously fascinated.

Allie couldn't help noticing that the stubble had grown back where the molasses had pulled it off Clay's chin. Now the hair lay like a golden haze across his jaw.

"Several have asked about occupations," she reported, glancing down at the notes she'd taken when she'd asked the other women for input that afternoon. "We had been given to understand that teachers were desperately needed, but you seem to think otherwise. They'd like to know where you see opportunities in Seattle."

Clay grinned at her. "Besides marrying a miner who's struck it rich?"

Allie shook her head. "How many times must I assure you, sir, that not every woman aboard ship intends to marry? And even if they do marry, they'd like to know how they can contribute to their new community. My friends are no more willing to serve as a decoration for their husband's parlor than I am."

Clay straightened in his chair. "Is that what you were in Boston? I'd have thought better of Frank."

Frank had treated her like a porcelain doll, fragile, precious. He hadn't shared his thoughts or his plans. She'd been the one most shocked when he'd declared he'd joined the army to fight in the war.

225

Except, perhaps, his mother. Mrs. Howard had glared across the table where Allie and Frank had been dining with her the evening Frank had made his announcement. But his mother's glare had never touched her darling son. It had been fixed on Allie.

Mrs. Howard knew, as many of the best Boston ladies had agreed afterward, that it must have been some fault of Allie's that had driven the normally docile Frank Howard to such a decision. After all, Frank had been wealthy enough that he could have paid some man to fight in his place if his conscience tweaked him.

Even thinking about her failed marriage hurt. How could she confess to Clay his brother's shortcomings or her own? Frank may have kept her out of his life, but she refused to be so disloyal as to blacken his memory. And she would never say anything to turn Clay against his own mother the way his mother had tried to come between her and Gillian.

"It doesn't matter," she started, but Clay reached out to take her hand.

"Of course it matters." His deep voice was laced with equal parts sympathy and indignation. "A husband and wife should complete each other, support each other. God gave Adam a helpmate, not an object

226

to be put on a shelf or worshipped from afar."

Her spirits seemed to lift with each word. How could he know exactly what was in her heart? "Oh, Clay, that's it entirely!"

Pink crept into his cheeks, and he dropped his gaze to their joined hands. "I like to think I've learned something in the years since we last saw each other."

She wanted to think she had, too. At first, she'd found Frank's diffident manner charming, but it had soon become a barrier that kept them apart. When she'd come to see it as merely another way to control her, she'd begun to realize how many men shared his view of women.

It was no different aboard the *Continental*. At times, she saw the same attitude from Mr. Reynolds and even the charming reporter, Mr. Conant. Certainly Mr. Mercer subscribed to it. How could she know whether Clay meant those beautiful words and would apply them to his own life? She hadn't met a man yet who could.

"I've learned a lot, as well," she assured him, pulling her hand from his. "And I'm sure your lesson tomorrow will teach us all something."

The air remained warm as they headed

south, so Allie asked Clay's students to meet again on the hurricane deck. She half expected another foray from Mr. Mercer, though she was more than ready to argue with him on the matter if needed. But their benefactor must have had others to harass, for class started with no sign of him.

"Think of Seattle as a set of rings," Clay advised them as they perched on chairs or chests around the edges of the deck, the breeze snapping the canvas over their heads. Several of the women had donned more summery gowns of floaty white organza with lace collars and shawls. Allie thought Clay must be thankful for the linen shirt he'd purchased in Rio and the lighter brown sack coat he wore on top.

He seemed particularly determined that day, sketching pictures in the air with his hands as he spoke.

"On the edges of the settlements, you have the Cascade Mountains with plenty of opportunities for trappers and prospectors," he explained. "Those gentlemen come into town a few times a year."

"A rather uncivilized existence," Catherine murmured to Allie.

Allie hitched Gillian closer on her lap. "And a lonely one," she murmured back to her friend.

"As you head west," Clay continued, gaze roaming his students as if to make sure everyone was attending, "among the foothills, you'll find coal mines. Good money in mining, but it's dirty work. Those families come into town maybe once a month, after they've been paid."

"My father worked the mines in Pennsylvania for a time," Maddie said. "The black soot has a way of worming into your skin and lungs."

Several of the women shuddered. Allie felt a similar revulsion. Besides, she'd never heard of a woman who trapped animals for their fur, prospected for precious minerals or worked deep in the mines. She certainly didn't have those skills.

"Next come the river valleys," Clay told them. "The land offers deep, rich soil, and the rivers make getting from place to place much easier than breaking new trails. Some areas still need clearing, but you'll find any number of people interested in buying the timber. Logging camps and farming outposts are cropping up all over, with two or more claims working together. Generally they send someone to town a couple of times a month."

More of the women brightened at that, but Allie still couldn't see herself in such a role. She'd never felled a tree, and the closest she'd come to farming lately was to arrange roses for the dining room table. Frank's mother hadn't even trusted her to tend to the thick bushes that bloomed along the front of the house, for all Allie had learned how to cultivate roses at her mother's knee. The Howard roses, it seemed, could only be tended by a true Howard.

"What about the city itself?" she asked Clay.

He smiled at her as if he knew her thoughts. "Seattle grew from the inside out. A number of the people have built fine houses along the tops of the hills. If the city prospers as we hope, those folks will soon need housekeepers and gardeners."

"And bakers and laundresses," Maddie declared with a grin.

Clay grinned back. "Quite right, Ms. O'Rourke. Perhaps a seamstress, as well."

A number of women nodded happily. Just as Allie had suspected, she wasn't the only one looking to ply a needle. But surely Seattle couldn't keep so many seamstresses busy. She supposed she might be able to serve as a housekeeper, but would her employer allow her to keep Gillian with her? And how would she care for her daughter if she was busy tending to a large household?

"And what of the town itself?" someone called. "Are there shops, playhouses, churches?"

"We have a few dry-goods stores," Clay answered. "There's a good hotel, and Mr. Yesler has a cookhouse at the mill he rents for civic meetings and traveling shows."

"And you have a university," Catherine reminded him.

She seemed so enamored of the idea. From Clay's earlier description, it didn't sound nearly as impressive as Allie would have once thought. Still, perhaps there was need for instructors. She might be able to teach history.

"Indeed, Ms. Stanway," he acknowledged with a nod in her direction. "But if you want more details on it, talk to Mr. Mercer. He helped construct the building, then stayed on as its president and only professor."

Allie felt as if each bubble of hope was popping around her. Maddie snorted. "Sure'n there's no surprise. The man's an opportunist if there ever was one."

"You'll find plenty of those in Seattle," Clay promised her as some of the women nodded agreement on Mr. Mercer's character. "And you may find opportunities that surprise you. Just know that you won't

231

find many jobs fit for a lady once you cross the skid road."

Allie frowned.

"What's a skid road?" Gillian asked from her lap.

Clay moved closer as if to speak to her alone. "It's the dirt track the loggers use to drag the logs down from the hills to Yesler's Mill, Captain Howard. And it's no place for a lady like yourself."

"Why?" she asked.

Clay's cheeks were turning pink again. Allie had pity on him. "I'm sure your uncle will explain, Gillian, if we let him talk."

Gillian settled back against Allie as if waiting. Clay tugged at the collar of his shirt.

"Let's just say that the businesses south of the skid road cater to the whims of the working man."

Allie wasn't sure what he meant, but Maddie shrugged again. "Whiskey establishments need tending and sweeping in any town. Such work pays the rent."

Immediately gasps echoed on all sides.

"For shame, Ms. O'Rourke," someone cried. "As if a good Christian woman would be found in such a place!"

Maddie's face turned nearly as red as her hair, and she turned to glare at the woman. "Begging your exalted pardon, to be sure.

But I'd rather take some low-thought job than see my brother and sister starve."

Allie reached out and gripped her hand in support. The other women might not notice, but she could see tears brimming in Maddie's eyes. Her friend didn't like to discuss what she'd left behind. Had she been forced to watch her family starve? Allie knew she'd have been willing to take most any job if it meant food and safe living conditions for Gillian.

As if her daughter thought so, as well, she crawled from Allie's lap into Maddie's and pressed a kiss against her cheek. "You're a nice lady," she said, her little face pinched as if she felt Maddie's pain.

"Sure'n you and your ma are the nice ones," Maddie murmured back, giving the little girl a fierce hug.

"A willingness to do what's needed to survive is the hallmark of the Seattle pioneers," Clay put in, his deep rumble silencing all other voices. "Those of us who call Seattle home now aren't afraid to roll up our sleeves or dirty our hands if it helps our families and friends." He nodded to Maddie. "I think you'll fit in just fine, Ms. O'Rourke."

Maddie hugged Gillian close and gave him a nod of thanks.

Allie was surprised when Catherine piped up. "What about me? I'm a nurse. You claim your doctor can't keep his hospital solvent. What am I to do?"

"We're a hardy lot," Clay agreed. "But every settlement has someone who can be called on to help nurse an injured man, bring a new baby into the world. Unfortunately they aren't generally trained to the task, so the mortality can be high. I expect many of them would be glad to have someone with more credentials available to help, so long as she didn't mind working on all types of people and getting paid with venison and homespun."

By the pallor on Catherine's face, Allie was certain her friend wasn't enamored of the idea.

Other voices rose, begging Clay to predict their likelihood of success, but Allie didn't dare ask him such a question. Each day it was becoming clearer to her that she would be hard-pressed to pay her way in Seattle. She didn't want to hear Clay agree with her assessment.

Clay was rather pleased with how the lesson had gone that morning. He'd shared the truth about Seattle, and Maddie's comments had helped him make his point about the attitude needed to succeed. He truly did think the redhead had the gumption to make good on the frontier. Catherine also had something to contribute, if she could let go of her highfalutin ways. And he was beginning to realize there was nothing Allegra couldn't do if she set her mind to it. That determination would make her future.

He offered her a smile as the lesson ended and she stood and retrieved Gillian from Maddie's lap. The smile she returned lacked its usual warmth. In fact, the lesson seemed to have troubled her, if her stiff movements were any indication. He watched as she led Gillian down the stairs near the smokestack.

"You're going about it all wrong," Maddie said, moving to his side.

Clay turned to frown at her. "I thought you enjoyed the lessons."

"Oh, I do," Maddie assured him.

"As do I," Catherine said, coming up on his other side. "But for such an accomplished teacher, you are remarkably obtuse."

Clay leaned his hip against a chest of life preservers and eyed the pair of them. Maddie's head was cocked, her hands on the hips of her green wool gown. Catherine was standing as tall and serene as always, though he thought a toe might be tapping beneath her lavender gown, if the sway of her skirts was any indication.

"So what am I missing?" Clay asked, crossing his arms over his chest.

Maddie raised a finger. "You're going out of your way to show Mrs. Howard that she won't fit in," she scolded.

"When you should be assuring her that she will always have a place at your side," Catherine added.

Clay straightened away from the chest and held up his hands. "Ladies, please! I'm not trying to court Allegra."

"Not the way you're going about it, you aren't," Maddie agreed.

"That's why we're here to offer our help," Catherine assured him. "We've come to know and admire Mrs. Howard, and we want to see her happy."

Maddie elbowed him in the side. "And she's taken a fancy to you, no doubt about it."

Clay glanced between them. The redhead was beaming at him, and Catherine was nodding her assent. Were they mad? Did Allie really have feelings for him? He couldn't deny the way his heart beat faster at the thought.

But the same problems reared their heads, hissing at him like a many-headed dragon.

He hadn't been able to settle down at Allie's side in Boston. What made him think it would be any different in Seattle? Besides, she seemed so set against marriage, so certain he meant his protection as control. And to keep from protecting her? Impossible!

"I'm honored if Allegra thinks well of me," he told her friends. "But I doubt she'd welcome my suit."

"Ho!" Maddie declared, peering closer as if she would see inside him. "I'd never have taken you for a coward."

Clay stiffened. Catherine pressed her hands together fervently. "Indeed, sir. Faint heart never won fair lady."

He should protest. He'd faced down his father, left everything he'd known to strike out on his own, given away a fortune with no guarantee of its return. He'd learned to deal with other cultures some people feared; survived windstorm, fire and flood. Him afraid?

Terrified, more like.

"Ladies," he said, "I'm just not husband material. I take risks few wives would countenance. I live simply in a two-room log cabin I built with my own hands. Every cent I make I reinvest for the future. I'm no longer the sort of fellow who courts women like Allegra Howard."

"Ah, but you could be," Maddie crooned, laying a hand on his arm and gazing up at him with her warm brown eyes.

"It isn't always money or position that draws a lady to a gentleman," Catherine agreed, setting her hand on his other arm.

"Though, mind you, those are nothing to sneeze at," Maddie countered.

"To be sure," her friend said with a warning look her way. "But more important is a gentleman's character. That is what makes us fall in love. You have a fine character, Mr. Howard."

Why didn't he believe that? Few Boston ladies he'd ever met agreed with her. He was Clay Howard, the wild man, the unpredictable, the disloyal. He'd put his own desires before family.

"You didn't care much for my character when we first met," he reminded Catherine. "What makes you think it any better now?"

She blushed and dropped her gaze. "I was mistaken, sir. I thought you were bent on mastering Mrs. Howard. I see now that you have ever only wished to protect her and dear Gillian. I find that most admirable."

He only wished Allegra saw it that way.

"So, what do you say?" Maddie asked, giving his arm a squeeze. "Will you try your hand, speak your mind?"

"Will you be guided by us in the best way to court Mrs. Howard?" Catherine pressed.

Clay shook his head. He'd never thought to take a wife in Seattle, even when men had suggested their daughters or sisters, rare as those were. Now, when he tried to picture his world with a wife beside him, the vision had one face.

Allegra's face.

Lord, is this Your will? You know I've tried to live by Your principles since I left home. You've taught me so much. I know Your book says it isn't good for a man to be alone. Everyone needs friends, helpmates. But a wife? And even if having her at my side pleases me, can I make her happy? Can I be the husband for her?

Every thought built an assurance inside him. He'd sworn to protect her. What better way than to offer himself as husband? She wouldn't have to worry about how to make her way in Seattle. She'd complained about being nothing more than a decoration for her husband's parlor. That wasn't the sort of wife he wanted; he didn't even have a parlor! But he did have enough income that she'd be free to try her hand at whatever sparked her interest. Surely that was what she deserved.

Clay took a deep breath and nodded. "I'm your man, ladies. Tell me, what do you advise?"

CHAPTER FOURTEEN

In the days that followed Clay's lesson on occupations, Allie couldn't help noticing a change in him. For one thing, even though the air started to cool as they sailed south along the coast of Argentina, he began sporting a tailored wool suit that was clearly of Boston make. He must have found someone to trim his hair, for it no longer brushed the back of his collar, which was stiff with starch. And not a trace of gold could be found on his square jaw.

"If I didn't know better," the widow Hennessy commented to Allie at dinner one evening, "I'd say he was bent on impressing a lady."

Allie wasn't sure. She couldn't see that he showed any preference for a certain lady's company, despite the number of fluttering lashes aimed in his direction. Indeed, he seemed to be going out of his way to be chivalrous to everyone, opening doors, pulling out chairs, tipping his hat or inclining his head when a lady passed him. He quoted poetry at the least provocation, earning him sighs of delight from the other female passengers.

"He even smells like lavender water," Allie marveled to Maddie one day after he had set out deck chairs for them and tucked blankets around their skirts.

"That's the mark of a gentleman, that is," Maddie informed her with a nod as Clay went to perform a similar service for two of the elderly widows.

"I miss Papa's brother," Gillian said with a sigh where she sat on Allegra's lap.

That was perhaps the most significant change in Clay. Where before he had teased Gillian, tossing her in the air and letting her perch on his shoulder, now he stood respectfully a few feet away and spoke in a calm tone as if he'd been promoted to Sunday-school superintendent. As he became more proper and stilted, so did her daughter. She didn't like seeing Gillian retreat into her shell.

And she refused to let him go back on his promise to her.

"I thought we had an agreement," she told him when he offered her his piece of the pecan pie Maddie had baked with the last of the nuts from Rio. "If I want more dessert, I am perfectly capable of asking for it."

" 'The chief joy of man is to serve the flower of womanhood,' " he replied.

Allie shook her head. "Quoting Vaughn Everard will not avail you, sir. Admit it. You are trying to help me again."

Green eyes met hers, surprisingly warm. "When it comes to helping you, Allegra, it seems I cannot help myself."

How could she be mad at him when he had such a charming answer to every question she raised, every argument she mustered? But the more diffident he became, the more distance she felt between them. His behavior was too much like Frank's.

Perhaps memories of her late husband were why she opened the trunk one night after Gillian and Maddie were asleep and drew out Frank's letters.

The paper was creased with folds, speckled with the dust of the battlefield camp where he had written them. In places, the words were stained by the drops of her tears. She and Frank had grown up together; she had considered him her best friend. But marriage had driven them apart instead of drawing them closer.

"It is perhaps louder here than I am used

to," he had written in the first letter she opened. "All around me men prepare for battle accompanied by the sound of distant guns. I think of you and Gillian snug in our home, and I am glad you are safe and well."

That was Frank. He never complained. But for the first time, she noticed the concern behind his words.

"We are fortunate to have a family," he'd said. "So many I meet have lost mother, father, sisters, brothers. If anything should happen to me, my dearest wife, I know you can count on Clayton to take care of you and Gillian. He was in California last our agents heard. Contact him. He'll know just what to do."

Even in the end, it seemed, Frank had never lost faith in his brother. Why couldn't she extend the same trust?

The thought was still on her mind the next day when she attended one of Mr. Mercer's worship services. The *Continental* had entered the Straits of Magellan, and dense forests crowded to starboard, rising to mountains in the distance, while rocky barren wastes stretched away to port. A fitful breeze darted along the deck, cold and lonely. She had thought the solemn surroundings might bring people to the service, but only some of the passengers joined in.

Though Allie still took comfort from the hymns and Clay's deep voice blending with her alto, she couldn't seem to focus on Mr. Mercer's flat reading of another man's sermon. She found herself closing her eyes and searching her heart.

Lord, why did You lead me here? I was so sure Your hand pointed to Seattle. Then Clay came along. Is he an obstacle I'm meant to overcome or a change in the direction You wish me to go? You must have had some purpose in bringing me here. I must have some purpose!

She sensed no words of comfort, no new direction. She opened her eyes, and her gaze lit on the books arranged so carefully on the shelves behind Mercer. Was that her answer? Perhaps she'd missed a treatise on occupations for indigent widows. Perhaps reading a novel would take her mind off her doubts. As the service broke up, she allowed Maddie to take Gillian for tea and went to see what she could find.

Clay drew up a few minutes later as she was thumbing through an encyclopedia of science and culture.

"Good afternoon, Allegra," he greeted her with a bow.

Allie sighed and slid the book back onto the shelf. "After all this time, are we not at

245

Allie and Clay?"

He grinned, and his stiff manner fell away to be replaced by a warmth that lifted her spirits. "Allie and Clay, is it? What happened to Allegra and Clayton?"

She stood to face him, brushing down the gray of her skirts. "They were buried under the weight of Boston society. I hear no one mourned their passing."

"A shame," he agreed. "But I quite like these new folks."

"Me, too," she replied. "Most days."

He cocked his head. "Most days? Why not all of them?"

She was tired of wallowing. "Everyone has an occasional moment of regret, sir. Now, why have you come to find me? I can't be late to class. I understand the next lesson is tomorrow."

His formal bearing crept back over him as his shoulders straightened. "We'll be anchoring off Point Tamar in an hour. Captain Windsor means to take a group ashore. I thought you might enjoy coming along."

Escape these walls and the thoughts that chased her around them? "I'd be delighted," she assured him. "Let me find Maddie and get Gillian ready."

His arm shot out to stop her. "Gillian

should stay aboard. There are too many ways she might get hurt."

His tone was brusque, as if he thought she'd argue. So now he didn't even trust her to look out for her daughter?

Anger flared. "In that case, sir," she told him, drawing herself up, "perhaps I should stay aboard, as well. After all, how could someone like me manage a foreign shore?"

He frowned at her, but she pushed past him for the stairs to the lower salon. If she was going to descend into misery, as least she could do so in private.

Clay blew out a breath as Allie disappeared down the stairs. He'd seen enough courtships in Boston and Seattle to know that his was not going well. But he was following all Catherine and Maddie's advice.

"Every woman appreciates solicitous attention," Catherine had assured him. "Show her you are more than a backwoods lout."

Funny. He'd always thought he was more than that.

"And offer her presents," Maddie had insisted. "There's nothing like flowers to turn a lady's head."

"Where would you suggest I find flowers in the middle of the ocean?" Clay had teased.

Maddie had grinned. "Oh, you're an inventive lad, so you are. I'm sure you'll find any number of things you can give our dear Allegra."

He'd tried. He'd offered her the choicest bits of food at the table, presented her with a poem hand-copied from memory and procured a book Roger Conant had refused to loan until now. He'd bestowed every solicitous attention he could think of aboard ship, but instead of warming to him, Allie had cooled.

And all this stiff posturing felt unnatural. He wasn't much enjoying pretending to be a person he'd thought he'd left behind. It was as if he'd squeezed into a coat two sizes too small.

"I don't know what I'm doing wrong," he confessed to Catherine as they waited for the officers to lower the longboat from the hurricane deck for the trip ashore. "Are you certain this is what she wants?"

"You must be patient," Catherine assured him, the cool breeze not so much as ruffling her pale hair as she twirled a lacy parasol over her head. "She'll come to see your stellar qualities."

Clay wasn't sure how, when those qualities were crammed into a starched collar.

Just then he caught sight of Allie walking

toward him. Over her gray gown she wore that cloak he'd first seen her in, the quilted hood framing her creamy face. One gloved hand held firmly to Gillian's as the little girl walked beside her in her plaid dress. He wanted to go to Allie, beg her forgiveness, promise never to act like a jackanapes again, in short to be the smitten beau she'd had trailing after her in Boston.

Then he noticed Reynolds walking at her side, her other hand on his arm.

"I managed to convince Mrs. Howard to join us," he bragged as if he'd negotiated a treaty with a warring nation. He gave his walking stick a twirl.

"Mr. Reynolds assured me that he feels perfectly comfortable with Gillian's safety," Allie said with a lift of her chin as if she dared Clay to say otherwise.

He would have liked to argue. He wasn't sure the rocky shore was anyplace for a little girl. Mountains crowded close to the narrow shingle, their sides darkened by forests so thick even light didn't penetrate. Part of the beach was shadowed by the ancient timbers of a massive sailing ship that must have wrecked upon the rocks. Allie would find it difficult to enjoy the rustic scenery if she had to spend every moment watching out for her daughter.

So he decided to look out for Gillian himself.

It couldn't be that hard, he reasoned, keeping an eye on a four-year-old. He'd spent enough time with her aboard ship to know that Gillian wasn't the most active of children.

But he soon found that there were a hundred ways for an inquisitive little girl to get into trouble. Those fingers trailing over the side of the longboat as it flew across the water could attract sharks, if any dared these cold waters. And what if she fell in? She'd drown or freeze before the longboat could come back for her.

"Come sit with me, Captain Howard," he said, lifting her off Allie's lap and depositing her on his own.

Allie frowned at him. Reynolds smirked as if he thought Clay was playing nanny.

The shore was even worse, for he quickly spotted dangers there. Gillian could trip over a rock on the pebbly beach, slip and fall into a tide pool. What if those shells she gathered were sharp and cut her? What if she wandered into the forest and was lost forever? He wanted to clutch her in his arms and never let go.

"She isn't made of glass, you know."

He turned from watching Gillian bend to

pick up a shell to find Allie beside him. Her hands were on her hips, and that militant gleam was in her eyes.

"No, but there's so much she doesn't understand," he countered, gaze going back to the little girl. "If something happened to her, I'd never forgive myself."

Even as he watched, Gillian began tugging on one of the redbricklike stones that littered the beach. The rock came free, and she tumbled backward.

His heart leaped into his throat, and he dashed to scoop her up. "Are you hurt, Gillian? Speak to me!"

Gillian frowned. "Why?"

Allie met him and held out her arms. "Here, let me."

Clay watched as she took her daughter, set her back on the ground and smoothed down the little girl's dress. All the while, Allie talked to her about the rock, about the giant ship looming over them, about the wonders of God's creation. Her tone and look assured her daughter everything was fine. Then she stepped back and watched as Gillian scurried away. Each step the little girl took up the beach, Clay felt himself tensing anew.

"You have to give her room to grow, Clay," Allie said beside him. "Believe me, I know that can be difficult. But would you plant a tree and cover it from the sun just to keep the birds from roosting in it? Would you lock a puppy in the cellar to make sure it never chased carriages?"

Clay felt as if the air came slowly into his lungs, crisp and cold. "How do you know when it's safe and when it's not?"

"You don't," she said, gaze on her daughter. "You do the best you can and pray." She raised her voice. "Gillian! That's far enough. Come and show your uncle what you found."

Gillian hurried back, fingers full of delicate little pebbles the color of amber. "Look, Uncle. Gold!"

Clay smiled down at her. "Very impressive treasure, Captain Howard. Do you think you should bury it to keep it safe?"

Gillian's frown returned. "No." She turned and went back to her search.

"Even she knows you can't hide something to keep it," Allie murmured.

Clay blew out a breath. "I'm no good at this, Allie. All I want to do is carry her around, show her the world, give her her dreams. I don't much like playing the schoolteacher."

"Is that what you're trying to do?" Allie peered up at him with a frown, then her brow cleared. "You are. All this formality, these fine manners. You're trying to prove you're still a gentleman."

"And failing," he admitted.

"No!" She lay a hand on his arm. "A few manners are quite nice, but please don't fall back into the patterns we knew in Boston. I made the choice to leave because I couldn't bear to live in that superficial manner another minute."

Clay couldn't help his smile. "Someone lock you in the cellar?"

To his surprise, she nodded. "No light, no air. All in the name of keeping me safe. And all that little dark space did was make me a girl afraid of her own shadow."

Frank truly had done her a disservice. Yet how could Clay blame his brother? He had the same feelings, to hold her close, to keep her safe.

"It's hard to imagine you afraid," he told her, "even back then. You ruled society."

"Our mothers ruled society," Allie corrected him. "I was a tool to that end. The Lord showed me a better way, and He has confirmed it a dozen times over. I won't go back to it, Clay, not for you, not for anyone."

Her conviction vibrated in her voice. How could he not applaud her? Yet he doubted many people would agree or even understand. He'd run away from such pressures, and still he struggled to understand how he fit in her new view of the world.

For if he couldn't protect her and Gillian, what place did he have at her side? Protection was the only thing he had to offer her.

He could not forget their exchange over the next few days as the *Continental* exited the straits and steamed north. The coastline dwindled to a smudge on the starboard horizon. Each day dawned bright and clear. He packed away his suit to be used on Sundays and special occasions and kept his skin coat for the cool evenings. He still opened doors and pulled out chairs for Allie and the other women, but she always cast him a look as if questioning his motives.

He couldn't blame her. He questioned his own motives. Protecting her for Frank's sake had seemed so noble. Courting her had seemed so perfect. But was he truly the right man for Allie, the man she needed by her side as she flew?

He still wasn't sure of his answer by the time Sunday came around again. They had finished listening to one of Mercer's services, where the fellow read a sermon from a book, and gone out on deck to enjoy the sun. Clay found it a lot easier to praise his Master surrounded by the wonders of creation than holed up in the upper salon.

The ocean stretched azure in all directions, rising to meet the blue of the sky. The only clouds were the sails of other ships in the distance, heading north, as well. The air smelled fresh and clean. Allie looked a part of the scene in her blue gown with its white trim. He reached for her hand and was pleased when she didn't pull away. With Gillian on his hip in her rainbow-hued gown, they stood along the railing in companionable silence.

Thank You, Lord, for this moment and all You've done for me.

"What's that ship?" Gillian asked, pointing.

It seemed larger than the others, and the smoke puffing up between the masts proclaimed it a steamer.

"I hope it's a man-o'-war," Maddie said as she joined them at the railing with a swish of her russet skirts. She grinned at Allie. "Full of handsome officers with coin to spare to take a lady about town."

"As our next stop is a decent-size town," Clay told her with a smile, "you just might get your wish."

Others ventured over, pointing and questioning.

"It's a race," one of the men declared.

"She means to beat us to port."

"Our *Continental* will see her sunk first," someone else predicted with a laugh.

Clay couldn't be so sure. There was something odd about the ship, the way it tacked as if moving to cut the *Continental* off from shore. He could see several of the officers above them on the hurricane deck, eyes trained on the horizon.

The passengers stepped aside to allow Captain Windsor room at the railing. He held his spyglass to his eye, and Clay had a mind to ask him to share, when Catherine moved up beside them.

"Here," she said, pulling off a set of mother-of-pearl-inlaid opera glasses from where they hung on the bodice of her brown dress and handing them to Clay. "See what you make of our rival."

Though he felt a little silly using the ladylike glasses, Clay raised them to his eyes, the golden chain tickling his wrist as it fell. What he saw made his blood run cold.

"It's a man-o'-war, all right," he said, lowering the glasses in time to see Maddie's triumphant smile. "But I don't think it's one of ours."

"Spanish," Captain Windsor agreed, and Maddie's smile faded. "They're in a spat with Chile. Nearly every port is under

256

blockade. Thankfully, Lota is not."

"What does he mean, Clay?" Allie murmured, stepping closer.

"It means we're caught in the middle," Clay replied. He couldn't stop himself from putting an arm about her waist. As if she realized the significance of the gesture meant to protect her, her eyes widened.

Captain Windsor snapped his spyglass shut and turned to call up to his burley first officer. "Full steam, Mr. Weinhardt, and all hands on deck. I want to beat her to the port before she attempts to board us. I will not surrender my ship or its cargo to His Spanish Majesty."

CHAPTER FIFTEEN

Allie clung to Clay as the deck burst into action. Sailors ran for their posts; ladies dashed to the railing or hurried to their staterooms as if to hide. She met Maddie's gaze over Gillian's head and knew that for once her friend had no idea what to do.

Clay did. He handed the opera glasses to Gillian and lifted her higher in his arms. "Keep your eyes on that ship, Captain Howard. Maddie and Catherine, watch for the port ahead. Call out every few minutes."

"Aye," Maddie agreed, turning her face toward the bow. With a nod, Catherine followed her.

"What would you have me do?" Allie asked.

Clay met her gaze, and she saw concern under the ready smile. "You have the most important job, Allie. Pray."

Pray? But praying seemed so small. Didn't he have more faith in her abilities than that?

She wanted to work, to fight. Spain bore America no love; she'd seen reports in the newspapers of missionaries captured, civilians imprisoned. What would she do if they separated her from Gillian?

Be careful for nothing, but in everything by prayer and supplication with thanksgiving let your requests be made known to God.

The remembered verse humbled her. Clay was right. Prayer was how she'd made it through the last few months. Prayer would keep them safe now.

Allie took a deep breath and prayed, eyes closed and hands clasped. She prayed for strength for the crew and passengers, for good fortune to reach safe harbor. She prayed for wisdom for the captain and those who helped him. And she prayed for protection over those she loved: Gillian, Maddie, Catherine.

And Clay.

Her eyes popped open, and she stared at the man beside her. He was all alert, eyes intent on the horizon, arms bracing Gillian. As her late husband's brother, he warranted her solicitous concern. But the emotion rising up inside her was far more than that.

Lord, please. I can't fall in love with him again. The woman I was was never enough for him. The woman you've made me will never conform to his vision of a wife.

Clay must have noticed her gaze on him, for he turned his head. His smile hitched up, and that dimple winked at her from his cheek. She wanted to hold that look to her heart.

"He's still there," Gillian reported.

Immediately, his gaze returned to their enemy. "She, Captain Howard," he told Gillian. "Ships are always ladies, though not necessarily well-behaved ones like you."

Gillian lowered the glasses with a frown. "Why?"

"The headland is in sight!" Catherine called back from the bow.

Allie sucked in a breath and reached to remove the glasses from around Gillian's neck. "Let Mama have a look."

She wasn't sure what she'd see, perhaps faces grinning in evil delight at their predicament. But even through the glasses, the Spanish ship seemed far away. Surely the *Continental* could beat her to port. *Please, Lord, help us!*

"Report," Clay ordered her.

Allie squinted through the glasses, trying to make out anything that might be meaningful. "She's poured on all sail as well as her steam. I don't see any signal flags hailing us. Wait." She focused on movement at the front of the ship. "There's a puff of smoke coming from the bow. And another." She lowered the glasses and frowned at Clay. "Does she have more than one engine?"

Clay shifted Gillian closer. "No. Those are some of her guns. She's warning us to stop."

But the *Continental* didn't stop. Clay and Allie no longer needed the opera glasses. They could see the ship swooping toward them, the proud colors of Spain flying from the highest mast. Maddie and Catherine took turns calling out progress: when they sighted the mouth of the harbor, when they could see the village inside. Allie felt herself tensing each time a cry was raised. Her fingers gripped the wooden railing, clinging to it as she clung to hope. Clay's hand came down on hers, firm and warm.

She drew in a breath. "I'm all right, Clay. We will win."

His smile said he believed her.

Always before, Captain Windsor had ordered the ship to slow as they entered port. This time, the *Continental* flew across the water, the land rushing toward them. Allie heard the engine ratchet back only as they neared moorage beside the dock.

Thank You, Lord!

Clay removed his hand from hers to set

261

Gillian down on the deck. Allie released the railing and was surprised to see it impressed across her palms.

"We did it," she said.

Clay's eyes didn't light. Instead, his gaze was fixed at the bow. Turning, Allie saw Maddie and Catherine hurrying back toward them.

"You should see the welcoming party," Maddie cried as she reached their sides. "They came a-running from every building in town, so they did, as if we'd scored a great victory."

Allie could only feel relief at their escape. She handed the glasses to Catherine. "You can stow these now, midshipman."

Catherine's blue eyes crinkled as she smiled. "Aye, aye, ma'am." She curtsied to Gillian. "With your kind permission, of course, Captain Howard."

But Gillian was frowning. "The boat is still rumbling." She stomped her little black boot on the deck as if to prove it.

Allie frowned, as well. Now that she concentrated, she could hear the low throb of the steam engine.

"Sure'n our good captain is prepared to make a quick escape if need be," Maddie guessed, glancing between her friends.

Catherine picked up her skirts. "I intend

to find out." She marched down the deck for the wheelhouse.

Clay laid his hand on Allie's shoulder. "We'll be fine, Allie. I could feel your prayers. We arrived here safe because of them."

Oh, if only that were true. She had prayed with all her might, but the Lord could surely only see her prayers as feeble, hindered by fears that refused to leave her even now. She pulled down on the white cuffs of her dress. *I lifted my petitions to You, Lord. Help me let go of these concerns, about the Spaniards, about the future, about Clay. Help me do Your will, whatever it is.*

"Her ladyship isn't pleased," Maddie murmured, and Allie saw Catherine hurrying back toward them.

"We're in the wrong port!" she proclaimed, eyes snapping fire over such behavior. "We passed Lota completely and docked at Coronel instead!"

Clay chuckled. "Good old Yankee ingenuity."

"This is no laughing matter," she scolded him. "Lota is apparently a free port. Coronel is under blockade. That's why everyone came running to meet us. They haven't seen a merchant ship in months!"

Maddie glanced around at the others.

"What are we to do? Will they be letting us stay in a blockaded port?"

"Not if we hope to see Seattle," Clay said grimly. "Captain Windsor has no choice but to make for open sea once more, try to backtrack to Lota."

"Can't we simply go on?" Allie protested. "Pick up supplies at a port farther north?"

"The ports nearest here don't have the coal we need," Clay answered. "If we don't refuel at Lota, we'll soon be reduced to sail alone, and that could slow us down sufficiently that we'd be late arriving in San Francisco."

Catherine shook her head. "Reaching San Francisco a week or so behind schedule seems preferable to fighting off the Spanish navy."

Clay met her gaze. "We'd reach San Francisco a week after our supplies of food and water run out. I don't know about you, Catherine, but I'd prefer not to live on fish and salt water for a week."

Catherine swallowed as if she felt the same way.

Allie raised her head. Already, she could feel the ship moving, the bow turning. "The captain's going to chance it," she said. "What can we do to help him?"

Clay reached out and pulled the opera

glasses off Catherine's neck. "Ladies, I'd advise you to barricade yourselves in your staterooms, but I doubt you'll listen."

"See how well you know us, Mr. Howard," Allie said. "We are going nowhere until we're safely in Lota."

They lined the railing, hands on the wood and gazes out to sea, as if they could will the *Continental* to the new port. She knew many more prayers joined hers this time.

The harbor of Coronel was shaped like a heart, with two bowls near shore divided by a low headland and the tip pointing out into deeper waters. As the *Continental* steamed toward the opening, the Spanish man-o'-war came to rest, blocking her way.

Clay was once again gazing through the glasses. "Allie, ladies," he said in his deep rumble, "take Gillian to the lower salon and get under the table."

Allie blinked at the odd advice. "What?"

"May I?" Catherine said, reaching for her glasses, and Clay reluctantly surrendered them to her. She took one look, and the glasses fell from her fingers to thud against her chest on their golden chain.

"She's opened every porthole," Catherine said, blanching as she stared wide-eyed at Allie. "She means to fire on us!"

As if to agree, something whizzed past the

bow and sent up a spray as it hit the water. Cries rang out all around.

Fear stabbed at her, made the day turn a brilliant white. Allie gripped Clay's hand. "Come with us."

He shook his head even as he retrieved Catherine's glasses with his free hand. "Captain Windsor will need all men to repel boarders. Barricade the stairs. Protect Gillian."

"Who's going to protect you?" Allie protested.

A whistle split the air, high and keening, and she heard the boom that had caused it. Something flew past to starboard, exploding as it hit the water. The *Continental* shook.

"Save us, Lord!" Maddie cried, clasping her hands as screams pierced the air. Nearby, one of the other women crumpled in a faint.

Catherine raised her head. "I'll see to her. Allegra, lead the rest to safety."

Catherine's brisk manner pierced the rising panic that had threatened Allie. She nodded agreement, and Catherine hurried toward the fallen passenger. Gillian's face was white, her eyes like saucers in her round face. Allie picked her up and gave her a fierce hug.

"It will be all right, darling," she promised.

"Go with Maddie now. I'll be right behind you."

Maddie opened her arms and took the little girl from Allie. She knew what she had to do, what Catherine expected of her, what she expected of herself. But if she was going to die this day or end up in a Spanish prison, there was something she had to do first.

She turned to Clay, tugged on his arm to take his attention from the enemy ship. His gaze met hers, and she saw his concern.

"Thank you," she said, "for listening to me and protecting Gillian. Please come back to us safe." She stood on tiptoe and pressed a kiss against his cheek.

Clay stood frozen as Allie's lips touched him. He caught the scent of the lavender she must use to wash her hair. More, he could feel her trembling against him, knew an answering tremor inside him. Though he realized he had to send her to safety, he wrapped his arms around her and held her close.

"Go below! Everyone!"

At the purser's cry, Clay released Allie. She stared at him as if the kiss had shaken her more than cannon fire.

He knew how she felt.

The purser hurried up to them. "Everyone belowdecks. Captain's orders."

Clay put an arm about Allie's waist. "Do we expect boarders, Mr. Debro?"

The young officer's face was white. "I fear so, Mr. Howard. See to your ladies."

It was a testimony to the state of Allie's mind that she did not protest as he led her down to the lower salon.

The women were gathered in tight groups, some crying, others praying with eyes closed and hands clasped. Catherine had managed to revive the woman who had fainted and get her belowdecks. Now the nurse moved from one group to another, offering smelling salts, checking pulses. Maddie and Gillian stood by the great table, and the little girl ran to Allie the moment their gazes met.

Allie picked her up and cuddled her close. "I'm here, Gillian. You don't have to be afraid."

Clay wished he believed that. From what he knew about relations between America and Spain, there was every reason for real concern should the Spanish capture the ship.

Maddie must have thought the same, for she joined them, rubbing the sleeve of her russet gown. "Are they coming for us, then? Will they be carrying us off to Spain and locking us up?"

Gillian's lower lip trembled, and Allie sucked in a breath and gathered her closer.

"Not while I live," Clay vowed. He knew how much Allie hated his protection, but he couldn't help himself. He waited for her to rebuke him, but she merely moved closer, her shoulder fitting so easily under his. He slipped his arm about her waist again.

Boots thundered above, and every gaze turned to the door leading up to the deck. Clay could feel Allie holding her breath. This was madness! He couldn't sit here, do nothing, while those he loved were in peril.

He set Allie back from him. "Wait here. I'll find out what's happening."

Her eyes were huge, like pansies in the snow of her face. He gave her a smile that he hoped would encourage her and turned to head for the door. One of the other women caught his leg as he passed.

"Don't go, Mr. Howard," she said with a sob. "What will we do without your protection?"

"Protect ourselves," Allie proclaimed, right behind him.

Clay whirled. "What are you doing?"

She ignored him to raise her voice and command the women. "Listen to me. Mr. Howard and I will determine the state of

269

affairs on the deck. As soon as we leave, turn the table on its side and barricade the main stairway. See if you can find something to block the other doors, as well. Ms. O'Rourke has a pistol, and Ms. Stanway can organize a guard."

Around the room, women raised their heads. Some looked aghast at her suggestions. Others nodded and began gathering themselves to act.

The woman who clutched Clay's leg just stared at Allie, openmouthed. Allie pointed toward Maddie and cried, "Go!" and the lady released Clay to hurry off and join the fight.

Clay shook his head as he and Allie started for the stair. "You have the temperament of a general, Mrs. Howard."

"Honed by years on the battlefield of society," she agreed. "You haven't seen a fight until you've tangled with a Boston debutante intent on stealing your beau."

Despite himself, he chuckled. "Does Maddie even know how to use her pistol?"

"Certainly," Allie said, head high. "She told me she shot it once for practice and never reloaded. But don't tell the others."

Especially the Spanish. A shame Clay's pistol was locked up, but then again he wasn't sure it was advisable to arm people who had no idea how to use a weapon.

He wasn't sure about Allie's presence, either. As they started up the stairs, he motioned her to silence. Then he lowered himself to crawl up the last few steps. She joined him, head just below his, blue skirts like a waterfall on the stair. Together, they peered out onto the deck.

A longboat must have brought the Spanish to the *Continental,* for a young officer and a crew of sailors were standing on the deck. The officer was clean cut, his patrician nose and raven hair proclaiming him a member of one of the finest families. But his crew was another matter, unshaven, unwashed, sunburned, older men with cutlasses held at the ready and pistols thrust in belts or bandoliers.

"If you can prove you have no support from the traitors in Chile," the officer was saying to Captain Windsor in English that held only a trace of an accent, "we will consider allowing you to pass."

Clay took a deep breath. Mercer may have snatched at money wherever he could find it, but Clay was fairly sure the emigration agent had never approached the Chilean government for support. So long as Captain Windsor's papers were in order, they might all live to see Seattle.

Clay slid back a few steps to keep the Spaniards from seeing him.

"I begin to understand why you do it," Allie murmured, crawling down the stairs to a stop beside him. "Protect us, I mean. When you care about someone, you can't bear to see them hurt, can you?"

"No," Clay said. "Not in the least. Is that why you kissed me, Allie? Were you worried about me?"

Her fingers gripped the edge of the closest step. "Don't ask me my feelings right now. I scarcely know them."

He touched her chin, drawing her gaze to his. "I have similar trouble, where you're concerned."

He couldn't keep himself from leaning closer. Her breath caressed his chin. His lips touched hers, the softness, the warmth. Could she really be his forever?

"How bad is it?" Maddie asked, creeping up on them.

Clay pulled away from Allie. His face felt hot, and he wasn't sure why. Maddie had encouraged him to court Allie. She should be glad to see his efforts bearing fruit.

"They are ruffians," Allie reported, and Clay hoped Maddie put her breathlessness down to the tensions of the moment. "But it sounds as if Captain Windsor can prevail."

Maddie peered over her shoulder for the deck. "What should we be doing to help?"

Before Clay could motion them lower still on the stairs, where the thrum of the idling engine would cover their conversation, Allie began to back down. "We must return to the lower salon, tell the others." She did not look at Clay as she rose to descend the stairs. Her skirts fanned gracefully behind her, but she moved swiftly, as if her message was urgent. Even Maddie frowned before following her.

Clay shook his head. He should never have kissed her. He'd obviously offended her. But though he knew it was wise to tell the women below stairs that they were safe, he couldn't help wondering if part of Allie's hurry was to get away from him.

CHAPTER SIXTEEN

Allie hurried down the stairs, wanting only to put distance between herself and Clay. She should not have given in to the fears of the moment and kissed his cheek, for it was clear that was what had encouraged him to kiss her now. She hadn't meant to flirt. She had to remember who she was now and where she was going, for her sake and Gillian's.

"Who goes there?" Catherine demanded as Allie and Maddie reached the bottom of the stairs, her blue eyes peering over the top of the table that now blocked their way.

"Allegra Howard," Allie reported. "And Madeleine O'Rourke."

"It's all right," Gillian piped up from behind the panel. "It's Mother."

Catherine and another woman slid the table aside just wide enough for Allie and Maddie to squeeze through. Gillian scurried over to Allie, who scooped her up and held her close, inhaling the lavender scent of her golden hair. This is what she needed to feel, this thankfulness for her daughter, this hope for their future.

Maddie retrieved her pistol from Catherine and took up her spot on guard. The other women hurried forward to meet Allie, begging to hear what was happening on deck.

"The Spanish officer is examining the *Continental*'s papers," Allie explained as she carried Gillian deeper into the room. "As soon as he's satisfied, we'll be free to go."

Cries of relief echoed on all sides. Allie wasn't sure how Maddie heard the noise on the stairs, but she could see her friend raising the pistol toward the doorway. "Who goes there!"

The women shushed, cowering back down around Allie. Gillian tensed in her arms. Allie raised her head, ready to meet whatever was coming.

"Clayton Howard," Clay drawled, stepping down into the lamplight and pushing back on the table to let himself into the lower salon. Several of the women ran to meet him, voices shrill as they begged for details.

"What, did they think I lied?" Allie asked Catherine with a shake of her head.

"Lies are bad," Gillian agreed, twisting in Allie's arms to see Clay. The silk of her curls tickled Allie's chin.

Gillian was right. Lies were a poison. Some made you think the world had changed when it was your own heart that needed changing. She wasn't ready to fall in love, to surrender her heart into another's keeping. She was merely thankful that the *Continental*'s engine woke from its slumber a few minutes later, signaling their freedom.

As the passengers raised a cheer, Clay approached her. "We should talk."

"No," Allie said. "We should not." She handed him Gillian and went to where Maddie and some of the other women were trying to right the table. Clay followed her, passed Gillian to Maddie and hefted the piece easily, carrying it to its place in the center of the room.

Allie set to work moving the chairs back to their places, as well. Surely the busier she kept, the less time she'd have to think about Clay.

But as if he intended to stay front of mind, he paced her. "You kissed me," he murmured, grabbing the back of the chair she had lifted as if to take the burden from her.

Cheeks heating at the reminder, she

tugged the chair out of his hands and staggered to keep from falling. "And you kissed me. I'd call us even."

Clay frowned. "Do you consider this a game?"

Oh, but he could be maddening! "I thought we were going to die," Allie whispered, mindful of the other women around them.

Clay's brows shot up. "That was how you preferred to spend your last minutes?"

"Yes! No!" Allie twisted the chair to scrape it across the floor. Clay came around and took it from her. She gave up and let him position it at the table.

"You have to stop helping me," she said when he returned to her side.

"No," he said, face grim. "You have to stop fighting me."

Allie puffed out a breath and turned to look for her daughter. She thought Clay might continue to follow her about the room, but he seemed to know he'd pushed her as far as she could go, for he headed back up the stairs for the deck.

"Man troubles?" Maddie teased her, passing with one of the last chairs. "Sure'n I'd be glad to advise you on how to solve them."

"I don't need help," Allie said. "From anyone."

She truly meant those words, and Maddie must have believed them, for she did not offer to so much as change Gillian for bed that night as they anchored at last in the harbor at Lota. Clay, too, took dinner in the upper salon, as if giving Allie time to think.

But thinking, she realized, only took her deeper into trouble. Clay had named Gillian Captain Howard. Allie rather thought the title should belong to her. She was the captain of her life. She'd set her course. So, she'd found a few questions along the way — how to support herself and Gillian in Seattle, what to do about Clay. She was the one who must find the answers.

First, however, she had to escape the harbor of Lota.

She knew from conversations among the officers of the *Continental* that the ship was to stay a week in the port. She was looking forward to seeing the little coastal town with its stucco buildings and wood-trimmed market. What she hadn't expected was for the town to come to her.

She heard the hum of voices from the lower salon before she even finished dressing in her gray gown with the black fringe. When she opened the door, Gillian beside her, it was to find that the *Continental* had been besieged.

"Have you ever seen so many handsome gentlemen in one place?" Maddie marveled as she and the rest of the women attempted to converse with six of the many Chilean officers who had rowed out to visit.

The gentlemen had shiny black hair and slender mustaches framing shy smiles, with red braid at their shoulders and across the chests of their dark dress uniforms. Their lilting praise drifted about the room like butterflies, dancing from woman to woman.

All around Allie, ladies perched with fluttering lashes, fluttering fingers, making the most of the opportunity to flirt to their hearts' content, as Mr. Mercer had apparently gone ashore before the Chileans had arrived. Matt Kelley had grabbed a biscuit and had gone into hiding.

Catherine remained aloof. "Poppycock," she told Allie before seeking safety with the *Continental*'s officers. "It's the same in the upper salon and on deck, but nothing will come of it. You mark my words."

Allie quite agreed, but she was too busy fending off the officer who had attached himself to her as she and Gillian sat beside the long table.

"And so you come from Boston, Mrs. Howard?" he asked, capturing her hand from where he sat beside her.

Allie pulled away. "Yes, and I have every intention of continuing to Seattle."

"No, no, such a fair flower cannot be left to whither in the northern cold," he protested, seizing her other hand. "You must stay here in Chile, teach our young women how to be great ladies." His grip was as sure as his smile.

"I don't like being chilly," Gillian said from her lap. She took Allie's arm and tugged her mother's hand back from the officer, whose eyes widened in surprise. "I don't like you, either."

Very likely such behavior stemmed from a concern for Allie, just as Catherine had said back in Rio. Allie knew she should scold her daughter, but she rather agreed with Gillian this time. The Chilean gentlemen were far too bold. All around the lower salon, they were kneeling, professing undying devotion, when they'd known the ladies of the *Continental* at most three hours!

Just then, Clay ducked into the lower salon. He had gone into town with Mr. Conant and Mr. Reynolds that morning, Maddie had reported earlier. Allie hadn't talked to him since the Spanish had let the ship go yesterday. She suspected she had overreacted, but his comment had made her feel as if she was being forced into a corner.

Now the three men stopped inside the doorway from the stairs, staring about. She saw the surprise on Clay's face quickly melt into disgust. She knew exactly how he felt.

Reynolds immediately excused himself. Conant took out his notebook and began making notes. Clay's gaze swept the room until it lit on Allie. She could almost see his struggle in the way he shifted on his feet. He wanted to help her, but she'd forbidden it.

Allie set Gillian on the floor and rose, forcing her beau to hop to his feet, as well.

"Mr. Howard!" she called, motioning to Clay.

His brow cleared, and he strode to her side. "Mrs. Howard, Captain Howard," he said with a nod. "Did you need me?"

He was going to make her say it. "Yes, Mr. Howard," she admitted. "It's a lovely day. Would you care to join us in a promenade on deck?"

"Delighted," he assured her with a grin as he offered her his arm.

She accepted it with one hand, taking her daughter's hand with the other, and hoped she didn't look as desperate as she felt.

Her would-be suitor expressed every intention of escorting her, as well.

From a good head above his, Clay gazed

down at him. "The lady has little need for one man's help, let alone two. Look for better hunting, sir."

The officer frowned at him in obvious confusion, but Clay swept Gillian up on his hip and led Allie away before her swain could recover enough to protest further.

"Thank you," she said as they climbed the stairs to the deck. "Another minute and I would have had to be rude."

"Then I'm glad to have saved you from that fate," Clay said with a wink to her daughter.

At least he was willing to forget their argument. Right now, she was more concerned about what was happening on the ship.

"I simply don't understand this," she said as she, Clay and Gillian reached the main deck. Here, too, noble Chilean gentlemen walked about, laughing and chatting with the ladies. "Is the town so lacking in female companionship they must flock to ours?"

"Not from what I could see," Clay replied, shifting Gillian up on his shoulders so she could gaze out over the water. "Maybe it's just the novelty of Yankee women."

Allie shook her head. "Novelty is seldom enough to interest a gentleman to this degree."

One of the more vinegar-tongued women

sashayed past with a mustachioed beau on each arm. She tossed her head at Allie as if to crow.

"You were saying?" Clay asked with a grin.

Allie threw up her hands. "If this is any indication of what Seattle will be like, perhaps we should stay in San Francisco."

"Perhaps you should." His voice had sobered, and Allie glanced his way. He had turned his gaze out across the waters of the harbor, over the other ships that rocked at anchor, but somehow she didn't think he saw any of them. "It's no Boston, but it's far more civilized than Seattle. The Howards have trading partners there. You'd have ready access to society."

There he went again! Why couldn't he understand her antipathy to society?

"I know you want the best of us, Clay," she managed to say. "I'm convinced that is Seattle. And I truly don't want to live anywhere the Howards have influence."

He turned to look at her, Gillian frowning down from his shoulders. "Even mine?"

Allie was spared having to answer him by the sound of Catherine calling her name. Turning, she saw her friend hurrying toward them, one hand on the flat-topped hat perched on her pale hair.

"You must help me," she declared as she

283

came abreast of them. "It's simply monstrous."

What now? Allie sent up a prayer for wisdom. "What's happened?"

Catherine took a deep breath, dropped her hand and pressed it against the lavender of her gown over her diaphragm, as if to catch her breath. "It was in the newspaper. The American consulate gave one to Mr. Mercer. A respected scholar and politician currently residing in America wrote home to tell his people we were coming and claimed we were all schoolmarms. He encouraged every man in Chile to try to keep us here, by hook or by crook. *That's* how badly they need teachers!"

Allie stiffened. "Surely no one would fall for such blatant manipulation."

Catherine shook her head. "A dozen women have already agreed to positions as teachers or housekeepers in distant villages, at exorbitant pay, I might add."

"Pay that may not materialize," Clay said, his deep voice serving to emphasize his warning. "Who's to protect them once they leave the ship?"

Allie felt cold all over.

"Even Madeleine's considering an offer!" Catherine cried. "We have to stop them! We must demand that Mr. Mercer act."

Allie shook her head. "It's no use appealing to him. They won't believe him if he tries to dissuade them. They'll think his demands no different from his posturing about fraternizing with the ship's officers."

"They don't believe me, either," Catherine lamented. "They say it's sour grapes because I didn't get an offer. As if I'd want one!"

Gillian's face scrunched. "I don't want sour grapes, either."

Clay patted her boot as if in agreement, but Allie puffed out a sigh. "There must be someone they'd listen to, some neutral party they'd respect."

"The American consulate?" Catherine suggested.

"They don't know him," Allie pointed out.

"Mr. Gardiner, the leader of the mission here?"

"He may very well encourage them to stay." Allie caught herself rubbing her chin the way Clay did when he was thinking and dropped her hand. Then inspiration struck. Her eyes swung up to meet his, saw his widen as if he knew she was about to ask the impossible.

"Clay!" she cried. "You'd be perfect!"

Clay stared at her. A dozen women about to

jump ship for a handsome face and the promise of hefty pay, and Allie thought he could do something about it?

"Your faith in me is humbling," he said. "But I doubt I have that kind of influence."

"More than you know," Allie assured him. "Besides, you have the authority of living in Seattle. You can explain to them that better opportunities lie ahead."

That was the problem. He couldn't convince himself that Seattle was the best place for many of these women. Even after teaching his lessons, he could see that some were too headstrong to be willing to bend their ways to fit in. Others were so trusting they'd be cheated out of their stake the first day they hit shore.

Of course, his feelings didn't mean that Chile was the best place for them, either. Many people in the interior were likely to speak only Spanish or a native language. The country had won its independence more than fifty years ago, but the incident with the Spanish man-o'-war was testimony that fighting continued.

"Let me talk to Captain Windsor," Clay offered. "Perhaps we can come up with something."

Allie smiled her thanks. He wasn't sure why she believed in him, but if she was willing to ask for his help for once, he wasn't about to let her down.

The captain was less encouraging. "Mr. Mercer already came to complain of the matter," he said when Clay approached him in the wheelhouse. "I have no authority to lock passengers in their staterooms unless I can prove a danger to the ship. Short of that, I cannot think of a way to keep them aboard if they are determined to leave."

Clay rubbed his chin. "There might be a way. Do you agree with me and Mrs. Howard that staying here could be dangerous to the women's safety?"

"Assuredly," Windsor said. "I would not allow my wife or daughter to remain where they could not speak the language and had no resources or friends to appeal to for comfort."

Clay leaned closer. "Very well. Then if the Chileans try to take them, here's what we'll do . . ."

Clay hoped he and the captain wouldn't have to put their plan into effect, but the week required to resupply the *Continental* seemed to stretch too long. Whether visiting the mission on the hillside above the town or haggling with sellers in the market, Mercer's belles remained the most popular women around. The consulate feted them; officers serenaded them. Two even fought a duel over the right to petition a certain lady for her hand. It was enough to turn any woman's head.

Allie and Catherine seemed the only ones immune. Even Maddie had made a conquest. Clay was with Allie and Gillian on deck when Maddie came to tell Allie the news.

"I'm to be the schoolmistress of Valmontera," she said, red hair nearly as bright as her smile in the sunlight. "And at pay twice what I ever earned, plus my own house. Sure'n it's more than I ever hoped for."

"And do you think perhaps it might be too much to hope for?" Allie asked, gaze searching her friend's for a moment before rising to Clay's. He could see the worry written in those deep blue eyes.

"I thought you wanted to be a baker, Maddie," he tried pointing out.

She shrugged, though her smile faded as if their lack of enthusiasm for her choice hurt. "I love baking, to be sure, but I've ever been after finding someplace I was wanted. I was a child when we left Ireland. . . . I don't remember life there. My da moved us about so much I never felt like anyplace was home. At least I have a fair chance here."

"You've a chance in Seattle, too," Allie said, pressing her hand. "I've come to think of you as family."

"Sure'n you're a dear for saying so," Maddie said, face softening. But even that did not change her mind, for she was one of several women waiting in the lower salon the next afternoon, bags packed, expecting a boat from Lota to take them ashore to stay.

Allie's pain touched Clay as well as she hugged her friend tight. "Please, Maddie, don't go. It isn't safe."

"And where has it ever been safe for an Irish lass on her own?" Maddie countered. Despite her brave words, Clay could see she returned both her friends' embraces tightly, then bent to kiss Gillian on the top of her head. The tremor on the little girl's lips was matched by the one on Maddie's.

Allie gazed at him as if begging him to intervene. He couldn't. If he and the captain were to put their plan into effect, he had to look as if he agreed with this travesty. She turned her back on him, and Clay followed her and Catherine up the stairs, with the other women trailing behind.

Mercer, however, had other ideas. He stood in the doorway, blocking the way to the deck. The sunlight outlined his reddish hair with flame. Clay stiffened when he saw what was in the man's grip.

"No one takes one of these girls unless they pass over my dead body," Mercer cried, brandishing a pistol.

Clay reached over Allie's head and wrenched the gun from their benefactor's hand. "Give me that before you kill someone."

As he came level with the man, he could see that Mercer's eyes were wild. "I feel as if I could, sir," he declared. "Indeed, that is just how I feel. I cannot allow any man to harm one of my ladies."

"Sure'n you've been planning a fate no worse than this," Maddie reminded him as she ducked under his arm to reach the deck. "Seattle, San Francisco, Lota, it's all the same to me. A lady must go where she'll be best appreciated."

Captain Windsor moved down the deck to meet them. "I'm afraid I must intervene. I cannot have such shenanigans aboard my ship."

"You see?" Mercer crowed as the other women pushed their way past him to the deck. "Listen to the captain if you will not listen to me."

Maddie put her hands on her hips. "I don't see how you can be ordering us about, captain or no. I didn't sign on as one of your crew."

Captain Windsor inclined his head. "Indeed you did not, Ms. O'Rourke. I was speaking to Mr. Mercer." A glance around her set the emigration agent to sputtering. "And I am no tyrant," Captain Windsor continued. "But you cannot leave today. Neither the tide nor the hour is favorable to ferrying all your belongings over to the town now. You and the ladies will have to wait until tomorrow."

The women exchanged glances as if they could not believe him. Clay held his breath, his gaze brushing the captain's. Windsor did not so much as smile.

Maddie peered over the railing as if to confirm the captain's words. When she straightened, she snapped a nod. "The tide's out, ladies. Tomorrow it is, then." She glanced among the captain, Clay and Mercer. "And I'd like to see the fellow who can stop me." She lifted her chin and her skirts and marched back down the stairs. The other women followed, with Mercer scurrying behind, still voicing his protests.

Allie let out a breath. "Well, at least that gives us more time to reason with her."

Catherine shook her head. "Reason cannot prevail here, I fear."

Clay could only agree. He excused himself from Allie, feeling her gaze on his back as he approached the captain. "Will you do as I suggested, then?" he murmured.

Windsor nodded. "I'll weigh anchor after midnight. By tomorrow, we'll be far out to sea. But I wouldn't want to be in your shoes, sir, when Mrs. Howard and Ms. O'Rourke find out that this was your idea."

CHAPTER SEVENTEEN

"Men," Maddie said the next day, "are nothing but bums, cheats and liars."

Mutters of agreement echoed around the circle of women who were sitting on the hurricane deck mending. The afternoon was bright; a breeze tugged at the sail above their heads. Those who had more summery gowns were dressed in organza and linen, their hair brushed back from their faces.

Allie couldn't help glancing to where Clay and Gillian were watching the waves for mermaids. At that angle, both her daughter and Clay were silhouetted against the sky, and it was a bet as to which studied the sea more seriously.

She had asked him to keep the women aboard. She'd expected him to argue with her friends, appeal to reason, extol the virtues of their original path. Instead, he'd resorted to trickery. Though part of her was thankful Maddie and the others were safe aboard the *Continental,* she could not like his methods.

He'd acted a bit too much like a Howard.

Mr. Mercer climbed the stairs from the main deck and strolled toward them, smile pleasant. Since the crisis at Lota had been averted, he had been in an uncommonly fine mood. He'd instigated a number of parlor games, as if that would keep his charges' minds off their shattered dreams.

"And away from the officers," Catherine had surmised.

Now he approached their little circle, hands clasped behind the back of his black frock coat.

"Ah, nothing gladdens the heart more than the sight of industrious women," he proclaimed, stopping to rock on the balls of his feet.

"The same could be said of an industrious man," Catherine replied, taking a careful stitch in the sleeve she was mending. "A shame I've seen so few this trip."

Several of the women tittered at that, and Mercer's face darkened. He turned purposefully away from her toward Allie.

"Might I speak to you a moment in private, Mrs. Howard?" he asked.

What, would he scold her for her friend's behavior? Allie couldn't imagine what else he had to say to her that couldn't be said before the group. They'd clashed often enough on the trip that no one had to guess where each stood on a number of topics. He simply couldn't understand that the more his grip tightened on his charges, the more inclined they were to slip through his fingers.

Still, a part of her was curious as to what he intended, so she asked Maddie to keep an eye on Gillian and rose to accompany Mr. Mercer down the stairs. She could see Clay watching her as they passed below his vantage point and entered the upper salon.

Several of the women were sitting and chatting. They, too, watched as Mercer led Allie to a little writing desk in a corner and bid her to take a seat beside it. He perched on the wooden chair and cupped his hands over one knee.

"I'm sure you have noticed, Mrs. Howard," he said, eyes intent on hers, "that I have incurred considerable expense in bringing our fair ladies west."

"Expenses for which you were reimbursed," Allie reminded him, "either by the ladies themselves or by the good people of Seattle."

He sighed, dropping his gaze to his laced fingers. "Oh, if only that were true.

Unfortunately, I have had to resort to using my own finances to support this worthy venture." He raised his gaze once more and leaned closer. "I'm sure you'd agree that such a circumstance is most unfair."

Allie could not imagine where he was leading. "Sometimes we must sacrifice to bring our dreams to fruition, sir."

He straightened and beamed at her. "We certainly must. I knew you would be quick to see the problem." He slid a piece of paper across the desk toward her. "If you would be so good as to sign this note, I will allow you to return to your sewing."

Allie frowned as she picked up the page, then heat flushed up her. "This is a promissory note! For five hundred dollars!"

Mercer's smile didn't waiver. "A paltry sum, I know, especially for a lady related to the Howards."

Allie pushed to her feet and dropped the note on the desk, feeling as if the paper had burned her fingers. "I may carry the name of Howard, sir, but I am no relation. And I refuse to pay you another cent when you apparently misplaced the money I originally gave you."

His brows rose with his body. "Dear lady, do not for one minute think I expect you to pay this money. No, indeed. I'm certain Mr.

Howard would be more than delighted to reimburse me the funds once the two of you are wed."

"Wed?" Allie could barely speak. "What makes you think I intend to marry at all?"

He went so far as to reach out and take her hand, which she jerked away from his touch. "Of course you will marry, Mrs. Howard. Do not think you can hide your feelings from me. One of our other passengers acquainted me with the story of you and Mr. Howard. I reunited you with your first love. I'm certain you agree that entitles me to some compensation."

"It entitles you to nothing!" Allie was so angry her hands shook. So did her legs, but that didn't stop her from backing away from him. "You, sir, are a charlatan! The money for me and my daughter has been paid, twice over. You will get nothing further from me or anyone with the name of Howard, if I have anything to say about the matter." She turned on her heel and stomped from the room.

What an unscrupulous man! She knew not all the passengers had paid full fare, and a few had racked up bills at the hotel waiting for the *Continental* to sail. Very likely he'd had to lay out some funds to keep the expedition going. But that promissory note was nothing less than extortion.

She took the long way back to Clay and Gillian, circling the ship, to give herself time to calm. *Lord, what am I to think when every day I'm faced with men who cannot act with honor, with compassion? Am I to entrust Gillian's future, my future, to such as these?*

Clay's face came to mind, that smile of his lifting, that dimple showing. She could not deny that he had helped many people on board the ship, especially her and Gillian. But at times he seemed controlling. She sighed. He was no Mercer, but she could not trust that he wouldn't act like the other Howards.

She'd thought she'd mastered her emotions by the time she climbed to the hurricane deck again, but her feelings must have betrayed her, for Clay took one look at her, set Gillian down and told her daughter to go sit with Maddie and Catherine.

"What happened?" he asked, a hand on Allie's elbow as he led her to the opposite side of the deck where the shadow of the funnel provided a little shelter from the breeze and the gazes of the others.

"Just another misguided conversation with Mr. Mercer," she reported. Around the funnel, she caught sight of their so-called benefactor leading one of the older widows down the stairs. No doubt he had other notes he wished signed.

Allie sucked in a breath. "It was horrid, Clay," she informed him, feeling her fists bunch in her gray skirts. "He asked me to sign a promissory note for five hundred dollars!"

Clay's brows came thundering down. "What! Why?"

"He says he's lost money on this venture," Allie explained, barely managing to keep her tone civil. "He thinks the men we'll marry will gladly make up the difference."

"They might at that," Clay said, then held up his hands at her scowl. "It's the truth, Allie. There are men in Seattle who'd happily pay any price for a good wife. From what I hear, some already have."

Allie narrowed her eyes at him. "What do you mean?"

"You know this is the second trip Mercer has taken, don't you?"

She nodded. "That was one of the reasons many of us felt comfortable following him. Flora Pearson says he brought out her father and sisters two years ago."

"She's right. Her sisters were two of a dozen women who journeyed with him then." He shifted on his feet as if he wasn't sure she'd like the next part of the story.

"His friends financed the trip, three hundred dollars each for a bride. I don't know who paid him this time, but I'd guess he accepted twenty to thirty commissions."

Allie stared at him, feeling as if the ship had commenced rocking again. "He said the people of Seattle helped pay the way for some. Was it only the bachelors, then?"

Clay's nod only served to fan the flames of her temper.

"And these men who paid their money, what do they expect?" she demanded. "Do they think they can march aboard the moment we reach Seattle, pick any woman they want?"

Clay shrugged. "I'd imagine a few will think just that."

She could scarcely breathe with the enormity of it. "We've been sold, like cattle!" She paced in front of him, hands clasped to keep from striking something. "Surely there is some recourse. No one can force us to wed if we choose not to. No one can tell us who to marry."

Then another thought struck. Allie spun to face Clay. He took a step back from her.

She advanced on him. "Mercer said you would pay my note. He claims someone aboard ship informed him of our past. He said you would be glad to help out because he'd reunited us. Did you pay him to bring me to Seattle?"

Clay had never seen Allie so angry. Her face was flushed, her eyes snapped fire and her shoulders were so high they might have brushed the lobes of her pretty ears. He didn't want to add fuel to the blaze, but he refused to lie.

"I've funded a lot of risky ventures in Seattle," he told her, "but only when I trusted the person who requested the money. I knew what he hoped to accomplish, and I believed in the principles of the venture. I don't agree with Mercer, on any number of points. I've said so on more than one occasion. I certainly don't trust him. Why would I underwrite his activities?"

Still she watched him, as if she expected to see the truth appear on his forehead in bright gold letters. "Perhaps because your family told you to. Perhaps it was the only way to trick me into complacency."

Clay met her gaze, held it. "Since when do I do anything to please my family? As it is, I had no idea you were heading to Seattle until my mother told me."

She took a deep breath as if to calm herself, dropping her gaze and her shoulders at last. "That doesn't mean there isn't a man waiting in Seattle, expecting me to bow down in gratitude for bringing me out as a wife. I won't have it!"

Neither would he. The reality slammed into him and knocked him speechless. Allie didn't want to marry; she'd made that perfectly clear. But Clay didn't want her to marry, either. Marry anyone except him, that is.

She had the fire to make it in Seattle; she had the determination. Her vision was so strong at times he was certain he saw it, too. He'd worried that he couldn't be the man she would need, but with her by his side, there would be nothing he couldn't do, even being a good husband. And he could be a father to Gillian.

Lord, help me be the father You would want me to be.

He longed to take her in his arms, promise to love her forever, to help her reach whatever dreams her heart devised. But now was no time to express his devotion, not with steam pouring from her ears faster than the *Continental*'s funnel.

"No one could hold you to a contract you never signed," Clay told her. "If any gentleman thinks otherwise, you send him to me."

Allie glared up at him. "I'd prefer to fight my own battles, sir. I just didn't realize this particular fight was coming. Why didn't you tell me?"

"I thought you knew. The pacts were common knowledge in Seattle. I'm sure I saw at least one article on them in the newspapers."

She sighed. "I tried to avoid the papers after they started reporting my disappearance." She glanced up at him. "Your family put a reward out for information on me, as if someone had kidnapped me."

"I'm sorry they treated you so badly, Allie," he said, meaning every word. "I wish I'd come home sooner so I could have helped."

She raised her chin. "You came at the right time, Clay. I was the one who had to help myself. Until I was ready to do that, nothing would have made a difference. I only wish I knew what to do now. I won't be coerced into marriage."

Or courted, either, he realized. Small wonder she'd bristled when he'd tried to play the gentleman. She didn't need a society beau. She needed someone who would believe in her, encourage her.

He wanted to be that person, even if it cost him.

"Stand your ground," he told her. "Neither Mercer nor his cronies can force

303

you to marry. You have the right to say no."

She took a deep breath. "We all have that right. But I still say forewarned is forearmed."

He glanced over his shoulder at the other women sewing so contentedly behind them. Perhaps none of them knew the fate awaiting them in Seattle.

"Maybe it's time for another session of the Seattle School," he said, "and I don't particularly care whether Mercer likes it."

"I'll gather your students," Allie offered, face set. "You get Gillian."

The plan agreed, Clay met with Allie and her friends a few minutes later, taking up his usual place with his back to the funnel on the hurricane deck. Apparently word had circulated about the purpose of his lesson, because the women shifted this way and that on their deck chairs, muttering, gazes dark.

"So, we've been sold, is it?" Maddie blurted out before Clay could speak. "Passed to the highest bidder like horses! Isn't that just like a man?" She narrowed her eyes at Clay as if she suspected him of being part of the pact.

"Why are you all so upset about the matter?" an elderly widow asked, glancing around with a confused frown. "Mr. Mercer said he picked me out especially for an older farmer looking for a wife. It's a comfort to know I'll be cared for when I arrive."

"And how do you know you'll be cared for?" Allie challenged, rising to face them beside Clay. Her strength was so loud he felt as if he heard a battle hymn. "What if this farmer is cruel or cowardly?" she demanded. "What if he lives so far from town you never see another soul for help? How can you know the character of a man you've never met?"

"Mr. Mercer met him," she protested. "He wouldn't hand me over to a monster."

Her statement set off a firestorm. Comments flew thick and fast on all sides, with finger-pointing and reddened faces.

"Ladies," Clay tried, only to hear his own voice drowned in the tumult. He took a deep breath and bellowed, "Ladies!"

They quieted, gazes stormy, faces set. At least they were all turned in his direction now.

"The truth of the matter is that you'll have offers aplenty when you reach Seattle," he told them. "You may have seen some of the statistics in the papers. Every girl over the age of thirteen is spoken for, and I hear tell in parts of the territory, men are offering the fathers of baby girls allowances in order

305

to marry the girl when she comes of age."

"That's barbaric!" Catherine cried.

Clay shook his head. "That's survival. A wife is a helpmate, a partner beside you, someone to talk to in the long, cold winter months. And the government gives a man twice as many acres if he has a wife at his side."

She shuddered. "Small wonder they think to bid over us."

"But don't you see?" Allie spoke up, meeting each woman's gaze in turn. "They need us. We don't have to settle for the first man who welcomes us on the dock or offers us a cottage."

"Think carefully before accepting any offer," Clay encouraged them. "Spend time with the fellow, ask around about him. Seattle is a small place. You'll soon hear enough stories to tell you what sort of fellow he is."

"And pray over the decision," Allie told them. "Give yourselves time."

Maddie glanced around. "But with this many women coming in, sure'n the good men will fall right away."

Clay chuckled. "You can't imagine, Maddie. Believe me, there are far too many fish along the sound. You can afford to wait for the right one."

"Or chart your own path," Allie added. "Mr. Howard has shown us a number of opportunities that might exist there. Make the most of them."

"Quite right," Catherine said with a brisk nod. "It's possible to function perfectly well without a husband."

The dinner gong sounded, and the women rose to go to table. Allie went to lift Gillian off Maddie's lap and take her down to the lower salon, but Allie's words lingered behind.

For every business venture, Clay had done just what he'd told his students. He'd spent time with the person requesting his help, listened to the vision, gauged the person's ability to fulfill it. He'd asked around, leaned about habits, drive. Only then had he been willing to take a risk.

Allie had spent the last two months in his company. She knew his beliefs, what he did, how he worked. What could he do between here and Seattle to prove to her that she should take a risk, on him?

CHAPTER EIGHTEEN

Allie found herself thankful for Clay's lesson as the ship continued north. Surely he was right — no man could arbitrarily claim them as wives once they reached Seattle. His assurances went a long way toward calming the other women's fears, as well.

In fact, the closer they were to reaching their destination, the more excitement seemed to be blowing along the decks of the *Continental.* All around Allie, her fellow passengers smiled, laughed and dreamed about the future. She wanted to feel the same hope, but she simply couldn't determine how she would make her way in Seattle, and she refused to think about how Clay might play a part.

He continued to be helpful and polite, but at times she caught him watching her as if he was about to say something of great import. Always when his gaze met hers, he'd smile and offer some observation, perhaps a snatch of poetry.

"Why poetry?" she asked one day as they were walking about the deck in the sunshine. Gillian was playing Scotch-hoppers with Maddie, and Allie couldn't tell who was having more fun jumping about the planks.

"I thought you liked poetry," he countered. "I seem to remember a dog-eared volume of Byron in your lap as defense against your mother's staid social calls."

Allie couldn't help smiling at the memory. "I was quite enamored of the English poets back then, and I've found others to enjoy since. I simply struggle to think of a man like you enjoying them."

"Perhaps because only a true gentleman enjoys poetry," he said.

His voice was tight; she'd hurt him. She rubbed her fingers along the strength of his arm, stopping him as they reached the stern.

"I didn't mean you weren't a gentleman, Clay," she assured him. "But poetry seems, well, pretty. I always thought it held greater appeal to women, for all men seem to write it."

He shook his head. "Poetry appeals to men, as well. It's powerful, unexpected. Look through the eyes of a poet, and you're sure to see the world differently." He pointed to the vista of sea around them. " 'Many waters cannot quench love, neither can floods drown it. If a man would give all the substance of his house for love, it would utterly be scorned.' "

The words seemed to echo inside her, yet she recognized their source. "But that's the Bible."

"And some of the most powerful poetry I've ever found. How can any man read it and not be moved?"

He was so certain of his convictions, gaze out over the waves, eyes glowing like gemstones. Part of her wanted to ask him if he felt as strongly about her; another part was afraid to find out.

She was standing along the railing one afternoon just before Easter, thinking hard, when Gillian scurried up to her. Her daughter had been reading a book with Catherine and Matt only a few moments before. Now she tugged on Allie's hand.

"Ms. Catherine says the moon is going to disappear tonight," Gillian said. "May we stay up to see it? Please?"

"She called it a lunar eclipse," Maddie explained, joining them by the railing. "Sounds like it will be quite the sight to see, especially here on the ocean."

"How late?" Allie asked.

"Catherine said midnight or so," Maddie replied.

Allie frowned. Gillian tugged her hand again. "Please, Mother? I'll be good."

Allie's heart melted, and she knelt before her daughter. "I know you'll be good, Gillian, because you are always good. It's a little late for you, but if you go to bed early, I promise to wake you in time."

Gillian positively glowed. She spent the rest of the day telling anyone who would listen that she was going to stay up for the eclipse. Clay and Matt were two of several people who evinced interest in joining her. So it was a large party that gathered on the hurricane deck that night to watch.

In honor of the event, the crew had taken down the shade sail, giving the passengers a fairly unobstructed view of the sky in all directions. The night was clear and warm; the moon was full, hanging round and pearly in the sky. Gillian, whom Allie had woken an hour earlier, yawned behind her hand as she sat on Clay's shoulder in her rainbow-striped dress.

"Look now," he murmured. "Something's about to take a bite out of the sky."

Gillian stared upward, eyes wide. As Allie watched, a dark spot appeared on the bright lunar surface, every bit as if some huge animal had munched off the side. Murmurs rumbled around her.

Gillian huddled closer to Clay. "Where is the moon going?"

"Nowhere," Allie assured her, reaching up to stroke her daughter's back, feeling the tension in it. "You know how when we walk on a sunny day, your shadow covers the deck? That dark spot is a shadow too, of the whole earth."

"You might say," Clay murmured, gaze upward as well, "that a little part of that shadow is you, Captain."

Gillian's mouth opened in an O of wonder.

Careful not to dislodge her, Clay reached for Allie with his free hand. She didn't pull away as he tucked her against him. She allowed herself the luxury of leaning into his embrace, listening to his deep voice as he explained the wonders of the cosmos to Gillian.

The shadow crept over the moon, little by little, moment by moment. Allie couldn't take her eyes from the sight. As the last sliver of moon disappeared, the entire globe turned orange. Allie gasped and heard others doing the same.

"Why did it do that?" Gillian cried.

Clay shifted her in his arms as if to comfort her. "The shadow can make the moon turn all kinds of colors, Captain. Blue, pink or orange, or so I've read."

"Pink is better," Gillian said as if she were capable of determining the color.

Allie could only stare at the vision. *That's my life, Lord. I had hopes of shining, but the darkness crept up on me. You've been leading me all along, and I have faith You'll make something this beautiful of my future.*

"You know a lot of things, Uncle," Gillian said, patting him on the shoulder as if he were a noble steed.

"Learned from books," Clay promised her. "You'll know as much once you read more of them. In fact, you'll know more than I do, because new books are always being written."

"I'm going to read them all," Matt declared. "And I'll share them with you, Ms. Gillian."

Gillian nodded as if she accepted his promise. But Allie stood arrested. Books! Of course! She could form the first subscription lending library. That's how she could contribute to the great city of Seattle. It was the perfect solution, giving her and Gillian a home, providing them with income. But achieving that dream would require an investment of funds she didn't have at her disposal.

She stared at Clay holding her daughter so gently. He'd said he funded ideas, helped people grow their businesses.

Would he be willing to invest in her?

Clay watched as the moon brightened. *That's my life, Lord, coming out of my father's shadow and into the light. I may not have stood so fixedly, but with Your help, I can. I hope You let me shine, for my sake and for Allie and Gillian's.*

He glanced at Allie to find her gazing up at him with her head cocked, as if she were meeting him for the first time. He didn't have a chance to question her, for several of the other women requested that he repeat his explanation of the event they were seeing, and by the time he managed to extricate himself, Allie had taken Gillian from him and retired for the night.

She came to find him the next day. He was standing in the bow with Reynolds. Once again, nothing but the blue of ocean and sky surrounded them. He was heartily glad he'd taken the overland route when he'd headed west the first time. Though more challenging, it had had far more variety.

"Looking forward to going home, Reynolds?" he asked to make conversation.

"Indeed," Reynolds replied with a smile as he leaned on his walking stick. "I'm quite partial to San Francisco." He raised his voice as Allie approached them, her swinging skirts nearly as blue as the sky. "And I hope to convince some of our lovely ladies to stay there."

Clay frowned. Funny. At times he was certain Reynolds held the ladies in disdain for leaving home. He couldn't imagine the man campaigning against Mercer for a chance to have them settle in his town instead.

"I hope for Seattle's sake you don't succeed, Mr. Reynolds," Allie said with a nod of greeting to them both. "From what Mr. Howard said, I think we are more greatly needed there than in San Francisco if your home has grown so big already."

"She's a shining city on a hill," Mr. Reynolds proclaimed. "But a few more gems in her crown would not be remiss." With a wink to her, he turned to stroll away, the clack of his stick against the wood fading with distance.

"So you're certain about Seattle," Clay said, watching her.

Allie nodded. "And I have a proposal for you."

A proposal? He knew she was determined to be her own woman, but surely she wouldn't propose marriage herself! He leaned against the railing, trying to still the rapid beating of his heart. What, was he the debutante now?

"Oh?" he managed to say, pleased he sounded so nonchalant.

She was hardly as calm. Her hands were knotting, and she shook them out even as she raised her head. He felt the deep breath she took before starting in.

"Mr. Mercer is bringing back a number of books donated for our use," she rattled off as if afraid she might forget a word if she didn't hurry. "I'd like to purchase them and start a subscription lending library in Seattle. If you invest, I'll pay you half of all profits until I've made up the investment, and a quarter of the profits from then on."

This was not what he'd hoped for, but he couldn't fault her thinking. Already the business side of him was tabulating likely costs, amortizing returns over a ten-year period. Still, he couldn't help teasing her. "You think we read in Seattle?"

Something fired in her eyes. "Some people must read," she said with conviction. "And

316

the people on this ship will only add to that number. With time, the subscriptions will grow."

Clay nodded. "They might at that. And Mercer is so desperate for cash you could likely convince him to sell at an attractive price." He straightened off the railing. "Bringing culture to the frontier. I like it. You have a deal, Allie."

He stuck out his hand, and she accepted it with a firm shake. He couldn't seem to let go of that fragile connection. Perhaps it was the movement of the ship, but he felt as if he and Allie were being pulled together, their faces closing until her lips were mere inches from his own.

She pulled back, face flushed. "Thank you, Clay. I won't let you down."

"You never could," Clay assured her, trying to find his way back from wherever his heart had led him. Logic, business, making money, aiding progress. Why did she have to have such kissable lips?

She dropped her gaze, tucking a strand of hair back into the bun behind her head. "You didn't think so much of me once."

"I've always been impressed with you," he insisted. "I may not have made this clear, Allie, but I admire what you've done — raising Gillian, setting off on your own. I know how hard that can be."

She glanced up. "Was it difficult for you, Clay? I was under the impression you couldn't wait to leave Boston."

He shrugged. "I missed it, and Frank. And you."

Her lips twitched as if she was fighting a smile. But the movement only drew his attention to her mouth again. He forced himself to gaze out at the ocean.

"Funny," she said. "I would have thought you'd meet far more interesting women along the way."

"None like you." His voice was deepening with his feelings, and he cleared his throat so she wouldn't guess the reason. "I understand Captain Windsor intends to anchor off the Galápagos Islands in the next few days. Would you and Gillian like to go ashore and see them? I understand they're unusual."

He returned his gaze to hers to find her smiling at him. "That would be wonderful. Thank you for offering." She bobbed her head and hurried back down the deck as if she feared he'd ask her something far more personal. He intended to do just that, when the moment was right.

His opportunity came when they reached the Galápagos a few days later. The islands did not disappoint. The shore where the company from the *Continental* landed was dotted with rough black rocks, the beaches covered with sand so white it reflected the sun. Beyond the beach lay hills tufted with waving grasses and strange twisted trees like the cactuses Clay had seen on his way west. Rising from the center was a massive volcano, its peak obscured by clouds.

Several of the women stayed closer to the landing spot, but Clay wanted to explore. He led Gillian and Allie along the shore, gulls and terns calling overhead, until they found a private little cove with sands whiter than snow and shallow water nearly as blue as Allie's eyes.

Gillian promptly began hunting for shells, while Allie perched on a black rock, spreading her blue skirts about her like the petals of a flower. Clay stood beside her. He knew his gaze should be on the little girl, but somehow he couldn't make himself look away from Allie. Her profile was serene, her concentration unwavering. She might have been a statue, except no statue had ever made his heart beat so quickly.

It was now or never.

"Allie," he said. "I've wanted to talk to you. These last few weeks aboard ship have made me think."

She laughed, a sound as soft as the waves against the shore. "I find it hard to believe that was the first time you thought, sir."

"I hope not," Clay agreed with an answering smile. Why was this so hard? The last time he'd asked her to marry him, he'd been calm, in control, sure of what he wanted.

Of course, the last time she'd refused. Small wonder his palms were damp. He rubbed his hands along the gray of his trousers.

She stiffened beside him. "Gillian! Come away from the water!"

He turned to find the waves lapping at the toes of Gillian's black boots as the little girl stared out at the water as if fascinated. She raised one arm to point out to sea. "But, Mother, I see a mermaid!"

Allie frowned, and Clay gave her his hand to help her down from the rock. Now he saw it, too, two warm brown eyes gazing back at them from a furry round face.

"That's not a mermaid, Gillian," he called. "That's the mermaid's pet lion."

"It's a sea lion, sweetheart," Allie agreed.

Gillian turned her gaze on theirs, clearly perplexed. The look struck him as hard as a rock. When had he ever seen her smile?

"What happened in Boston?" he murmured to Allie, gaze on the little girl who now trudged toward them as if the world was devoid of wonders. "Who hurt Gillian?"

Allie sucked in a breath. "I'm sorry, Clay. I didn't want to tell you."

"I can't believe Frank would be cruel to his own daughter." The words came out harsh, but he couldn't stop the disappointment in his brother and the anger at the injustice.

Allie shook her head. "No, Clay. Never Frank. He loved Gillian. He even wrote to her while on campaign, telling her stories about the people he met." She took a deep breath. "It was my fault."

Clay seized both her hands, feeling them cool in the warm air. "I won't believe that, either. I've seen how much you love her."

Her face was nearly as pinched as her daughter's. "But for a time, I didn't stand up for her. I let myself be guided by another voice, your mother's. She seemed so certain strong discipline was necessary. Spare the rod and —"

"Spoil the child," Clay finished, the ugly memories circling him like a flock of ravens. "I remember. I used to think it was my fault she was always disappointed in me. I must have been particularly wicked, because I always needed punishment. The tutors never had to raise a hand to Frank."

"That's because Frank never disobeyed," she replied, voice choking. "Until the day he decided it was his duty to help in the war. Your mother was beside herself. I think that's why she insisted that everyone be so hard on Gillian. She wanted to remove any chance that her granddaughter might disobey and leave her, as well."

Gillian had stopped to pluck a shell from the sand, turning her discovery this way and that so that the coral color glowed in the sunlight. Was his mother so used to bending society to her will that she demanded similar obedience from everyone in her family? She'd certainly used Clay with her story about losing Allie. She hadn't even mentioned her granddaughter! He felt his hands fisting, thinking of anyone being so cruel to Gillian.

Or Allie.

"And yet that very discipline made you run away," he realized. "You gave up everything for Gillian."

She shook her head. "Don't make me a martyr, Clay. I wasn't too fond of your mother's rules myself, especially after Frank died. I suppose I wanted my freedom."

Clay gazed out over the crystal waters. No wonder she fought him at every turn, why she refused to marry again. She couldn't take the chance that the man or his family would harm her daughter.

His gaze returned to hers, and he took a step back from her. "Then be free, Allie. Do whatever pleases you for once."

She laughed. "Here, now?"

Clay spread his hands. "Why not? You broke away. You earned it."

Her laughter sparkled brighter than the sand. "You're right. I did. Gillian!"

He wasn't sure what she was about, but as her daughter joined her by the rock, she had her sit on the sand and set about removing her boots and stockings.

"Turn your back," she told Clay, who turned, bemused, to gaze out over the volcanic wastes. The rustle of cloth gave him a hint of what she was about.

"Clay!" she called, and he looked back. She'd removed her own shoes and stockings, as well, hitched up her petticoats to bring her skirts a good six inches off her feet. Gillian likewise stood with her legs bare, staring down at her toes as if she wasn't sure where they'd come from.

Allie's eyes were bright. "Come play," she said.

Laughter rumbled up inside him, and he bent to remove his boots and socks. A few minutes later, and he was running down the warm sand for the cool water.

"Isn't this marvelous?" Allie asked, and he could see her pink toes wiggling in the sand as she stood in a few inches of water. She held out her hands to her daughter, who stood beside her kicking at a wave as if she wanted it to go away. "Come on, Gillian. Let's dance."

The little girl regarded her with a frown, as if she wasn't sure such things were allowed. "Why?"

Allie's hands fell, and Clay could see the effort it took to keep her smile in place.

Clay waded to Gillian's side and bent to tweak a curl. "Come now, Captain Howard. What will the mermaids think if they see you so serious? You might scare them away."

"I think you might be right," Allie said. "Mermaids are known for having fun." She bent and scooped up a handful of water and tossed it upward like a fountain. Though it came nowhere near her, Gillian retreated.

"Mother," she scolded, sounding all too much like her grandmother. "That wasn't nice."

"No harm done," Clay told her. "It's all right to play, Gillian. Like this." He loped along the beach, each step splashing water up his legs. When he was sure he was out of

324

reach from Allie, he turned and stuck out his tongue at her. "Nah, nah. Can't catch me."

"Well!" Allie put her hands on her hips and looked to her daughter. "I say we most certainly can catch him. In fact, I think it's our duty to catch him. What do you say, Gillian?"

Gillian glanced between Clay and her mother. Something inside the little girl was fighting for supremacy.

Please, Lord, help her be who You made her, not what my mother tried to make her.

Gillian raised her head and nodded. Slowly at first, then gaining speed, she hurtled down the waves toward him.

Clay ran.

Round and round they went, up and down the beach, always in the shallows for Gillian's sake. Allie's laugh sent his heartbeat faster than the run. He knew the splashing salt water was likely ruining his wool trousers, but he didn't care.

"Got you!" Gillian dived for his legs, up to her knees in water, and hung on tight.

"I surrender!" Clay declared, raising his hands over his head. The smile aimed up at him was priceless. He couldn't keep himself from bending and sweeping her up, tossing her above his head.

And she laughed, a giggle as warm and golden as the sun beating down. Allie froze at the edge of the waves and pressed her fingers to her lips.

Clay hugged Gillian close as he waded to Allie's side.

"I caught him, Mother!" Gillian crowed.

Moisture sparkled on Allie's cheeks, and he didn't think it was seawater. "Yes, you did, Gillian. Well done."

Gillian bounced in Clay's arms. "Let's do it again!"

Clay set her down on the sand. "All right, Gillian. But this time, how about I catch you?"

She giggled again and ran off up the beach.

"Thank you," Allie said. "You gave me back my daughter."

"I'd like to give her a father, too," Clay said, voice tight in his throat. "I've fallen in love with you all over again, Allie."

She sucked in a breath, pressed her lips together as if to keep from speaking. He plunged ahead anyway.

"I want you beside me in Seattle. I never needed a wife who sits on the sofa looking charming while she entertains. I don't own a sofa, and I doubt I'll ever entertain like our parents did. You've shown me what it can be like to have a helpmate, a woman I love who will stand with me, support me just as I support her. I know you don't want to marry, but is there anything I can do or say to change your mind?"

In answer, she stood on tiptoe and pressed a kiss against his cheek. "I'll consider your proposal," she murmured in his ear. "But first you have a promise to keep."

Clay frowned as she lowered herself again. "What promise is that?"

Allie pointed up the beach where a small figure was growing smaller every second. "You have to catch a mermaid, sir, before she gets away!"

CHAPTER NINETEEN

Allie had never felt more alive as they returned to the ship. Gillian's eyes still glowed with the adventures of the day, and Allie knew she would always remember hearing her daughter's laughter floating in the golden air.

She also knew who had brought about the changes in Gillian. From the first, Clay had encouraged her daughter to play, to dream. And though he had distrusted Allie's dreams in the beginning, she thought he finally understood why Seattle was so important to her.

She was beginning to understand why he was important to her, as well. She could always count on him to be waiting if her strength failed her. But marriage? And to a Howard?

Father, how am I to answer him? My heart beats with his, but my mind says beware!

As they reached Allie's stateroom, Clay

bent and kissed her cheek.

"I look forward to hearing your answer," he murmured, and that deep voice vibrated with hope. With a nod to Maddie, who was waiting in the doorway, he headed for the stairs to the upper salon, his salt-crusted trousers snapping with each step.

"And what answer would that be now?" Maddie asked as Allie entered the room to change herself and Gillian out of their own salty clothing.

"I'll explain later," Allie said, all too aware of Gillian's presence. She knew her daughter adored Clay, but she didn't want to encourage her to believe in so tenuous a future. It wasn't until she had settled the little girl to sleep that evening that she had a chance to talk to her friend.

"You should have seen Gillian today," she murmured as she watched the even rise and fall of her daughter's chest under the wool blanket. "She had so much fun!" She and Maddie were wrapped in their flannel nightgowns and sitting on the bench across from the bunks.

"Sure'n her dress tells the tale," Maddie said. "I'm not looking forward to washing out all that sand and salt!"

Allie couldn't summon the guilt that would once have accompanied that statement. "And I don't care! I saw her smile today, Maddie. I heard her laugh."

Maddie clasped her hand and held it tight. "Praise the Lord for that!"

"There's more." Allie pulled back her hand and rubbed it with the other. "Clay asked me to marry him."

"And?" Maddie fairly bounced on the bench. "Well? How did you answer?"

"I didn't," Allie confessed. "I told him I had to think about it."

Maddie nodded, curling her legs under the red flannel once more. "Good. You've no need to be rushing into anything."

Allie couldn't help a laugh. "I've known him since I was born, and we almost married six years ago. I'd hardly call that a rush."

Maddie's eyes crinkled. "It makes a fellow humble to be kept waiting, so it does. Just be certain this is what the Lord intends for you before agreeing."

Allie couldn't argue there. She'd always felt this trip was God's leading. Could it be He had intended her to reunite with Clay all along?

She thought and prayed about the matter as the next two weeks passed and the *Continental* continued her course north. Each day, she felt more annoyed with herself that she could not settle on an answer. Where was the strength she'd worked so hard to build? Why couldn't she reason out the right response?

Clay, for his part, did not press her, though it seemed to her he spent even more time than usual in her and Gillian's company. His hand reached for hers as they stood by the railing looking for mermaids with Gillian, his voice joined with hers at worship services. Gillian's laugh became an everyday occurrence as Clay chased her around the ship, teased her at meals and read to them in the evenings, his warm voice drawing in others as well.

"Sure'n the fellow's smitten," Maddie assured Allie with a wink.

Allie found it hard to doubt Clay's devotion. She found it equally hard to question her own. Clay challenged her, made her think about her plans, her approaches, helped her see the best path for her. When he gazed at her, she felt like the most beautiful, talented woman in the room, which was saying a lot considering the beauty and talent among the ladies of the Mercer expedition.

Yet something held her back. Marriage meant bending her will to another's. Having just escaped such a trap and with her strength still new, how could she submit herself again, even to Clay?

She was getting heartily tired of her thoughts chasing her in circles. The next stop, she knew, was San Francisco. Surely Clay deserved an answer by then.

Knowing her intentions was one more reason for her stomach to start fluttering when the purser announced at breakfast one morning that they would reach the famous city by nightfall.

"We're almost at the end of our journey," Maddie said, eyes shining. "I can see those streets of gold now."

"You are confusing San Francisco with utopia, Madeleine," Catherine said with a smile. "But I am looking forward to seeing this great metropolis myself."

So was Clay, it seemed, for he was already extolling the virtues to Gillian as they finished the meal.

"Islands more fair than the Galápagos," he promised her, "with plenty of trees and rocks to climb and shells to collect. And playhouses to watch stories come to life."

"We'll be staying for a week so Captain Windsor can bring more food and coal aboard," Allie told her daughter. "We can see all the wonders if you like."

Gillian nodded with a smile. "Yes, please,

Mother."

Mother still. It was the last vestige of her trauma in Boston. But Allie held out hope that the word *Mama* would return one day, perhaps when they saw some of Clay's wonders.

Which started that very afternoon.

Through a rising mist, the *Continental* approached American soil for the first time in months. All the passengers lined the railings, hats and hankies at the ready.

"They call this the Golden Gate," Clay told Gillian as the *Continental* passed between two tall wooded headlands into the bay. "It's the gateway to all the gold found in the hills outside San Francisco." Her daughter was up on his shoulder as usual, peering about her in her plaid dress, while Allie stood beside them in her blue-and-white gown and Matt squeezed between.

Maddie, who stood with Catherine on Allie's other side in her best russet dress, gave her friend a nudge. "Now are you seeing what I meant about gold?" As Catherine smiled and shook her head, Maddie pointed to a rocky isle that appeared to be blocking their way. "And is that one of your favored isles, Clay?"

"No, that's Alcatraz," Clay answered. "It holds a military garrison with more than one hundred cannons to protect the entrance to the bay."

Matt whistled. Gillian looked impressed, but at Clay's fact or her friend's whistle, Allie wasn't sure.

Maddie grinned. "One hundred cannons ought to take more than a hundred soldiers to handle."

"Few of whom are allowed to visit the city at any time," Clay assured her with a smile.

Allie was craning her neck for a glimpse of San Francisco itself. Everyone had been talking about this Boston of the West, Mr. Reynold's shining city, Maddie's golden land. From the deck of the *Continental,* all she could see were stocky stone and clapboard businesses crowded together in shades of gray, as if someone had started building at the water's edge and hadn't stopped until they reached the highest hills. There were no trees, no grass in sight, the land baking under the warm spring sun. Though wide board sidewalks lined the lanes, the streets were made of dirt, and every passing wagon or carriage raised dust that hung in the air.

This was the great metropolis?

"Look at the wharf, will you now?" Maddie said, pointing to one of the many docks that stuck out into the bay. "Who'd have thought the whole town would come out to meet us? It's like when we reached Coronel all over again, so it is."

Allie could see the crowds now, too. Not a square inch of planking was visible along the dock. As the *Continental* made berth, willing hands tied off the ropes, waved in greeting.

"But they're all men," Catherine marveled as the other passengers flapped hankies and cheered their arrival.

She was right. Allie could see bowlers and Stetsons bumping each other as their welcoming party jockeyed for position.

"Throw down the gangway!" someone yelled, and the cry was immediately taken up and chanted. Men climbed on each other's backs to get closer to the ship. As if he didn't like what he saw, Clay lifted Gillian from his shoulder and set her down next to Allie. Matt hurried off for the bow as if to gain a better vantage point.

Allie pulled her daughter close as Clay put an arm about her waist. For once, she didn't fight his protection. She had a sinking feeling she was going to need it.

She couldn't help her sigh of relief when Captain Windsor appeared at the railing. His long face was grim; his gloved hands gripped the wood as if to assert his right to the space.

"This dock belongs to the Holladay shipping line," he informed the waiting men, voice stern with command. "You have no authority here, and you are preventing me from off-loading."

"Then throw the ladies over the side," another man yelled. "We'll be happy to catch them!"

Allie saw Catherine and Maddie exchange glances and heard other women gasp.

"We won't let that happen," Clay murmured beside her.

"We most certainly will not," Allie agreed, and Catherine snapped a nod, as well.

"No lady will leave this ship until you clear out," Captain Windsor insisted as if he had heard the exchange.

"Then let us aboard!" the man demanded, and his comrades chorused their agreement as they pushed closer to the edge of the dock.

"Sure'n they'll tumble in," Maddie said with a shake of her head.

"And if they do, their friends will walk across their bodies," Catherine predicted. "We may need to go below, ladies."

Allie couldn't make herself move.

"I'll give you fifty dollars in gold," someone shouted.

"No, one hundred!" another man yelled.

"Five hundred!"

"A thousand!"

"Glory be," Maddie said, eyes wide. "You really can strike it rich in California."

Clay turned to the captain. "Put me ashore. I'll find the police station, bring back help."

"I can't lower the gangway," Captain Windsor replied, frown on the men blocking them. "They'll only rush it. As it is, I may have to enlist your help to repel boarders." Then he raised his voice and pointed ahead. "Ho, Weinhardt, get those men off the bowline!"

"What nonsense!" Catherine cried. "Have they no self-respect?"

"No wives, more likely," Maddie replied. "Though, mind you, I've never been much for desperation. It makes a gent do crazy things."

Allie shook her head. Already the men on the dock were casting about as if looking for another way aboard. Some had cut the ropes holding the supply boats to the wharf and were making ready to put out into the harbor. Did they intend to capture the *Continental* like pirates?

As Captain Windsor finished directing his

staff to protect the ship, Allie caught his arm.

"Must we stay here, Captain?" she asked. "Can we take on the supplies we need and simply sail on to Seattle?"

He touched his cap in respect. "I'm afraid not, Mrs. Howard. My orders are to go no farther than San Francisco. You will all be let off the ship shortly. It will be up to Mr. Mercer to find another way to Seattle."

Clay stiffened even as Allie washed white.

"Now, see here, my good man," Catherine said, raising her chin. "We paid our fare to Seattle."

"If you'll forgive me for saying so, ma'am," the captain replied, "most of the people on this ship paid less than the actual price, and your Mr. Mercer failed to make up the difference per the contract he signed with the Holladay line. You can't blame Mr. Holladay for taking what measures he must to keep his company solvent."

"Solvent!" Maddie cried. "Sure'n you've fed us nothing but salt beef and beans for three months! I don't see how that could have cost your Mr. Holladay such a fortune."

"If you have an issue, madam," Captain Windsor said, face stiff, "I suggest you take it up with Mr. Mercer." With a nod, he strode off, calling orders to his crew.

"This is outrageous!" Catherine fumed. "What, are we to make our way north on foot?"

"I won't," Maddie said. "There must be more than one man in that rabble who has need of a baker or a laundress. My future's made right here."

Clay waited for Allie to protest, but her gaze roamed the crowd. She was so pale her skin matched the white collar of her gown. Now she turned her gaze to his, and he felt as if he could see her concerns written in the expansive blue of her eyes.

"You said they wouldn't force us to marry, Clay," she reminded him, "but what do you call this? They're like wolves after sheep. Will Seattle be worse?"

"No," Clay promised her, "for the sole reason that we have a smaller population. You'll likely have a welcoming committee in the dozens rather than the hundreds."

By the deepening of her frown, the fact did not comfort her.

He had to admit it didn't comfort him, either. San Francisco was held up as the center of commerce and culture along the West Coast. If this was how the bachelors behaved here, he wasn't sure he wanted to see what would happen in Seattle.

Captain Windsor refused to let anyone leave the ship, so Clay escorted Allie and Gillian back to their stateroom, then spent the rest of the evening patrolling the deck with the crew. Word must have reached the local police, for a contingency arrived as night fell. The constabulary set up a perimeter around the ship, ordered the boisterous welcoming party to cease and desist. By midnight, all that remained were the watchful policemen. At least that meant Clay could get some sleep.

But even then sleep was hard to find. He'd seen the dismay on Allie's face as the *Continental* steamed into the harbor. The sight of San Francisco had darkened her dreams. Once, he would have pressed his case, encouraged her to take the next ship to Boston. But after finally understanding what she'd faced there, he couldn't in good conscience send her back. And in all truth, he didn't want her to go. He wanted her at his side.

But is Seattle truly the best place for her, Father? She faced dangers to her daughter in Boston, but the dangers in Seattle are no less real. She'll have to deal with a lack of doctors, possible skirmishes with the tribes, fire and floods. Am I just bringing her and Gillian to

340

where they'll have to brave more heartache and hardship?

Immediately a verse came to mind. *Greater love hath no man than this, that a man lay down his life for his friends.*

He'd always believed that. Look at how Frank had laid down his life protecting others. Look at how Allie had left all she'd ever known to protect her daughter. Clay had built a new life for himself in Seattle. Now it seemed that life could be dangerous to those he loved, which meant he had to lay it down. If the answer to his prayer was to find another home or even take Allie and Gillian back to Boston, face down his mother and cousin, his own past, then so be it. He was ready to lay everything down and look to the future.

He'd talk to Allie in the morning, and they'd make the decision together.

Allie held Gillian close as the night crawled by. Clay had tried to warn her Seattle would be different from her expectations. She simply hadn't believed him. She'd been sure some part of him was trying to scare her back to Boston. But after seeing San Francisco and all those men crowding the ship, she could no longer deny the truth. Seattle would be more primitive than this.

How could she keep Gillian safe in such a wild, lawless place?

She felt cold all over and pulled the covers around her and her daughter. A subscription lending library might provide income, but her livelihood suddenly seemed the least of her worries. She'd refused to be daunted until now, sure she could master any challenge. But what did she know of struggle? She hadn't done more than embroider and arrange dinner parties before running away from Boston.

Her body began to tremble, her heart to pounding. Her breath came short. Fear wrapped around her tighter than a blanket. Why?

The Lord had brought her safely here. These fears, these worries, they weren't hers. They'd been planted by Mrs. Howard and her poisonous nephew, whispered in her ear even as they assured her they were acting in her best interests. They wanted her weak so she would do their bidding.

She was not that person anymore. She closed her eyes, dug deep for the verses she had heard over the years.

Be strong and of good courage, fear not, nor be afraid of them: for the Lord thy God, He it is that doth go with thee; He will not fail thee, nor forsake thee.

For God has not given us the spirit of fear but of power and of love and a sound mind.

Her breath evened out, her pulse slowed. She did not have all the answers, but she had the answer. God had set her on this path. He would not forsake her. She did not have to fear the future. God had given her the power to take this journey, a sound mind to make decisions. He'd sent her helpers along the way — Catherine, Maddie.

And He'd sent her Clay. She had seen him as a specter of her past, a barrier to her future. Yet he had the shoulders on which she could lean when her own strength failed. Together, they could accomplish things neither did well alone. Look at their collaboration on the Seattle School, their efforts when the Spanish had attacked the ship.

She'd railed that he could not see her for who she was, but she'd been just as bad. She'd continued to compare him to the Clayton Howard she'd known, instead of seeing the man he had become. He wasn't a tool of his family; he'd forged his own future. She should never have kept him waiting for an answer.

She loved him. Once, she'd admired him from a distance. Now, she felt as if she truly knew him, and everything she saw she

343

admired. Unlike his mother and cousin, he thought of others besides himself. She had only to consider his kindness to those aboard, his willingness to pitch in where needed, his patience with Gillian, to know his character. She'd tell him how she felt in the morning, that she was willing to follow him to Seattle or wherever the Lord led them. At last she fell asleep.

And woke to Maddie's hand on her arm.

"It's time you were up, sleepyhead," she said with a smile. "Mr. Mercer has finally proven his mettle. He's arranged for us to stay in a fine hotel, until he can find a ship going north. That handsome Mr. Debro says transportation of a sort will be here shortly."

That necessitated a flurry of dressing and packing. They had put away most of their belongings the previous night after the captain's announcement, including packing up the books Allie had purchased from Mercer with a promissory note from Clay. Now the beds had to be stripped, the linen stowed. But Maddie and Allie worked together, with Gillian giving a hand where she could, and soon they dragged their trunks out into the lower salon where a burly drayman stood waiting.

"These are going to the International and

Fremont Hotel," Maddie instructed him, brushing down her green wool skirts.

He tipped his cap before reaching for the strap of Allie's trunk. "That may be where yours is going, miss, but I have orders to take this one to Main Street."

Allie paused in shaking out her own gray skirts to put out a hand and stop him. "Why? Has Mr. Mercer split our company in two locations?"

"I wouldn't know, miss." He tugged on the strap as if to take the luggage from her.

Maddie latched on to the trunk. "Oh no you don't. That's all she has in this world. Until we know where you're taking it, it's going nowhere."

"There's no need for concern, ladies," said another man who had just entered the lower salon and was approaching their doorway. He was thin and dapper in his fitted brown coat and trousers of yellow-and-brown plaid. He tipped his top hat respectfully and nodded to Maddie and Allie in turn before smiling at Gillian, who was waiting in the doorway of the stateroom.

"Forgive the interruption, Mrs. Howard," he said to Allie. "I'm here on behalf of your family. I know Mr. Clayton Howard has been working on his mother's behalf to see you safely this far. It's time you and Ms. Gillian were sent home, where you belong."

CHAPTER TWENTY

Clay came into the lower salon in time to hear Allie lighting into someone. He'd dressed in his suit again that day, trousers pressed and collar crisp, intending to escort her and Gillian to the hotel, where he hoped to have a chance to talk to Allie about their future. But he took one look at her standing there with her hands on the swell of her gray gown, silk fringe trembling and eyes blazing, and he knew something was very wrong.

"I'm sorry you feel that way, Mrs. Howard," the newcomer was saying. A small man, he had already taken one step back from her and now took another, hands worrying the brim of the hat he was holding. "But I'm only doing my job."

"What's this about?" Clay asked, coming up beside them. He nodded to Gillian, who was standing in the doorway of their stateroom in her pretty plaid dress, hanging on to the doorjamb as if afraid to move away.

Maddie, who was sitting on Allie's trunk for some reason, her green skirts belled about her, leveled a finger at him. "Mr. Howard, I am highly disappointed in you, so I am. I thought you loved this lady!"

"It's all right, Maddie," Allie said as Clay frowned. Her voice was firm, her head high. "I know Clay can't have ordered this." She met his gaze forthrightly, but her own gaze was clouded with concern. "Clay, this man says he was employed by your family to bring us back to Boston. He says you made the arrangements."

"That's a lie," Clay declared, but the fellow whipped out a sheet of paper from his coat pocket.

"It's the truth!" He pointed to the words on the sheet. "This came from Gerald Howard himself. See the signature?"

Clay took the paper, and Allie gathered close to read it. Even Maddie hopped off the trunk to take a look.

" 'Detain the Howard women in San Francisco and help my family representative aboard ship return them to Boston,' " Maddie read aloud. She glared at Clay. "Well, and what do you say about that?"

"Those are Gerald's words not mine,"

348

Clay replied. He could feel his frustration growing, but he refused to let it brush Allie. There had to be some way to prove his innocence.

He turned to find her regarding him nearly as solemnly as Gillian usually did. His dastardly cousin had put doubts in her mind, and he wished the fellow was in front of him now so Clay could make him recant.

"I paid your way to Seattle, remember?" he tried. "Why would I do that if I was determined to return you to Boston?"

"Perhaps you were trying to earn our trust," Allie said. Her hands tugged at the fringe edging on her skirt. "You implied as much yourself."

"You were playing a game with us, now, was that it?" Maddie accused him.

"No." He couldn't let Allie think that. "I'm still not sure Seattle is the best place for you, Allie, but I know it's wrong to drag you back to Boston." He turned to the man, whose balding head came up as if expecting orders.

Clay was glad to give them. "Tell my cousin Gerald that Mrs. Howard and Gillian are safe with me, but they'll be deciding where they call home, not him or my mother."

The man glanced among them, and Clay

knew he saw determination on all sides. Even Gillian scampered out of the doorway to cling to her mother's skirts and glare at him.

"I don't like you," she said, as if there could be any doubt.

He seemed to think that summarized everyone's feelings, for he clapped his hat on his head. "Very well, Mr. Howard. You'll be the one to take responsibility for all this."

Maddie shook her head as he stalked away. "I beg your pardon, Clay. I should have known you'd never treat Allie so shabbily."

"Of course he wouldn't," Allie agreed. Her brow remained knit. "But what did you mean, Clay, that you still had doubts about Seattle? I thought you agreed I could handle myself there."

Maddie took Gillian's hand. "Come along, Captain Howard. Let's say farewell to your ship and give your mother time for a quiet word with your uncle." With a look at Allie, she led the little girl away.

Other women moved past, intent on seeing their own things safely off-loaded. Clay gave instructions to the drayman, then took Allie's elbow and led her to a table by the wall. So many times they'd sat here, talking about the past, planning how to teach the others about the future. Now it was their own future that concerned him.

"I don't question your abilities, Allie," he told her as they took their seats for the last time. "I saw your face when we sailed into port yesterday. This wasn't what you expected."

She dropped her gaze, hands bracing the smooth surface of the table. "No. I know you warned us, Clay, but somehow the vision wasn't real until I saw it rising up in front of me. It's so wild, so remote, so dusty."

He nearly chuckled aloud at that. Dust was the least of their worries in Seattle.

"I understand how it can seem that way," he promised her. "And I understand why you didn't believe me. You told me about my family, and somehow I couldn't believe they'd treat you and Gillian so cruelly. Now I've seen it for myself. Gerald had no right to order someone to detain you."

She rubbed the sleeve of her dress. "I'm glad you were here to help us stand up to that man. Do you think he will be the last? Will your family accept your word?"

Clay smiled at her. "I'd like to see them try to stop us."

She smiled at that. Clay reached across the table and took her hand in his. "I won't

351

let anything happen to you, Allie."

She rubbed her free hand over his, her smile turning soft. "You can't promise that, Clay. We don't know what tomorrow will bring. But I will go where you lead."

He leaned across the table, and she met him halfway, lips touching, hands clasped. This was where he was meant to be, at her side, wherever the future took them.

He pulled back, and she laid her hand against his cheek. Clay took her fingers and pressed a kiss against her palm.

"How about we collect Captain Howard," he said, "and make our farewells to the good ship *Continental*?"

Allie laid her hand against the white-paneled wall. "I will miss her. But I'll be glad to see trees again instead of endless waves."

"You'll have to wait until we reach Seattle to get your fill of forests," Clay advised her. He rose along with her, then tucked her hand into his arm. "But we should be able to find something interesting to do in San Francisco while we wait. Consider it an adventure."

The adventure, however, came to them before they ever left the ship. Clay and Allie had just reached the deck when Maddie moved to meet them.

"Mr. Debro is only allowing folks off by twos, so he is," she complained. "Sure'n you'd think we'd sailed on the ark!" She peered behind them. "Where's Gillian?"

Allie frowned. "I thought she was promenading with you."

Maddie shook her head. "Mr. Reynolds said you were looking for her. I gave her into his care."

Allie stiffened, but Clay was done seeing danger at every turn.

"Reynolds probably just wanted an excuse to pay his respects," he told Allie. "We must have left the lower salon by one route while he and Gillian came in another." He turned to Maddie. "Check the starboard entrance, Maddie. We'll take port."

Maddie nodded, and they all hurried off.

Clay could feel Allie's tension beside him. She called her daughter's name as they descended to the lower salon, but no little voice greeted hers in return. Only a few women were left in the lower salon, and none had seen Gillian.

Now Clay felt the tension, as well. Reynolds might be opinionated, but evil? He had to have some logical reason for detaining Gillian.

"Mrs. Howard?" Mr. Debro approached them as they reached the deck again. His papers were once more in hand, as if he was taking great care to ensure none of his passengers or their baggage went astray this time.

"Ms. O'Rourke tells me Ms. Gillian is missing," he said. "I cleared her to go ashore a few minutes ago with Mr. Reynolds. He had authority."

"Authority!" Allie cried. "Whose authority?"

The purser glanced back and forth between the two of them. "Mr. Reynolds assured me he had both your permissions. He said he was acting on behalf of your family."

Allie felt as if the ship had gone to sea again, the deck heaving. She clutched Clay's arm to keep from swaying.

"We assumed you were the Howard representative aboard," she murmured, voice as weak as her knees. "It must have been Mr. Reynolds. That's why he was so quick to make himself known to us, why he always wanted to take Gillian ashore. He was looking for the opportunity to kidnap her!"

Clay put an arm about her waist, steadying her. "We'll find them," he promised, and she could hear the steel behind his deep voice. "I may have been disowned, but I should have some influence on the family representatives here in California. I'll bring in the law if I must."

Allie nodded, not trusting herself to speak, for she knew if she opened her mouth the most likely thing to come out would be a wail.

Lord, please, protect my little girl! Don't let Gerald or Mrs. Howard take her from me!

Mr. Debro cleared her and Clay to leave the ship immediately, and they hurried down the gangway and onto the wharf. The long, wide planks stretched from deep water in to shore, their lengths already scoured from the cargo and passengers who had passed this way. Laborers worked to load the ships waiting alongside the *Continental,* sending much-needed supplies to the territories and north. To Allie, none of that cargo could be half as precious as her daughter.

"This way," Clay said, taking her hand and leading her through the maze of crates and barrels. Stacks of lumber nearly two stories high blocked her view. Men shouted to each other, calling orders, directing traffic. A little girl could be so lost in all this!

Allie was thankful Clay seemed to know his way. He brought her out of the forest of goods onto Folsom Street, taking her carefully across the crowded avenue and up along the stone buildings lining it.

"The two most logical places for him to go are the Howard offices just above the docks," he explained, "or the headquarters on Main Street."

"Main Street," Allie told Clay, giving his hand a squeeze. "That's where that man wanted my trunk to be delivered. But why would Mr. Reynolds take her, Clay? What does he want?"

Clay's look was grim. "My guess is he hopes to hold her until you agree to return to Boston."

Allie clung to his hand and to her hope. She waited for her fears to climb, prepared herself to fight them. But the anxiety she might once have felt seemed to have vanished in the mist covering the city. The memory of it was just as nebulous.

Thank You, Lord. I know it's Your doing. I won't let fear paralyze me again. You deserve better, and so do Gillian and Clay.

Clay turned the corner onto Main Street. They passed banks with wrought-iron lacework on the windows and tall buildings proclaiming the names of prominent lawyers and real estate agents. Ladies in stylish taffeta gowns and gentlemen in black coats and top hats strolled the boardwalk as if their business there could never be pressing. Some paused to frown as Allie and Clay hurried past.

On the corner stood a white stone building braced by columns of veined marble, brass door swinging open for customers.

"On the corner of Main and Howard," Allie marveled. "How fitting."

"I never claimed my family wasn't pretentious," Clay said as he held the door open for her. "Once we amassed our fortune in shipping, we never let anyone forget it."

The heels of their boots clattered against the marble tiles as they crossed the foyer and climbed the stairs for the second floor. There a wide balcony opened on to glass-topped doors with the name Howard painted in gold on the polished wood.

"Stay close," Clay advised as he reached for the brass knob.

Allie could barely snap a nod of agreement before he pushed the door open.

Inside lay a waiting area lined with massive oil paintings in gilded frames and leather-upholstered benches tufted with brass pins that twinkled in the light. Allie didn't have a chance to notice anything else, for Gillian was perched on one of the benches, and her eyes lighted at the sight of

Clay and Allie.

"Mother!" Gillian hopped off the bench, and Allie rushed forward only to have Reynolds step between her and her daughter. His face, once so pleasant, was as hard as the stone of the building. One hand gripped his walking stick as if he meant to use it on her.

"That's far enough, Mrs. Howard," he said. "You have no authority here."

"Only the authority of a mother," Clay said, moving to her side. His hand on her shoulder was firm, confident. She knew she could count on him.

"Gillian," she called, trying to see around Reynolds. "Are you all right?"

"I don't like that man," Gillian said. "He said we'd look for mermaids. Everyone knows mermaids are on the water."

Her little voice was so indignant Allie didn't know whether to laugh or cry.

Clay raised his fists. "Let Gillian go, Reynolds," he demanded. "You have no right to take her, and I'll be happy to tell the Howard agents that."

"I sent them out to lunch." Reynolds's smug smile felt like a slap. "It's just the three of us. And I have every right to Ms. Howard. You see, Frank Howard's will leaves his daughter in the care of her closest male relative. With your father gone and you disowned, her closest male relative would be my employer, your cousin Gerald Howard."

"That can't be right," Allie argued, but Clay stiffened.

"This isn't about returning Allie and Gillian to Boston, keeping them safe, is it?" he said to Reynolds, voice hard. "My mother may want her granddaughter back, but my cousin wants Gillian because she inherited Frank's estate."

Allie stared at him. Of course! Mrs. Howard wanted control of her granddaughter, but Gerald, the odious Gerald, cared more about the Howard fortune.

That had to be why he'd persisted in courting her even after her many set downs. The bulk of the fortune was entrusted to Gillian. If Gerald married Allie, he would have been Gillian's guardian. No one would have questioned his right to dip into the trust. When Allie left with Gillian, he'd had to resort to drastic measures to retrieve them.

Reynolds was focused on Clay. "Stupid choice, if you ask me, leaving your money to a child. Only men have the brains to handle money."

"Particularly when they're dealing cards

or rolling dice," Allie countered, cold all over. "More than one wife has been left destitute by a husband who handled money like that."

"Mr. Howard's no gambler," Reynolds said. "He knows how to manage money, even if he has no idea how to handle an uppity female like you. Now it seems your little girl is going back to Boston on the next stage. If you want to be her mother, you'd better get a ticket."

"You're mean!" Gillian cried.

"Mind your manners," Reynolds barked, not even bothering to look her way. "I thought your grandmother taught you better."

"My grandmother is mean, too!" Gillian darted around him and ran for Allie, who hurried forward, holding out her hands.

Reynolds lunged for them, but Clay intercepted him, grabbing him in a bear hug that crushed the walking stick between them. As Allie hugged Gillian close, Clay wrestled Reynolds to one side.

Gillian safe in her arms, Allie backed away from the two struggling men. Clay's muscles were bulging under his suit coat, his face grim.

"Give up," he told Reynolds through gritted teeth. "You're beat."

Part of her wanted to run, to take Gillian into the city and disappear somewhere the Howards could never find them. But she knew if she and Clay were going to have a future together, she had to stand her ground and have faith in him.

Just then, Reynolds twisted and turned, grunting as he managed to break free.

"Stay back!" he warned, stumbling away from Clay and raising his walking stick. "I have the law on my side!"

"I doubt that." Clay kept himself between Reynolds and Allie and Gillian. "You've committed a kidnapping. And even if I overlook that and just consider Gerald's actions, I think the court would have to determine which male relative is closer, a cousin or a brother."

Allie sucked in a breath. She should have known. Frank would never have left Gillian to Gerald's care. When he'd written his closest male relative, he'd meant Clay!

"Your father disowned you," Reynolds reminded him.

"But his brother didn't!" Allie cried. "He believed in Clay to the end."

"A shame he didn't put that in writing," Reynolds said with an ugly laugh.

"But he did," Allie insisted. "He wrote me letters from the battlefield. I have them in my trunk. He said if anything happened to him, he knew Clay would take care of us. I was the one who didn't believe him, until now."

She was never sure afterward, but at that moment it seemed something dark sloughed off Clay's shoulders. She knew he stood taller.

"It's over, Reynolds," he said. "Might as well admit it. You're lucky we don't bring charges."

"You can't prove anything," Reynolds replied. "And as for Mr. Howard's rights to the money, a judge might have something to say about that. You Howards pay them well enough. I imagine your cousin has one all ready to rule in his favor."

"Ah, but the case could as easily be tried in Seattle," Clay said. "I'll take my chances with my lawyer. Now, what will it be? Do I turn you over to the police or will you carry a message back to my family?"

Reynolds eyed him, lowering the walking stick until it struck the floor. Allie clung to Gillian, ready to fight if she had to, yet knowing Clay would be fighting alongside her. She had never seen him so sure of himself, hands at the ready, face set with determination.

Reynolds shook his head. "Very well. What

message should I give your cousin?"

"Tell Gerald that Gillian is my concern," Clay said, voice as hard as Reynolds's look. "Her inheritance will stay in trust, just as my brother intended. Gerald will have to settle for managing my mother's money, which ought to be enough for any man. Remind him that if he tries to take me to court over the matter, I can countersue for my own inheritance and tie up the money for years."

Reynolds nodded thoughtfully. "Smart fellow."

Clay shrugged. "I'm a Howard. Tell Gerald there will be no more threats to Mrs. Howard or her daughter, or I will return to Boston and see to the matter personally."

Reynolds paled, but he nodded again.

Clay stepped back from him and held out his hand to Gillian. "Come on, Captain Howard. I don't know where to find mermaids in San Francisco, but I've eaten pie at a fine restaurant near your hotel. I could use a slice of something warm right now."

"Me, too," Gillian said.

Clay's other hand slipped around Allie's waist as they turned for the door. She wanted to hug him and Gillian close, never let them go. Because of him, they had a

363

chance for a future.
She could hardly wait.

Chapter Twenty-One

Allie stood on the wooden deck of the lumber schooner, Gillian on one side, Clay on the other. The *Washington Fir* was a far more graceful ship than the *Continental;* with her six shorter masts and flatter bottom, she skimmed the waters like a seagull homing for port. Allie was thankful its captain had been willing to carry a large number of the Mercer expedition north with their belongings, including the boxes of books for her lending library. Mr. Mercer had stayed behind with the last of their company, who would be following in a few days.

Allie, Catherine and Maddie had spoken to him before they left, taking over a corner of the hotel lobby screened by potted palms and furnished with wicker chairs with red chintz seats.

"We have become aware that you were

paid to bring us out as brides," Allie told him.

He beamed at them. "No need to thank me, ladies."

"No need at all," Maddie agreed. "Does the cow thank the butcher for filleting him so nicely?"

Mercer blinked. "But I —"

"Enough, sir," Catherine snapped. "Your game is done. We will be party to no such arrangements, and neither will any other woman on this expedition."

"We simply wanted you to know," Allie said as he frowned. "Because if the stories about your dealings are true, I imagine you'll find quite a few gentlemen out for your head when we reach Seattle."

He paled and reached up to loosen his collar. "Yes, well, I am certain my behavior on this trip reflects my character."

Allie was certain he was right. She was glad to have reached Seattle before him so she could witness his reception on his return.

Catherine and Maddie had also confessed that they had encouraged Clay to court Allie.

"We did not intend to interfere," Catherine promised. "We had only your best interests at heart."

"And isn't that exactly what Clay said when he first met us on the pier?" Allie countered with a shake of her head. "You didn't think much of his approach then."

They had apologized profusely, but Allie had merely hugged them close. "Just know that your support means the world to me. I can't wait to see what we bring to Seattle!"

Now Catherine, Maddie and the others ranged along the railing with her in the May sunshine as the ship followed the tide south down the shoreline of Puget Sound. They were all dressed in their best gowns, Catherine in a tailored brown suit with black braid across the chest, Maddie in her russet gown and black lace shawl crossing her shoulders and Allie in her blue gown with the white edging. She had Gillian wear her plaid outfit, a flat hat perched on her golden curls. Matt stood nearby, wearing a new coat Allie had sewn him from one of Mr. Debro's old uniforms. Anticipation rippled through the group as the waves rippled around them.

"There!" Clay shouted, pointing, and every eye turned to the clearing that was coming into sight around the point. Ships rested at anchor in the little harbor, sails furled and masts nearly as tall as the trees behind them. Houses and businesses dotted the hillside, straight and firm, with plenty of room to move among them. Allie could see people along the streets, hurrying down to the wharf. Others thronged the dock, men and women alike, hankies waving like banners to welcome them.

Ten days from San Francisco through stormy seas had landed them at this sheltered shore.

"So this is Elliott Bay," Catherine mused. "And look at the trees!"

Though much of Seattle's waterfront and the hill behind it had been cleared of timber, stands of fir still scraped the sky along the ridges and fanned out on either side.

"Where's that fancy new university Catherine is always a-talking about?" Maddie asked.

"There," Clay said, pointing to the white cupola rising above the town.

"That's where I'll go to school one day," Matt promised.

The entire town was less than one-tenth the size of San Francisco, with muddy streets and not a building taller than two stories. Yet Allie felt as if hope flew like a flag over the settlement. She could hear the cheers of the citizens as the captain ordered the crew to trim the sails in preparation of landing.

Everything was about to change, yet she knew one thing that would never change. She handed Gillian to Maddie and tugged on Clay's arm. "Mr. Howard, a word with you, please."

Clay moved back against one of the sturdy chests that lined the deck of the schooner. He hadn't donned his suit that morning. Instead, he looked much as she'd first seen him in New York. His heavy fur coat made his shoulders look massive as he leaned a hip against the chest, his brow raised.

"Something wrong, Allie?" he asked.

She took a deep breath. She'd been planning this moment since the day he'd rescued Gillian in San Francisco. They'd been so busy at the hotel as they waited; it had been like shopping at a sale at Jordan Marsh, Boston's finest fabric store. Men and women had crowded the hotel lobby day and night, offering Mercer's maidens marriage or employment, warning of the dismal life waiting for them in Washington Territory. To Mr. Mercer's dismay, some dozen women had been persuaded to leave the party. However, thanks to Clay's lessons, most had remained true to their vision.

Allie's vision for her future, on the other hand, had changed, and all because of the man beside her.

"You asked me a question back on the Galápagos Islands," Allie said. "And I never gave you an answer."

Clay went still, as if every part of him waited. "I thought we'd agreed. You came this far. I couldn't be prouder of you and Gillian, Allie."

She smiled at him. "I'm proud of us, too, and so thankful to reach Seattle at last! But we would never have made it without you."

He shrugged. "I don't see that I did all that much."

"You wouldn't. That's one of the reasons I admire you."

He drew in a breath. "What are you saying, Allie?"

"I'm saying yes. Yes, Clayton Howard, I love you. Yes, I will marry you and work beside you to make Seattle the New York by and by she was meant to be. If you will have us."

"If? Allie, nothing would make me happier!" Clay pulled her close and kissed her. The warmth of his embrace left no doubt in her mind that he felt the same way she did. When he held her like this, she knew there was nothing they could not conquer.

" 'She walks in beauty like the night,' " Clay murmured against her hair, " 'of cloudless climes and starry skies, and all that's best of dark and bright meet in her aspect and her eyes.' "

He cradled her close, kissed her temple. She'd fought so hard for her independence and almost missed the chance to depend on someone in love just as he depended on her. She could imagine long nights by the fire, reading, talking; days spent planning and working together. The world was so much bigger than she'd thought in Boston. Anything was possible.

Thank You, Lord, for bringing us back together!

The schooner's horn woke her from her dream.

"Mama!" Gillian cried. "Look, mermaids!"

Allie gasped and hurried to her daughter, lifting Gillian in her arms. With Clay's arms steadying her, her heart full, she gazed out at the water, where porpoises rode the bow wave of the ship as the *Washington Fir* slid into port. She didn't want to spoil her daughter's delight by explaining that they were not the fin-tailed mammals she'd been hoping for.

"They're welcoming us," Clay said, taking Gillian from Allie and lifting her higher to give her a better view. "We're almost there."

"No," Allie said, wrapping her arms around both of them. "We're almost home."

Dear Reader,

Thank you for choosing *The Bride Ship,* the first in my Frontier Bachelors series. If you enjoyed the story, I hope you'll consider leaving a review on a reader or retailer site online.

I was born and raised in the Puget Sound area, and the story of the Mercer expeditions has been near to my heart since I was a child. Roger Conant was indeed a reporter for the *New York Times,* and he left a journal that has been published as *Mercer's Belles.* I owe a great deal to his chronicles for the background of this story.

One fact I did stretch a little. While there is a Howard Street in San Francisco, it was not named for Clay's family.

If you'd like more information on the Mercer Belles, please visit my website at www.reginascott.com. You can also find me online at my blog at www.nineteenteen.com or www.facebook.com/authorreginascott. I love to hear from readers!

Blessings!
Regina Scott

QUESTIONS FOR DISCUSSION

1. Allie is determined to be the strong one. When should we rely on God's strength instead of our own?

2. Allie doesn't want to tell Clay how controlling his mother could be. Is there a reason to keep family secrets?

3. Allie and Clay both struggle to know how to treat Gillian so she will grow emotionally. How can we encourage the emotional growth of others?

4. Clay feels he abandoned his family by going west. When is it right to strike out on our own?

5. Clay worries that the frontier is no place for a civilized lady. Are there any places today women of good character should avoid?

6. Allie has several friends in the book. Who was your favorite and why?

7. Maddie is willing to take any job to help support herself. Are there jobs you would refuse? Why?

8. Catherine struggles to reconcile her ideals against the reality of the journey and the frontier. When should we adjust our ideals for the situation?

9. Gillian is afraid of "being bad." What constitutes being bad today?

10. Asa Mercer held a limited view of the capabilities of his charges, a view that was unfortunately widespread during that time period. What role should Christian women hold today?

11. Mrs. Howard sought to control everyone around her to ensure that she was never left alone. What is a better way to ensure we have people to care for us?

12. The women of the Mercer expedition dreamed of a new beginning in Seattle. Where would you live if you could and why?

ABOUT THE AUTHOR

Regina Scott started writing novels in the third grade. Thankfully for literature as we know it, she didn't actually sell her first novel until she learned a bit more about writing. Since her first book was published in 1998, her stories have traveled the globe, with translations in many languages, including Dutch, German, Italian and Portuguese.

She and her husband of over twenty-five years reside in southeast Washington State with their overactive Irish terrier. Regina Scott is a decent fencer, owns a historical costume collection that takes up over a third of her large closet, and she is an active member of the Church of the Nazarene. You can find her online blogging at www .nineteenteen.blogspot.com. Learn more about her at www.reginascott.com, or connect with her on Facebook at www.facebook .com/authorreginascott.

The employees of Thorndike Press hope you have enjoyed this Large Print book. All our Thorndike, Wheeler, and Kennebec Large Print titles are designed for easy reading, and all our books are made to last. Other Thorndike Press Large Print books are available at your library, through selected bookstores, or directly from us.

For information about titles, please call:
  (800) 223-1244

or visit our Web site at:
  http://gale.cengage.com/thorndike

To share your comments, please write:
  Publisher
  Thorndike Press
  10 Water St., Suite 310
  Waterville, ME 04901